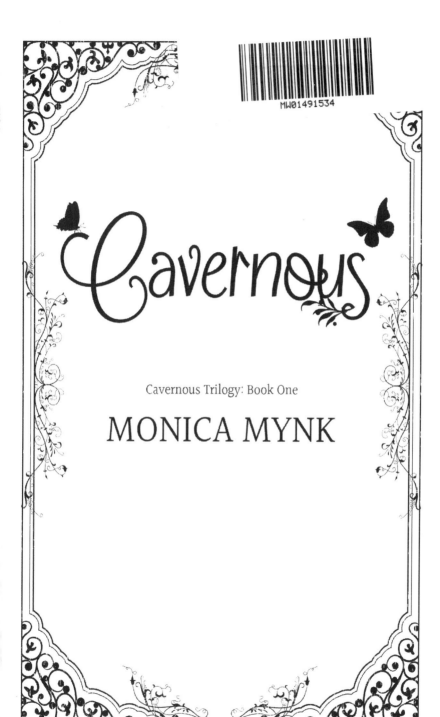

Cavernous

Cavernous Trilogy: Book One

MONICA MYNK

Edited by Deirdre Lockhart, Brilliant Cut Editing
(http://brilliantcutediting.blogspot.ca).

Cover and interior images by Christa Holland of
Paper & Sage Design (http://paperandsage.com).

Published in the United States of America by
Prodigal Daughter Publishing
416 Wellington Way
Winchester, KY 40391

PRODIGAL DAUGHTER PUBLISHING

Dedication

To my patient husband and my beautiful children
To God whose promises are new every morning

My people are destroyed from a lack of knowledge. Because you have rejected knowledge, I will reject you from being priest for Me; Because you have forgotten the law of your God, I also will forget your children. Hosea 4:6

Chapter One

THE OLD grandfather clock chimes nine thirty, its echo searing the last of my frayed nerves. I follow a trail of wax to a chipped piece of Mom's Fiestaware, two feet from the porch swing. Though it's July, flickers in windows across the street make it feel like Halloween and set my teeth chattering. The whistling wind overtakes my flame, bringing an unseasonable chill. It causes the shutters to knock as though they, too, can sense my dread.

Where is Mom? Dad's earlier words still haunt me. *She'd never be late without calling.*

A passing car illuminates silhouettes of trees, whose limbs tangle and snap in their frenzied dance. The car doesn't slow, but it spotlights my older sister sitting on the swing with the boy I've loved for two years. Amber's wrapped in his muscular arms and caressing his silky brown hair. I think her tongue is somewhere down the middle of his throat. Ick. And apparently she's not worried at all about Mom.

Wish she'd hurry up and go to EKU for the semester. At least I didn't have to watch them when she was at college.

Ethan yawns and stretches, working himself free from her grasp. One side of his shirt's untucked and wrinkled, and he stuffs it back into his jeans. "I should leave. Gotta work an eight-to-four tomorrow." After planting a lingering kiss on her, he pats my shoulder. "Bye, Callie. Hope your mom gets home soon."

"Bye." My skin tingles where he touched me.

I bite my lower lip as lightning brightens the whole block, revealing the rural Kentucky skyline. Debris from our last storm swirls over sidewalks and skitters across the blacktop. Amidst pelting rain, Ethan hurries down the concrete steps to his black Mustang and disappears into the shadows.

Amber's perfect lips, swollen from his kisses, contort in a wistful pout. "He's so good to me."

"He's too good for you." The now-roaring wind masks my words. I shiver with the bitter cold, an odd end to such a warm summer day.

I'm too young for Ethan, of course. That's what Mom said. Quit moping. He's nineteen, I'm seventeen, and I'm not allowed to date anyone who's not in high school. And, I can't go out with anyone who can drive which means I can't date at all. Never mind Amber's twenty and she didn't have to follow these crazy rules.

I slam the screen door. Must be nice to do whatever you want. Although, I'd really love to hear Mom's nagging right now. Where is she?

In the living room, I fluff already-plump pillows and dust the polished coffee table. Amber let wax spill all over the kitchen counter, so I scrape it with a butter knife. She also knocked over a rack of Mom's crocheting magazines. Squinting in the candlelight, I alphabetize them the way Mom likes.

The power blinks on at the same time an enormous crack of thunder sends me jumping. Amber rushes inside as the electricity fades back into darkness. "The storm's getting bad, Callie. And I'm hungry."

Mom's been missing four hours. Priorities, Amber. Blowing hard, I puff my cheeks and count to ten. "Yeah, me too." I head to the kitchen, grab a jar of peanut butter, and slather it on slices of multigrain bread. "I'm worried. Maybe we should call Dad again."

Flickering candlelight crawls across her face, creating a landscape of shadowy slopes. "Maybe." She takes a sandwich and downs it in four large bites.

I try his cell. Whatever keeps Dad from answering must be important. Mom wasn't in an accident. At least I hope not. He'd tell us. Besides, wouldn't the police have called?

Another hour passes. The power returns, but wind still jostles the windows. Amber cowers on the couch, watching the radar on our old-school, boxy TV. A hint of her tawny hair peeks from under a blanket, and she resembles a Middle Eastern princess with her striking green eyes and perfect skin. She yawns, long and drawn-out like a cat.

I touch my own face, running my fingers over acne, and catching them in my drab brown locks. "You should go to bed. I'll wake you if there's any news."

"I think I will." She stretches again and drops the blanket to reveal the low-cut tank top she wore under her jacket. Of course, said jacket spent most of the evening draped over the kitchen chair since Dad wasn't home. She's going to end up pregnant before my eighteenth birthday. By the boy I love.

"Monster." I stalk back into the living room, my head filling with sinister thoughts I'd never act on—shoving her off steps, and tripping her as she crosses my path.

Thunder crackles as if in answer, and I glance at the sky with a sheepish grimace. I get it. Thinking it in my heart's just as bad. Forgiveness and compassion... easier said than done.

I turn off the TV and flop down on the couch so hard it unsettles the cushions.

A piece of white plastic catches my eye, poking out from the depths of the couch. I reach for it, knocking it farther under Amber's seat. "Get up a second."

She dives under the blanket.

"Amber. Get up." I scoop below the cushion and lift, uprooting her slender frame.

Loose change and junk food crumbs litter the burlap covering, as well as a tube of Mom's favorite lipstick and a gas station receipt.

8

Her purse must have spilled, and she was in such a hurry she didn't notice. I grasp her plastic driver's license, photo side down.

As I raise the edge, my heart skips a beat. West Virginia, not Kentucky. I turn it over, revealing Mom's face underneath a dark wig, distorted by heavy makeup.

Thunder rumbles in the distance while I hold the fake ID under our CFL lamp incase light makes a difference. Elizabeth Lamb. It appears legit, with a barcode and organ donor signature on the back. The plastic's even scratched a bit. How long has she kept this secret?

It's dated a year ago.

When Dad comes home at nine, I show him the license, keeping Amber's shenanigans quiet. He careens forward, misses the chair, and lands on the carpet.

With my hand extended, I help him into the seat, wincing as he grips my fingers tighter than he should. He sits still for a moment, and then releases me, swinging his arm in a wide arc across the table. The license flies to the floor. "Why, Callie? Why would your mom do this to us?"

"Wish I knew." Kneeling, I pick it up and set it back on the table, unable to keep the quiver from my voice. "Sorry, Dad."

Squeezing his chin with one hand and holding his neck with the other, Dad inspects the ID for about thirty minutes. Then he scoots away from the table, bends over double, and rests his elbows on his knees.

I've seen him cry one other time, at Grandma's funeral, and it was nothing like this—a total breakdown in heart-wrenching sobs. Returning to the armchair, I let out silent wails of my own.

After a few minutes, he excuses himself to the room he shares with Mom, which I'd think would be the last place he'd want to be. His scuffles thud through the wall. He's probably searching everything she owns for any sign she's been hiding another identity. With nothing else to do, I crawl into my bed and cry myself to sleep.

Around eight the next morning, the phone rings.

Dad staggers out of his room, glances at the caller ID, and starts the coffee. "Is Amber awake?"

"I tried a few minutes ago, but she didn't budge."

"I'm going to run by work." He grabs his bulging leather satchel. Papers stick out in all directions. "I've requested a leave of absence, and I'm getting my courses in order."

"Okay, we'll be fine here. You want breakfast?"

"Nah."

I follow him to the porch.

Dad nods to a woman next door who drags two resistant little girls to a minivan. Four houses down, an older man in a fluffy blue robe walks out to get the paper. Doors slam, men in suits hustle, and car engines rev. Against the skyline, tractors putter across the fields, the part-time farmers returning to their subdivided homes after a few hours of morning labor. Typical day on Sycamore Street.

Dad mutters to himself as he stands between the car and the door. He watches me until I go back in to the kitchen then falls into the seat.

As I fill a bowl with cereal, I blink away more tears. Is Mom having an affair? The ID picture seems to imply it. Detailed eye makeup and red lipstick take years from her already stunning face. Darker hair highlights her creamy skin, and the slight curl of her lips gives her a sultry air. An affair is a definite possibility.

Three knocks rattle the front door, and I drag myself into the entry to answer. Mrs. Whitman and company stand on the porch with a box full of baked goods and plastic containers of food. "Morning, Callie. We've been praying."

"Morning, Mrs. Whitman. Mrs. Spencer, Mrs. Parker, Mrs. Bates." I dole out hugs, my soft cotton tee catching on their gaudy polyester prints. Two still have hair in rollers. "Thank you so much."

Mrs. Whitman shoves past me into the kitchen and sets the box on the counter. "This should keep you guys fed for a couple of days. We'll be by with more sometime later this week."

"It took forever to get here. Traffic's backed up on the freeway for miles." Mrs. Bates wipes a dramatic arm across her forehead. "I don't know how I'll get to the hairdresser."

"Speaking of hair…" Mrs. Spencer lifts one of my matted locks and wrinkles her nose. "Go take a shower. It will help you feel better."

"I'm sure you're right." I force a smile. "Thanks for stopping by."

Mrs. Whitman shuffles around the kitchen, opening cabinet doors and glancing at the pile of mail Mom left on the counter. "What's the smell? A candle?"

"Come on, Mary," Mrs. Parker says. "Let the poor girl rest. She's had a rough night."

They tug Mrs. Whitman toward the door, and she pulls away. "What kind of candle, dearie? I'd love to get one."

I sniff, detecting leftover pizza and the faintest hint of weed. "Um… pine?"

Mrs. Spencer also takes in a deep breath. "Have you been smoking marijuana?"

"No." Pressing my lips together, I cross my arms over my chest. "No, I don't do drugs."

"It's the college girl," Mrs. Bates says. "The sister. Leroy always said she was trouble." She turns to me. "Is your sister still here?"

Leroy has no idea. "Amber's asleep. I couldn't get her to wake up this morning." I walk over to the door and hold it open. "Thank you for the food. I'll let you know the moment we hear something."

"Is she breathing?" Mrs. Whitman starts down the hall to the bedrooms.

Mrs. Parker links arms with her, dragging her toward the door. "Mary, we can visit later this week. Let's go. We've got the women's club meeting, and Ellen has a hair appointment."

Mrs. Whitman harrumphs and follows the other ladies to the porch.

Outside, summertime dew covers the ground, and it smells like earthworms. I permit myself a tiny laugh as the ladies take ginger steps through the wet grass to Mrs. Whitman's car, which is parked too close to the edge of the driveway. Hope she doesn't hit the mailbox when she backs out.

When the church ladies are gone, I put plastic containers in the refrigerator and tuck baked goods in our breadbox. Knowing Mrs. Whitman, they'll taste terrible. Still, my stomach rumbles, so I help myself to four slices of banana bread. The dry crumbs catch in my throat, and I chase them with two full glasses of milk.

After breaking down the box and taking it to the recycle bin, I return to the armchair and concentrate on wiggling my feet. My cell rings, a number I don't recognize. "Hello?"

"Oh, good, Callie. Michael Harding, from church. I've been trying to reach your dad."

I draw in a deep breath and release it. "He's at work. Do you have news?"

"Sorry, no. I wanted to be sure everything is okay. I heard them dispatch an emergency crew to your house on my scanner. An unresponsive woman. Do you know anything about that?"

"What?" Sagging into the cushion, I lean my head over the arm of the chair. "Everything is fine. At least I think it is. Except Mom." My breath catches. "Could she be outside?"

"When will your dad be home?"

I shake my head and pace the kitchen. "A couple of hours. What do I do?"

"We'll check the yard. I'm on the way."

Nothing out the windows. I stick my head out the back door. "I don't see anything."

He blows a burst of air into the phone speaker. "Is Amber home?"

"She's still asleep."

"Well, you might want to wake her. Be there soon." He disconnects before I can reply.

I stare at the blank cell screen. My teeth chatter so hard, my whole body shakes. Is Mom lying in the yard? I can't imagine answering the door. What else could go wrong?

"Why?" I speak through clenched teeth. A sob jumps out, and I lift my gaze to the ceiling. "God, why did you let this happen?"

No answer. A grease spot I've never noticed stares back at me, and I feel icky, dirty.

I run to my room, grab clothes, and head into the bathroom to undress. Then I hesitate. What if I'm naked when the police get here?

After a few seconds of debate, I take the quickest shower in my entire life. I'm standing in the hallway with dripping hair when an ambulance screeches up the drive.

The drugs.

I race to Amber's room and give her shoulders a violent shake. She rolls over, groans, and closes her eyes again. Did she hide them? And if not, will they take her to jail? Will they take Dad to jail?

Footsteps pound the porch, shadows cross the window. I take a deep breath, and after staring a minute, go to the door.

When I open it, Mrs. Whitman drags a young, bald-headed paramedic from an ambulance to the porch stairs while Mr. Whitman waits in their car.

The paramedic narrows glassy eyes. "We have a report of an unresponsive woman at this residence."

Mrs. Whitman beams at me. "I called them and told them you couldn't rouse your sister."

"Oh. I…" Smoothing my sopping wet shirt, I take a deep breath before raising my eyes to his. "She was drunk and high. I think she's hung over, but she's not unresponsive."

The paramedic's jaw flinches.

"We don't usually have drugs in the house. But she bought weed from the pizza guy last night."

Dad whips into the drive behind the Whitman's Cadillac and the ambulance, his SUV jutting into the road. He jumps out and races to the porch, his thick black hair bunched up on top like he's been pulling it. He first eyes the paramedic, next Mrs. Whitman, and then me. "What's going on?"

Amber staggers from her room, her pupils dilated. "Whoa." She reeks of incense.

"She's been doing drugs." Mrs. Whitman points a finger straight at Amber's nose.

The paramedic sighs. "Have you?"

"Nope." Amber sashays into the bathroom.

The lock clicks, and the veins in Dad's neck bulge. He snatches the skeleton key, storms into Amber's room, and starts digging through drawers. "You are in so much trouble."

"Get out of there," she calls through the door. The water runs, and she comes out draped in a towel, her eyes blazing. "Leave my stuff alone."

Dad brushes past her into the hallway, holding up a bag of weed. "Care to explain?"

She clutches her towel with one hand and slaps the bag with the other. "That's Callie's."

I cross my arms over my chest. "I've never done drugs a day in my life."

"She's lying." Amber runs into her room with Dad a few steps behind. She steps over the clothes he threw in the floor, grabs an oversized t-shirt, and slips it on over her towel. Fake gasping, she grabs the bag of weed and dumps it on the floor. "I don't know where this came from."

"I don't believe you." Dad stands in the doorjamb as she tosses clothes in a suitcase.

"I'm so leaving." She zips the luggage and tries to get past Dad, but he blocks her. As she lunges toward him, she drops the bag and pounds him with her fists. "I hate you!"

When the paramedic helps restrain her, she lets out an earth-shattering scream, which sets Mrs. Whitman pacing the hallway.

"Maybe you should wait in the kitchen." I link arms and tug the poor old lady away.

Wide-eyed, she nods and sits at the table while I return to the chaos.

Amber squirms in the paramedic's arms. Dad runs his hand through her underwear drawer, and pulls out a handful of plastic bags with herbal residue. By this time, firefighters storm through our open front door, and one calls dispatch to report a domestic disturbance.

A few minutes later, an officer drags Amber out the front door to his cruiser, charging her with disorderly conduct. Dad trails a couple of feet behind him. Mrs. Whitman and I follow.

Mr. Whitman stands beside his car, reading a newspaper like nothing's happening. After the emergency vehicles leave, his wife rushes to him. "Bill! It's over. Let's get out of here."

She races to the passenger side of their Cadillac, slides into the seat, and slams the door. Mr. Whitman gets in, but before he can back around Dad's SUV, Ethan pulls into the driveway.

Shaking my head, I head to the living room couch, grab the remote, and switch to CNN.

The anchorman dissolves into a photo of the US President and Vice President, which then cuts to a huge street riot. The remote slips from my fingers, and I clutch the edge of the couch.

According to the caption, both men are dead.

Chapter Two

IT'S SUNDAY, four days since Mom disappeared. Dad and I are staying with Michael and Angela Harding, a middle-aged couple from church, until the police finish their investigation. Somehow, Dad's a suspect in her disappearance. We've been glued to the television, while chaos spreads across the nation city by city. Gunfights in the street, rioting, fires, and looting—it makes me feel like I'm trapped in some kind of Old West movie.

Amber's still in jail. Dad could have posted bail, but he decided she'd be safer there than trying to get her out on the streets, especially after someone blasted a Molotov cocktail into the church and blew out part of our auditorium. Suits me fine.

Since they live out in the country in an enormous house, Michael and Angela have offered to hold a service and meal in their home. Half the church youth have piled into their basement while their dads sit around the living room discussing how we'll handle the chaos. Their mothers mill about in the kitchen. Even several older couples are here, including the Whitmans, Parkers, Spencers, and grumpy old Mrs. Bates.

I don't feel like being sociable, so Angela lets me help in the kitchen. It's going to be an amazing meal—southern-fried chicken, butterfly pork chops, chunky homemade mashed potatoes, thick roma beans braised in a tomato sauce, and fluffy butter biscuits, perhaps made of air. Mrs. Whitman tries to boss Angela about changing her recipes, so Angela sets her to making banana bread. We all cringe when she insists on adding a single banana instead of several.

Angela's huge assortment of pans allows her to cook enough food to feed an army. And the counter space—feet of it! More than enough room for each woman to contribute to the meal. It reminds me of Ephesians 4:3, which we studied in class two weeks ago, keeping the unity of the Spirit in the bond of peace. We're not afraid of the chaos, serving together in Him.

As the men's voices drift in from the living room, I shudder. Maybe I am afraid.

Michael leans against the arched frame separating the living and dining rooms. "No one but essential government offices operating. Like during the ice storm last winter."

Dad rests against the opposite frame leading from the living room to the bedroom hall. "Rodney Simpson tells me things are even worse in the eastern counties. Families on either side of the secession, just like the Civil War."

I swallow hard. Secession? War? What does he mean?

Lorie, a local hairdresser, shucks steaming cornhusks. "Ellen Bates is mad at me. I couldn't get her hair set before we closed."

Next to her, a woman I don't recognize dredges chicken in flour and drops it into a huge fryer. "When is Ellen Bates not mad? She can't stand my kids."

Mrs. Whitman huffs and slaps her spoon against the side of her bowl. Banana dough flies across the kitchen. There goes the peace. "Ellen's a good woman. She loves kids. You young women think you're better than us. You should go fix her hair."

As the two ladies face off, I hide in the corner, stirring chocolate chips into a huge bowl of cookie dough.

Ethan's mom bursts into the kitchen, nostrils flaring. "My son is out on the road in this mess. His dad let him go by the jail and visit the little hussy since her father told them to keep her."

The kitchen stills, and the women all turn to me. Angela offers her a spoon. "Here, Brenda. You can do the gravy."

"Don't worry." I dump even more chips into the already-full bowl. "I feel the same."

Brenda's chest deflates, and she glares at me before accepting the spoon. I know what she's thinking. I'm the one who introduced them in the first place. Don't think I haven't regretted it for years. Don't think I haven't regretted a lot of things.

Tears stream down my face and splash onto the counter, missing the cookie dough by millimeters. But I hold Brenda's gaze until she averts her eyes.

One of the ladies hums a few lines to "Amazing Grace." Before long, they're all singing, and the tension eases. I'm paralyzed, forgetting to stir and trying to calm my racing pulse with even breaths.

Angela takes the cookie dough and leans close to my ear. "Go in the bedroom and rest for a while if you want. We've got this."

"Thanks." I slip away, pausing by Dad at the edge of the hallway.

"It's the best place for her until things settle." He backs into a lamp, knocking it over, and then rights it. "I'll try to go get her tomorrow or have an officer bring her by. At least she's not out on the road. There were men with rifles roaming the streets. Roger, you were crazy to let Ethan go to the jail."

Michael nods. "When I got to the bank yesterday morning, it was empty, but by the time I left, eighty or more people crowded in the lobby, two workers, and none of them in a good mood."

Roger scowls. "He's a grown boy. What could I do?"

"Don't forget the explosions," adds another man. "I'd have stepped in, even if my kid was old as Ethan. It's too dangerous out there."

Roger's face pales. "What explosions?"

"Started three days ago on the north side of town. Surprised you haven't heard, but then again, you work out of town." Michael hands him the newspaper. "We had four or five today. Earlier, around lunchtime near those abandoned factories."

A shadow crosses Roger's face. "Well, there have been things going on in Lexington, too, but..."

Larry, one of the church elders, pats Dad on the shoulder. "Still no news from Ella?"

"Nothing." He runs his teeth across his lower lip. "She had me fooled."

Roger drops a page of the paper and bends to pick it up. "She had us all fooled. And so did your daughter." When he reaches a stand, he glances at the paper and hands it to Dad. "Did you see this article? People disappearing all over the Commonwealth. Like families packing up and leaving town without even a word of goodbye. Where are they going? Could Ella have been going the same place?"

Dad sighs. "Ella had a lot of online connections with strangers. They were always mouthing off about the President and political stuff." He unfolds the front page to show the whole thing. "A mob at the capitol staged a protest yesterday morning demanding we go forward with the secession and join the other states."

I crane around shoulders to see the headline. Below it, a picture shows throngs of men and women rushing the capitol gate, a mix of suited professionals and flip-flop-clad women. With crazed eyes and gritted teeth, they wave picket signs. Down with the Establishment! End the Oppressive Regime! Mom might not be the only one who's lost her mind.

Ethan's dad holds up another page. "Here's the rest of it. They were griping about eating processed food and breathing toxic air. Teen pregnancy and medical mayhem. Secession is supposed to let them put a stop to it all."

Larry snorts. "This so-called Alliance is supposed to fix all our problems with a magic wand. I'd love to see it."

Michael nods. "The reporter cites economic challenges and the federal government's inability to fix them as the reason for secession, blasting government shutdowns and the bickering that hinders productivity of federal committees."

Good grief. Lawyer speak. I clear my throat. "We studied secession in one of my classes, but my teacher said it would never happen."

Michael scratches his chin. "None of us thought it would happen. This is what I overheard at the bank. Might not be a lot of truth to it, but there were secret meetings behind Capitol doors. Libertarian stuff, but extreme. Threats of a political uprising. Prominence of the so-called Redemption Party. And I'm talking about from Republicans and Democrats alike."

I'm quiet for a minute, my gaze hopping between red flicks in the carpet fibers. "What do you mean?"

Michael places a light hand on my shoulder. "States file petitions to secede all the time. Several every year. Most times, they are contested applications. They'd never pass. I'm not so sure about this time."

"Oh." I reach for the paper. "Can I read it?"

"Here you go." Ethan's dad hands it to me, and the men return to discussing politics while I move to the front porch.

I sit on the steps and spread the paper, flipping pages until I spot a full-page ad captioned Know the Enemy. It features a crude drawing of a single mom toting a fat baby on each hip. Chin rolls and puffy cheeks distort her face. Each baby drinks from a slime-covered bottle labeled FDA Approved.

Gagging, I turn my head.

Ethan comes up the walk from the side of the house. He stops beside the paper and wrinkles his nose. "Disgusting."

"Yeah. It's pretty gross."

He scans it, his brow wrinkling. "We were studying stuff like this in my college class last semester. It's propaganda. The mom is trying to get the money that's out of her reach, and the babies are struggling to hang on."

"What does it mean?"

He frowns. "I'm not sure. What does the bag say?"

"Federal aid."

"Hmm." He points to her foot, which is tangled in a thick chain, pinning her to a heavy weight. A cigarette smolders under the weight. "I think they're saying if we allow certain changes at a local government level, it will put a stop to the abuse of federal aid programs. But that's the thing about propaganda. It's often open to interpretation."

Grinning, he sits on the step next to me. "My professor would be proud."

On a normal day, I'd be unnerved to be so close to him, but I can't tear my attention from the bottom of the page, where the word *unity* forms a big arch over a seven-starred flag. Below the flag, calligraphy letters spell out a phrase: the Alliance of American States.

I brush a strand of hair out of my eyes. All kinds of crazy images flash through my mind. It sticks on one of the paintings I studied last year in humanities. Delacroix. *Liberty Leading the People.*

Mom threw a fit when she saw it in my textbook—a topless woman waving a flag as she stepped over a bunch of dead bodies. I tried to explain it represented much more, but Mom wouldn't hear it. Instead, she marched into the school and gave the principal an hour-long lecture on modesty and teen pregnancy.

My teacher claimed the painting showed a battle between humanity and identity, and suggested it's impossible to have true freedom without the occasional uprising. Mom accepted the critique and dropped the complaint. Could the painting have been the beginning of a personal crusade?

"It's bad out there." Ethan gestures to the smoky horizon. "People are acting crazy in town."

I cringe, picturing his mom's icy glare. "Yeah, your parents are worried. Your mom might never speak to your dad again."

He laughs. "She might not anyway. Dad's good at getting himself in minor trouble. But there are a lot of cops out. Things are settling down."

"Good."

"I went by the jail. I had to be there for Amber." Ethan's eyes are lifeless. "She's a mess."

"She's an idiot."

He shakes his head. "People don't understand her. She's got a lot going on."

"Yeah, like addiction and alcoholism. Did you know she was doing drugs, or did you lie?"

He picks up a pebble off the step and tosses it into the grass. "I knew she was drinking too much. I didn't know she was smoking that much weed."

A drop of rain hits my nose, and a menacing cloud rumbles. "So you don't think she was doing worse drugs?"

"Nah." He faces me. "You don't need to be so hard on her, Callie. She could use a few more friends."

"I don't owe her anything."

A clap of thunder rumbles, and a cool breeze brings the faint scent of smoke. Judging from the skyline, he's right. Town has settled.

"She's your sister."

Crossing my arms, I scoot a few inches from him. "All she's ever done is get in the way of things I've wanted."

More drops spill, and he holds his hand out to catch them. "Jealous much? You're the one who had all the opportunities. Amber's had to work for everything."

"She's never worked a day in her life. When she comes home from college, I always have to do her laundry and clean up her messes. And what does she do at her job? Watch soap operas and answer phones? Mom and Dad send her money every week, and she still calls and asks for more. And then they send it to her, and they can't get things I need."

I've raised my voice, but I don't care. Heat floods my veins and pulses through my heart. "I can't even go for my license because of her."

Ethan shrugs. "She can be a slob. And selfish. But that's not a good enough reason to hate her. Every time I'm over there, you're snappy and rude. And to be honest, it's getting old."

"She ruined my life."

He stands and steps toward the door. "You ruined your own life. You've turned into an old grouch. What did she ever do to hurt you so bad?"

The answer forms on my lips, and I stare at him, willing myself to say it. As I open my mouth, an unmarked police car whips through Michael's gate and speeds down the driveway.

"She—"

The thunder and spinning gravel drown my words, and there's a good chance he wouldn't have heard anyway. I duck around him and run into the house. "Michael, there's a cop out here."

Ethan follows me in, his expression grim. "Two. Carrying weird military rifles."

"Go to the basement," Michael snaps. "Everyone. Now!"

The women race to turn off the stove tops, and the men hurry them down the steps. Ethan and I stand paralyzed in the hallway as the two officers approach the screen door.

Without knocking, they barge in. One trains his rifle centimeters from Michael's nose. My mouth opens for a scream that never comes.

Michael backs against the wall next to Dad. "Can we help you?"

The taller man snarls, tugging the waist hem of his uniform coat. He resembles a soldier, almost a Union man in Revolutionary red. "Agent Kevin Wiseman. Is Martin Noland here?"

Dad holds his arms up in front of him. "I'm Martin. What do you need? What agency are you from?"

"I will be transporting Ms. Noland to West Virginia. Her father's orders."

Face tightening, Dad lowers his hands. "I'm her father. Is this a joke?"

At the same time, Michael steps forward. "Under whose authority? Where's your badge?"

West Virginia? No way. My chest burns as I clench my fists, falling into Ethan's restraining arms.

Agent Wiseman lowers his rifle and pulls a folded manila envelope from under his arm. "According to this DNA test, she's not your daughter."

Angela, still bustling around in the kitchen, drops a full platter of chicken.

Trembling head to toe, I dodge the crumbs scattering across the floor. Of course he's my father. And yet… the driver's license … No, it can't be true.

"I don't believe you." Dad crosses his arms and stands tall.

Wiseman hands him a piece of paper, which he scans, his face blanching.

All I can see is a blend of colors—the red flecks in the carpet, the gray steel of the gun, and the gold trim on the agent's pants—swirling into a twisted mess. It takes a few seconds to realize I've doubled over in Ethan's arms, and my hands grasp his legs for dear life.

Smirking, Wiseman snatches the paper and tucks it into the envelope, then removes another page. "Her real father has filed for and received custody."

Dad steps in front of me. "Not possible. When was the hearing?"

"We sent you a notification, and you didn't bother to show." Wiseman hands him the document, and Dad falls against the wall, steadying himself with quivering hands.

Snorting, the other agent turns to me. "Your father has made provisions for you to attend the Monongahela Military Academy. We're leaving immediately."

Ethan's strong arms loosen their hold of my rubbery ones, and he steps forward with clenched fists. The second agent aims his rifle, and Ethan relaxes his posture. "Can she at least have time to process it? Or to say goodbye?"

"I—" My gaze darts between Dad's gaping mouth and Wiseman's rifle.

"I'll be waiting in the car. You have five minutes to gather your things and say your goodbyes, or we'll have to resort to bigger extremes."

"But most of my things aren't here."

He points the rifle out the front door and shoots across the yard. "Five minutes, and no more. Resistance will not be tolerated."

Chapter Three

WHILE ETHAN GLARES, Agent Wiseman pins me with his arms, twisting to the side to avoid my kicking feet.

Dad swings at him, catching the tip of his jaw with his fist.

"Martin, you're going to get us all shot." Michael struggles to restrain Dad.

Bared teeth, brown from coffee stains, punctuate the tension distorting Dad's kind face. "They are not taking my daughter."

Wiseman drags me across the threshold as his partner nails Dad with pepper spray. Restricting me with one arm, he retrieves a small brown bottle from his pocket with the other and twists the cap with his teeth.

"Let me go!" I wiggle free from his grasp and stumble backward onto the porch.

He pours liquid over a rag and comes at me again. Poison?

I scoot away until my spine bumps against the house. He lunges toward me and covers my nose and mouth with his hands, forcing me to inhale the strong, sweet-smelling liquid. When he tosses the bottle to the ground, Ethan charges to my side and brings his hand to my cheek.

I struggle for consciousness. Tears fill my already-hazy eyes. I may never see him again. I have to tell him. "I… love you."

His eyes widen. There's the understanding I'd hoped for. Why I hated her. Why I felt betrayed by him.

"And she… she knew…" His face swirls into a blur. "She stole you away."

When I wake, my head aches, and my vision remains blurry. I think I'm in a moving car. What have they done to me? I blink several times to adjust to the light, and then try to move my hands to feel my way around the setting. No such luck. Cool metal restraints secure my wrists, and I tug with all my might to no avail. How dare they do this to me! I'm sitting upright, so I wiggle my knees, bumping them against a metal cage.

The back of Wiseman's head comes into focus. He's grasping the steering wheel with white knuckles. Creep. I narrow my eyes in the rearview mirror. "Let me out of here!"

Wiseman winks over his shoulder. "Sorry, sugar."

He stops the car. His partner opens the door and dodges my helpless kicks. Grabbing the waist of my jeans, he holds them away from my hip. I scream and jerk away, but not before he jabs a sharp needle into my flesh.

More drugs? It burns to my toes, like I stepped into a tub of acid. I open my mouth to scream again, but I'm frozen. My world grows hazy. I grit my teeth, and everything fades.

This time when I wake, Wiseman drives through a wrought-iron gate and parks in front of a four-story brick building. Austere in a way, it resembles a hotel, other than the chain-link fence with razor wire surrounding the perimeter. Is it a prison? Would Mom have agreed to send me here? "I'm not going in," I say, but my words come out muffled.

Wiseman gets out and stalks around to my side. He sneers while freeing my hands. "You don't have a choice."

I can't even muster enough breath for a gasp. Clenching my fists, I make a lame attempt to lunge past him, but he digs his fingers into my shoulder. Blood pulses through the veins in my neck, throbbing like a beating drum.

He can't stop me from scowling, so I do, imagining myself punching the smirk right off his face.

"So we're clear, we have the authority to shoot you if you try to fight us." His partner grabs my wrist and spins me to a standing position. They walk on either side taking turns shoving me toward the entrance.

Authority from whom?

A blonde woman with impeccable posture waits at the foot of a long set of stairs. Her thin wrinkles twist in a sideways frown, and her crisp blue uniform with gold trim matches Agent Wiseman's red one. "You're late."

"Sue me." Wiseman nudges me forward. "Delivered as promised."

The woman makes a 90-degree pivot and leans closer. "Miss Noland, your room will be on the third floor. Uniforms are on the bed, and we'll bring your luggage after we've inspected it. Personal items will go in storage until your graduation. Please place your bags over there." She points to a corner where a big stone fireplace stands. "Are we clear?"

I stand straighter. "I don't have any personal belongings. They didn't let me get any."

She strikes my cheek. The blow turns me sideways, toward Wiseman and distorts my vision. I embrace the pain, fanning the flame building inside me. When I roll my head to center, I raise my hand, but she's poised and ready to slap me again. "You will not take a defiant tone with me, young lady."

She uses the back of her hand. Three large rings dig into my flesh, and what might have been a short jolt of pain becomes enduring. I see spots. Reaching blindly, I touch the railing. Time to be humble. "Yes, ma'am."

"Is she ready?" A tall redhead joins us, her toothpick arms pointed straight to the floor, jutting out of a blue uniform with silver trim. Still wincing from the slap, I follow her to my room. She unlocks it and hands me the key. "I'm Nina. Try to blend if you can."

"Where am I?"

We both step forward to enter at the same time. Nina brushes my shoulder, which still aches from Wiseman's grip. "Monongahela Military Academy."

I scratch my fuzzy head. Wiseman described this place, didn't he? Trying to remember brings Michael's explanation of secession to mind, and I frown. "Is this a new school?"

"No, it's been here a while. Maybe eight or nine years. The people who run it are big Alliance supporters, though. So it's always been under their influence." She leans close and drops her voice to a whisper. "Things have gotten worse since the secession. They aren't um… regulated anymore. So they get by with certain things. Be careful."

She lifts her shirt to show me a grapefruit-sized bruise on her abdomen.

I gasp. "What did you do?"

Tears fill her eyes, and she shakes her head. "I spilled a drink. An accident, but—"

"Lights out!" The voice carries down a long hall, but there's no visible speaker.

Nina's shoulders straighten, and she moves to the door.

"How do I blend?" Trembling, I scan the room. Uniforms are folded on the bed, as promised, along with three pairs of pajamas and new packs of underwear and socks. It's similar to Amber's dorm, with two twin beds and dressers. A small mirror hangs behind a Formica counter and a stainless steel sink.

"Do what you're told." She glances over her shoulder in the direction of the voice. "You'd better hurry."

Rubbing my temples, I tilt my head from side to side. "Any chance I could get Tylenol?"

"You could, but you'll pay for it." She points to a chart on the wall. "They use this to help you keep up with your balance of merits and demerits. Asking for a pain reliever is a sign of weakness, so it would be a demerit. You'd have to work in the kitchen to earn merits for balance." Her laugh sounds harsh. "You don't want to be in the negative, trust me."

"Okay. So, what do I wear tomorrow?"

"You'll wear the gray uniform tomorrow and pretty much every day. Plan on being up by five." She points to the alarm clock on the nightstand. "It's already set for you."

The woman shouts again, and I grimace. She's closer, and I need to go to bed. It's going to stink to sleep alone in this crazy place. "No roommate?"

"Not tonight. But we still have three more days of student arrivals, so you might get one then." She points to the window. "Don't ever try to climb out or open it. They wired it like an electric fence."

My hands go limp at my side. "So I guess there's not much use in fighting."

"No." She steps toward the door as a heavyset woman wielding a thick, wooden cane stalks past. Her knees are knocking. "I mean it. Don't mess with her," Nina whispers.

As she leaves, the heavyset woman snatches Nina by the arm, raising her cane above her head. "Why aren't you in bed?"

"They sent me to bring the new girl—" Nina's screams fill the hall as she slams the door shut behind her.

My head hits the hard pillow, and I slip under the covers with my clothes on, hoping my jagged breaths don't give away my cries.

Dear Lord, please keep this woman away from me. Give me faith and strength to endure. Watch over Dad and Amber. Help me understand why I'm here. I know it's Your will. I should add thanks for blessings, but I can't say the words.

My door slides open a crack, and I hold my breath. The light flips on, but I keep my face muscles steady and my eyelids tight. I count thirty painful seconds before the brightness dims and the door thuds closed again.

Tears slide down my cheeks and into my ears, wetting my hair and pillow. I hold myself, rocking on the mattress and praying the woman doesn't return.

I try to think of anything peaceful and familiar. Ethan springs to mind, weeks after his parents moved in a few streets down from us. We raced across the rolling green hills behind our church, bent over in hysterical laughter when we tied—my first time hanging out with him.

His enthusiasm for life drew me, the way he'd break out in sudden song and whisk one of the older church ladies around the fellowship hall. I loved riding next to him in his fast car through the horse and cattle farms and making the other freshmen girls in my youth group jealous when he chose to sit beside me in class. None of them ever got attention from the seniors.

For a couple of months, he took me everywhere. Dad had to go out of town for a conference, so Mom let him drive me to school and church. We picked up leaves from the yards of our elder members, worked together on helping build a community teen center, and took a bunch of toys to the children's hospital. We smiled, we laughed, I loved. And I think maybe he did, too.

Then Amber showed interest, and he forgot I existed.

I roll my cheek across the wet pillow and turn on my right side, wincing as I brush the spot where Wiseman's partner gave me the shot. I've been kidnaped, drugged, and beaten. What will come tomorrow?

My eyes close for a few seconds. The door handle clicks, and bright light floods my room once more. Footsteps grow closer, and making my heart throb like it might explode. Somehow I manage to control my breathing.

A cold hand brushes my cheek, and I shiver. The fingers are too thin to belong to the heavyset woman.

"She had a headache. Good thing it didn't keep her from sleeping," Nina whispers in a tiny, quivering voice. "I think she'll adjust."

I hear a rattling, maybe a bottle of pills, and something being placed on the nightstand. When the footsteps retreat, I open my eyes a sliver. The blurred shadow of a tall dark-headed man hovers at the foot of my bed.

My entire body goes numb, except my racing pulse and pounding head. The sheets smother me, but my arms won't lift to move them. Several minutes later, when I'm finally calm, I flip on the lamp next to my bed.

There, on the nightstand, is a small cup of water and two white capsules. Thank God. I grab the pills and swallow, chasing them with the water. As I switch off the lamp, a wave of dizziness takes over my consciousness.

Chapter Four

DOWN THE HALL, doors slam and feet patter. I peer through a crack, seeing several girls about my age running into the common bathroom, all wearing identical white bathrobes. On a trunk at the foot of my bed, there's a small plastic tub with body wash, flip-flops, and a loofah sponge resting on top of the same white robe. Creepy. It wasn't there last night, and I never heard anyone else come in.

I change, but not fast enough, because I end up last in line for the shower. Ducking my head under the ice-cold water, painful jolts pulse through my skin like electricity. I slather on a drop of the unscented body wash and rinse as much as I can stand, finishing in less than two minutes.

An empty shelf sits beside the shower with a sign above it. Towels. With a sigh, I wrap the robe around my wet skin and trudge back to my room with dripping hair.

The heavyset woman runs at me, wielding her cane. "New girl, you're getting this floor sopping wet. Wipe it up, now."

"What am I supposed to wipe it with? There aren't any towels." I cringe, not intending a sharp tone.

Her cane raps against my temple, and my eyes water. This is not my fault. I clamp my lips together and kneel to wipe the floor with the hem of my robe, leaving small pools of water behind me.

"Foolish, foolish girl." The crook of the cane strikes my shoulder, and sharp pain shoots through my whole arm. "Go to your room and get dressed before you miss breakfast."

She mumbles to herself as I scuttle into my room and pick up the gray uniform skirt. Beneath it, I find a pair of white tights and worn leather loafers a size bigger than what I wear. Though I hurry to dress, no one remains in the hallway when I walk down the stairs toward the cafeteria. The smell of burnt meat drifts down the hill. Hope everything's not ruined.

The main building of the school is housed in a repurposed church, and I have to pass through the lobby to get to the cafeteria. A grayish film covers the faux-oak paneling, and the dingy orange carpet holds its shape when someone steps on it. Ugh. I reach out to steady myself on the rail.

The woman approaches again and waves her cane in my face. "Touch that and you'll be polishing wood all afternoon." Eying my unkempt hair and sideways skirt, she leans her cane against the wall. "You're a mess."

She snatches my hair at the roots, twists it into a knot that matches her own, and pulls it tight enough to induce the tears I've fought to suppress. When she sees them, she jerks a hand towel from her waist and rubs my eyes so hard my skin burns. Her sharp movements cause me to stumble, and I take a few steps forward to regain my balance.

Gripping the waistband, she turns my skirt a couple of inches, aligning the zipper with my spine. "Not great, but it will do for today. Now get to the cafeteria before there's nothing left."

The charred stench burns my nostrils. Wrinkling my nose, I scan the crowded room. The students face forward, expressionless, and fork food into their mouths without a word. And yet the room is not silent—scraping utensils, sighs and coughs, clearing throats play their melody against the hum of the machines. No one will meet my eyes.

Three students stand ahead of me in the line. I fill my tray with the last scrape of scrambled eggs and a couple fragments of what might have been turkey sausage. Then, I take what appears to be the last remaining biscuit, though it's more like a stone. Whatever it is, it's whole grain, and there's no offering of anything to spread on the dry bread. No salt, no pepper, and no butter. My stomach rumbles. Guess I'll have to eat it anyway. Can't be worse than Mrs. Whitman's banana bread or that whole grain pizza Mom's always trying to make.

The thought of Angela's fried chicken and the hearty meal I didn't get to eat set my mouth watering. Maybe I can just pretend this food tastes good. I grind my teeth and squeeze the tray. Can't let my thoughts drift, or I'll lose it.

The girl in front of me holds her forward gaze steady, so I mimic her body language as I search for an empty seat. When I find one, no one acknowledges my presence, but they stiffen. I turn as two men in stiff red jackets with gold trim making their way through the room. They inspect each student with extreme scrutiny.

Someone pinches my leg. "Don't look at them." The girl next to me hisses. "Sit. Straight ahead, best posture."

I plop down and focus on a piece of chipped paint that adds interest to the dingy concrete wall. Taking minuscule bites of cold scrambled eggs, I force even breaths.

One officer stops two tables from us. He grabs the collar of a tall blond-headed boy and pulls him to his feet. A hushed whisper crosses the room, the sound of collective stifled gasps.

The boy ducks his head and follows the officer out of my line of sight.

Rubbery eggs stick in my throat. I wash them down with warm, almost mushy milk that reminds me of what Mom used to give me for a stomachache. It does nothing to ease my current nausea. Thinking of Mom brings tears. I bite my lips and blink them away. Why would she do this to me?

A siren blares. The girl at my table links arms with me and drags me toward my dorm. "Come on. I'll show you the ropes. They don't tell the newbies anything around here."

"Thanks."

The other students disperse, descending the hill like ants. The girl and I follow, pausing by the dorm entrance to let another student in ahead of us.

"I'm Maggie." She stops at a wooden door and opens it to reveal an enormous closet. "I do the bathrooms if you want to help. Keep busy and don't let Reva see you standing still."

"I'm Callie." I nod across the room toward the hefty woman who smacked me with the cane. "That's Reva?"

"Yep." Maggie hands me a thick sponge and a pair of rubber gloves. "Now come on, and whatever you do, don't make eye contact."

My heart races as we pass Reva, but she doesn't acknowledge me. I follow Maggie into the bathroom and scrub every surface until blisters bubble my hands. Sweat drops drip from my forehead to the dingy floor, blending with the soap. I miss Dad so much. And I even miss Amber.

"Callie." Maggie grabs my arm and stills it. "You can stop now. It's all clean. Time for class."

I take one more swipe at the drab tile and mold-stained grout. The room still smells like old socks. "Okay." When I stand, big gray circles cover my knees.

"You'll get used to it in a day or so," Maggie says. "In class, we don't speak, just like lunch." She frowns, glancing at her bruise-covered knuckles. "Unless the teacher calls on you. And then, you respond right away, whether you know the answer or not."

"Thanks for everything," I give her a genuine smile.

"Oh, Callie…" she whispers, nodding to the ceiling, where a camera has been watching our every move. "I forgot to tell you. Whatever you do, promise me you'll never, ever frown or smile. Expressions of anger and happiness are forbidden here. We strive for complete control of our emotions."

The muscles around my mouth relax, though the ones around my heart tighten. "Understood."

Reva marches in to inspect our work, taking a couple of moments to gripe about how worthless we are and what a pitiful job we've done. She prods me toward the door with her cane, and I fall into the line of students walking out of the dorm and uphill to the church.

A bald man sits at a desk in the lobby, typing on a laptop. Maggie nudges me toward him. "He'll help you register for classes." She disappears into the crowd.

He looks at me through bifocals and gives a curt nod. "You're a sophomore, I see. Older than grade level, so I'm assuming you've repeated a year?"

"I should be a senior. I'd made up enough credits." My cheeks warm. "But yes, sir. I had mono in the sixth grade and missed too many days to pass." When he frowns again, I chew on a fingernail.

"Mono." More pecking. He leans forward and squints at the screen. "Your grades are on the low side of average."

That's generous. I haven't tried in school since Amber started dating Ethan. No wonder Mom agreed to send me to this rotten school. "Sorry. I'll work harder."

"You'd better." The computer beeps. He reaches under the table to retrieve a USB cable. "I'm going to print your schedule." He jabs his finger toward three crates against the wall behind him. "There are pencils, highlighters, and notebooks there, and you can help yourself to five of each. We'll get you a book bag and textbooks by the end of the day."

"Thank you."

A woman rushes from a nearby office. "Here you go." The folder quavers as she hands it to him.

He passes me the paper from the printer, and I find my first course.

He's got to be kidding me. "I've already had Algebra I."

Shaking his head, he makes a tsk sound. "You didn't earn a B or higher." He points to the paper. "You'll also repeat English I, US History, and Biology."

I have a mind to scream, but Reva walks by, her cane in tow. Forcing a couple of deep breaths, I blow air across my upper lip. "Does this mean I won't get to graduate on time?"

Before he can answer, Reva grabs my wrist. She scans my schedule and drags me toward the classroom. "If you're late, we have to shovel in the horse barns on the farm. The whole dorm has to help." Lowering her grip to my palms, she squeezes the blisters, bringing tears to my eyes. "My charges are always on time. You got that?"

My pulse thunders in my ears. "Yes, ma'am."

I meet her eyes, and she whacks the back of my head with her cane. "Go on, girl. Get your stuff and get to class."

The classroom is nothing like I've expected. It seats twenty, all the students sandwiched together in four tight rows of chairs with no desks. One in the center is empty. I crawl over legs and slip into it just as the blaring siren goes off again.

After a few discreet glances around the room, I follow the other students' lead and turn to a blank page in my notebook. They copy notes from the board, and I do the same. Without desks, we all have to hold our notebooks in our laps to write, which kills my shoulders and back.

The teacher, a thin, muscular woman with a faint mustache paces the room. She grips a metal ruler so tight the skin around it has turned white.

Once, I stop writing and stretch my hands. She leans across the students next to me and smacks them with the cool steel. After that, I grit my teeth and write on.

When we finish notes, the teacher announces we'll each work a problem for the class. "Our new girl will go first." She nods to an easel, then hands me a marker and an index card. Good. It's a topic I know.

I copy the problem at the top of the easel paper and examine it.

"Go on." The teacher waves her steel ruler. "Solve it."

My throat is suddenly dry. "Well, the problem says rearrange the equation to solve for height. It's a sphere."

A boy in the back of the room snickers.

"Um... cylinder, not sphere." My cheeks blaze, and I grasp the thick cotton collar of my uniform. "To isolate the h, you'd divide the volume by pi times the square of its radius."

The teacher points to my seat, with no indication of whether or not she's pleased by my answer. She hands another student a card and asks him to work the next problem.

We progress like this for two full hours, students standing in awkwardness at the front of the room while their classmates give them stoic stares and copy the problems in their notebooks. Every so often, the teacher hits someone's hands with the ruler.

At the end of class, we're ushered back to the dorms for a thirty-minute study time.

Reva glares at us, snatches Maggie out of the line, and raps her with the cane.

I straighten my shoulders and face forward, not breathing until I've closed the door to my room. Halfway through the ninth of my fifty homework problems, the siren rings again.

Maggie is waiting by the door. "Come on, Callie, we're going to be tardy for English."

We run down the hall, brush past Reva, and make our way to the classroom door just as the siren rings. Too late, we slip into our seats as the teacher picks up his ruler from the desk.

Chapter Five

ALTHOUGH MAGGIE and I arrive late to class, the English teacher only gives us five pages of extra homework. Annoying, but doable.

Like the Algebra teacher, he makes us work problems in front of the class, this time diagraming sentences. After two hours, we take a ten-minute break and head to US History. At least we have desks.

"Welcome, Ms. Lamb. I'm Mr. Sanders." A tall, bulky man with a buzz cut shakes my hand, squeezing it so hard he leaves a red mark.

"Um… My last name is Noland."

"According to my roster, your name is Lamb." He glances at a clipboard. "The other students have already been in their classes for a week, so you can catch up during free time."

"Sounds great." Not. There goes my extra homework time. Guess I'll be up all night. If they'll even let me stay up later for homework.

Mr. Sanders's muscles bulge out of his olive-colored T-shirt. Was he in the Army? Would a soldier abandon America for the Alliance? How did things go so wrong?

Two hours of sifting through Alliance propaganda leaves my eyes glossed. Mr. Sanders releases the rest of the class to free time and removes several used transparencies from a manila folder. "Copy these. Let me know if you have questions."

Great. More notes. I take out a fresh piece of paper and glance at the first transparency. "What does this mean? America was not founded as a Christian organization. That's ridiculous."

"Just write, Ms. Lamb."

Noland. "But I thought you said I could ask questions. It says we fell from grace through greed and self-seeking and all deserve punishment. What kind of punishment?"

Lips pinched, he shuffles a stack of papers on his desk. "Maybe questions aren't such a great idea."

I bite my tongue and copy the words. Prohibition failed. But, it was due to government weakness, and the Alliance plans to reinstate it. Nonsense. "Why do you think the states were able to secede?"

He yawns, stretching his mouth so wide I see his tonsils. "Congress came to an impasse, a checkmate, if you will." He writes the word checkmate on a whiteboard and underlines it twice. "We were blowing money on failed policies, and our national debt had become staggering."

My pencil squeaks as I continue copying notes. "If we were in so much debt, then how could the states afford to secede? Wouldn't we lose a lot of money for education and healthcare and stuff?"

When Mr. Sanders presses his lips together, he looks like a frog. "We had a lot of corporate backing and private investors. You see, running a government is like managing a business. Except the president is the CEO, and the people are the investors."

My brow furrows. Running a government is not like managing a business; at least I don't think it should be. I didn't pay much attention in US History the first time around, but even I know the President shared power with the legislative and judicial branches. Those checks and balances are important. Is he saying the Alliance doesn't have them?

I hold my pencil between my middle and pointer finger, twisting it back and forth. "What kind of government would you say the Alliance is? Still Democratic?"

He looks at the ceiling as if he sees the answers there. "Our founders studied all forms of government and tried to put together leadership that took the best qualities of each."

Right. Avoid my question. I shake my head. "When? How?"

"They met on the Internet and had secret meetings under the guise of a religious organization. That's all I know."

I gasp. Why is he telling me this? "Do we have a president?"

Mr. Sanders slams the dry erase marker on his desk. "Have you been taught nothing?" He leans into the hallway. "Do you people think I'm a miracle worker?"

I drop my gaze to the carpet.

He storms back into the room and pulls a chair before my desk, sitting where he can face me. "Sorry. I just get frustrated. They want me to rewrite your history from scratch. The Alliance leadership is comprised of ten delegates from each of the seven states." He clucks his tongue. "Do you know which states make up the Alliance?"

I scrunch my nose, trying to recall the ones I saw on Michael's TV. "West Virginia, Alabama, North Carolina…"

"Yes, yes, and yes."

"Ohio."

"Yes."

Curling my toes, I scan the walls for a hint. "Oh, Kentucky. Where I'm from."

He frowns. "Yes." He looks over his shoulder and leans in closer. "But they have a strong resistance."

I cover my mouth, stifling a gasp. Could that be true?

"Well?" He taps the dry erase marker on my desk. "Do you know the others?"

"No." I brace myself, expecting him to slap my knuckles.

A gray-haired woman with the most beautiful porcelain complexion pops in the room. "You'll have three more new students tomorrow."

"Virginia and South Carolina." Mr. Sanders stands and places his hands on his hips. "I can't keep doing this for the duration, Louise. I have a wife and kids, you know."

Louise smiles and pats his shoulder. "I know you do. But you signed an agreement." She turns on her heels and sashays from the room.

"Glad she's gone. Stupid woman. I hate this place."

My jaw drops, and I point to the ceiling. "Aren't you worried about the camera?"

He shakes his head. "I disabled it. Made it look like a mouse chewed through the wire. They haven't discovered it yet."

Mr. Sanders is not long for this job. Hope no one will suspect he's told me secrets. I start copying again. "Ten delegates from each state, so you're saying there are seventy people in charge of the whole government. Right? Is there not a head leader?"

"We're in the election process. There's an interim president, and we'll have a permanent leadership installed in the next six months. Maybe sooner."

I note it on my page.

"Miss Lamb, I suggest you read chapters six through ten in your textbook and prepare for a quiz tomorrow. You're dismissed."

"I don't have a textbook yet. They said you'd give me one."

He hands me a thick document bound by a plastic binder. Alliance-written, Alliance-issued. "Here you go. Now you're dismissed."

"Wait. Can you at least tell me why? My whole world has been turned upside down, and I don't understand any of it."

"Isn't that the truth?" He picks up a manila folder and rifles through it. "You know as much as I do. Maybe more. We had that chemical spill. The President was shot, and all of the sudden everything went haywire."

"But what went haywire?"

He walks over to the door, closes it, pulls another chair up to mine, and lowers his voice. "Here's what I know. One day I was a teacher at a regular high school, and the next day I was told to show up here. They held me at gunpoint and gave me two choices—take this job or find another state. I can't afford to uproot my family, so here I am."

"Why are you telling me this? Won't you get in trouble?"

Shrugging, he laughs. "Maybe. But some people believe in the resistance. Do you?"

"You're not making any sense."

He stands and pushes the chair back into the row. "You need to leave now, and we can't talk of this anymore. You're a smart girl. You'll figure it out."

He grips my arm so tight I can still feel it when he lets go. I wince as he ushers me to the door, opening it a sliver. "You'd better not come into my class unprepared tomorrow, young lady. Do you hear me?"

When he swings it open wider, he faces the camera and gives me a slap on the shoulder.

I glance up and down the empty hall. "I'll do better tomorrow. I promise."

As I round the corner to the stairwell, Maggie falls in step. "How was tutoring with the Sandman?"

"Weird." I show her my notes. "He gave me a bunch of extra chapters to read and said I'd have to take a quiz over them. Alliance history and stuff." Like the Alliance is old enough to have a history.

"I had to do that last week."

I raise my eyebrows. Did he tell her secrets, too? So many questions I want to ask, but I try to think of something safe. "How long have you been here?"

She touches each finger on her left hand with her right pointer finger. "Um… about two months. Before all the crazy national chaos." A sudden sheen fills her eyes. "My parents died. I had nowhere else to go, so I did summer school. A friend helped me get in so I could have the scholarship."

"Oh. Sorry to hear that." I reach for her shoulder to hug her, but retract when she pulls away.

"I'm over it now. No use in dwelling on the past when you can't change anything."

"What kind of scholarship?"

She inspects her hair and teeth in the glass door of the dorm lobby. "The scholarship is for anyone who completes the program. You can get your entire college paid for, but you have to go to an Alliance College. All you have to do is complete the whole program."

"Wouldn't you have had your college paid for anyway if your parents died? I thought you'd qualify for grants."

"In the US, maybe, but here? I don't know. I was scared, and this seemed like a good way out."

We walk up the stairs to my bedroom, and Maggie holds vigil at the dorm window while I try to work more math problems then pause. "Hey, can I ask you something?"

"Sure." She rubs at a spot on the window with her sleeve.

"Did you know anything about the Alliance before you got here? Like had you been told anything?"

"No, why?"

"I was just curious. Mr. Sanders thinks I should already know all this stuff."

She spins, hoisting herself onto the windowsill. "They never tell us anything." Her legs swing, bumping against the concrete wall in a rhythm. One, two, three-and-four. One, two, three-and-four. "Hey, do you want me to do some of your math for you? Our handwriting is pretty similar, and I already finished mine."

My jaw drops. I'd have never considered cheating at my old school. Well, I guess maybe if I had cared about how well I did in class. But now, with a beating hanging over my shoulders... "Well, I guess so. If you want to. But... What can I do to pay you back?"

Maggie laughs. "Just you being here is enough. It's nice to have a friend. None of the other girls ever want to talk to me."

I can understand why. Maggie is dangerous. She straddles the fence, staying just on the edge of compliance. I work on my English as she races through the math problems. When the siren rings for supper, my homework is finished. We eat, do our chores, and slide into bed by nine.

My door opens a crack, and I try to hold my quivering hands steady under the sheets. Two sets of footsteps tap the ceramic tile, stopping by my bed.

"I'd hoped she'd be awake," says a high-pitched male.

"We can rouse her if you'd like, sir." Reva pulls the covers away from my neck, exposing my gray Alliance-issued pajamas.

The man coughs. "It's not necessary." His voice trails. "She's beautiful like her mother."

Mom? My heart jolts. I clench my jaw, forcing myself to lie still. Where is Mom? Does this man know? Why would she want to send me here?

"She's transitioned very well. Look, she's completed her homework. She's a hard worker."

"Of course."

Cold fingers brush my cheek. I shiver and blink. The man doesn't seem to notice. He twists a lock of my hair and lays it gingerly against my shoulder.

"We should go before we wake her," Reva says.

"You're right." He sighs. "Perhaps I should come tomorrow."

"Give her some time. Tomorrow may be too soon."

Moist lips touch my forehead. Chills surge through my veins. Cool hands tuck the blanket up around my neck. Disgusting.

"I'm not sure I can wait."

Chapter Six

THE MYSTERY MAN doesn't return. Anticipation keeps me from sleeping, though when I do, I dream of escaping and returning to Dad. For two weeks, I've woken early, starting earlier than the last. Today, when I enter the bathroom, the digital clock reads 4:00 a.m.

I'm ready and waiting in line for breakfast before anyone else, but I can't stop yawning. After scarfing my food down, I race back to the dorm to finish my chores. Maybe I can sneak in a nap before class.

"I think you're starting to get the hang of this place." Maggie's reflection appears out of nowhere. Or maybe I was just too tired to see her approach.

Turning my head away from the camera, I sneak a grin. "Yeah, I've been first in line to the showers twice now. And I've had my chores done early every day this week."

Maggie glances out the restroom door into the hall. "Reva's coming. Not such a big deal for you, I guess. She likes you."

"Nah, she just likes that I work hard. If you worked harder, she'd leave you alone, too."

Scrunching her nose and twisting her lips, Maggie prances over to the sinks and starts wiping them out with a paper towel. She's jealous, and she should be. Reva has stopped caning me since I suggested cleaning the grout with baking soda and peroxide.

The cane appears in the doorway before Reva does. "Maggie, your bed isn't made. Hurry, five minutes until inspection."

Maggie ducks out of the cane's reach, runs past Reva, and jets out the door.

I scrub even harder.

"If you keep this up, you aren't going to have any hands left." Reva leans her cane against the sink. "It's cleaner in here than it's been in thirty years."

When I give her a forbidden quizzical look, she kneels to meet me at eye level and places a light hand on my shoulder. "I grew up in this church," she whispers. "Glad to see someone take pride in it."

She shifts her eyes toward the camera, which watches everything but the inside of the stalls, and gives my shoulder a light pinch. I yelp, though I don't feel anything.

"Get back to work, girl."

Her sudden transition piques my curiosity, but I cannot press her further. I pick up a toothbrush, and she goes down the hall to harass someone else.

I don't mind. Cleaning has become a safe retreat from my academic routine. Here I fantasize about escaping. Notes, study, clean, quiz. Notes, study, clean, quiz. Day-in and day-out, we start at 5:00 a.m. and learn until 5:00 p.m., and then chores until they send us to supper and bed.

The warning siren rings. Ten more minutes. I poke my head out the back door to dump the water. Farther down the hill, several students shout and run outside one of the male dorms.

"Help!" A boy runs up toward the cafeteria, where the dorm supervisors are huddled together. "Ben's not breathing!"

The supervisors follow him and crouch around a crumpled figure. One shakes his head and enters the dorm, returning a minute later with a sheet and a camera. He snaps a picture and then covers the body. Someone else yells up the hill for the students to quit gawking.

Reva blasts by me out the door, running faster than I thought she could. She stops short a few feet away, meeting another supervisor.

"What's going on? Who is it?"

"Ben Wilhelm. They think he's dead."

Ben Wilhelm. My arm hairs stand on end. I just met him yesterday.

She straightens. "I don't understand. He was fine just a couple hours ago."

"Mike says alcohol poisoning. He caught him with a bottle two weeks ago after his home visit."

Reva pivots, casting a glare toward the church. She speaks through clenched teeth. "You know, Mae, they're tainting it now, just like they did back in the prohibition." She tries to whisper, but her voice carries. "Hank told me they're spraying cannabis and tobacco fields with poison, too, but the owners are desperate and selling it anyway."

Mae shakes her head. "I don't like any of this. Not at all. Not even a little bit."

"The Alliance is not going to be pleased," Reva says. "We should call the officers. And his parents. What will we tell them?"

"I don't know. You'd better do another quick check before inspection. You guys are first today, I heard."

"Great." She takes a step toward the dorm, and I hustle back to my room to get ready for my classes.

As I unlock the door, I try hard to hold an expressionless focus, but my head throbs from my pounding pulse. A line from an old song pops into my head, about being prisoners of our own device. Did this boy know he'd risk death by sneaking a drink? Did he wish to die?

Tears sting my dry eyes as soon as I close my door. I've got to get out of this place. I slip fresh tights over my aching knees and grab my book bag.

"Last call for chapel." Reva's hollow voice echoes.

I walk with her to the church. When we enter the stark white auditorium, I join the other students in a somber row of submission.

Art, the chapel leader, launches into the routine of chants.

"Beyond the azure, beneath the dome, from sea to land we make our home." I mouth the words. The boy next to me is loud enough for both of us. "We live to serve; we serve to live. To fellow man, our all we give." Meaningless dribble.

When we finish chanting, Art launches into a twenty-minute tirade about respecting authority. Sure, whatever. But I hold my shoulders back and nod like everyone else.

Other than the memorization of Scripture, it's nothing like my old church. We memorized all the time. When I was five, Dad decided our youth group should enter a Bible bowl competition. He put together two teams, sticking me on one as the fourth player.

Dad never thought I'd do anything but fill the space, but I memorized the entire book of Ephesians word-for-word with the rest of them, and we won. The judges made me recite it, not believing such a small girl could know so much. After that, we went back every year, and I learned all four gospels, the prison epistles, and the book of James. Now, the Alliance wants us to memorize censored chapters, and I'm starting to forget the full ones.

I can't pretend I was a perfect Christian before this, but at least I knew what I was supposed to be. Other students have no idea. The Alliance has reduced our faith to impossible-to-reach virtues—thou shalt not smile, thou shalt not frown, thou shalt not ever have any fun.

At the end of Art's sermon, we stand and raise our Bibles—the thinner Alliance version. Even though all the books are there, some have fewer chapters and verses, and there are additions. We study passages related to things like respecting authority and acts of kindness and service, but there are no lessons about God or Jesus, and no mention of salvation.

"And now," Art flips pages, "the Book of James."

I keep my face trained on his. In my head, I recite what I can remember of the first chapter before chanting with the group. The

Alliance version starts with verse two and leaves out the part where James calls himself a servant of Christ.

Consider it pure joy, my brothers and sisters, when you face trials of many kinds…

Yeah, right. This place brings nothing like joy. I think of Ben's stiff body, motionless on the sun-scorched grass. Not joy. Fear and death.

A double-minded man is unstable in all his ways…

They skip the part about patience from Christ.

Art holds a colorful comedy/tragedy mask in front of his face. "In our time before the Alliance, we were faltering. A divided country with two missions, destined to fail.

"In six short months, we've started reducing teen pregnancy, cut back on heart disease, and made great strides in helping our citizens overcome their vices and addictions."

Overcoming vices. Yeah, by poisoning people. Wonder how they cut pregnancy. Did they kill the babies?

A screen lights up behind him, showing a large graph. "We've forced restaurants to stop contributing to obesity with portion control. As you can see, even in this short time, our nation has lost a staggering ten percent of our body weight. We'll be forgiven for gluttony and shine anew in our disease-free world."

He advances the slide. "Further, we've lost twenty percent body weight at our school. Look around at your thinner selves, conquering obesity one healthy meal at a time."

I knew they were controlling our portions, but where were these numbers coming from? As far as I know, I've never been weighed. Looking up at the cameras, I shudder. Talk about Big Brother.

Art resumes the recitation, skipping to verse twelve. I struggle with this one, because the cut is in the middle. "Blessed is the one who perseveres under trial," I call out in chorus. *For when he is tried, he shall receive the crown of life, which the Lord promises to them that love Him.* "Every man is tempted. Do not err, my beloved brethren."

Ben's stiff face appears on the screen, framed by a bed of grass. The students gasp, myself included.

"Consider your brother, a son who erred. Look at what happened to him."

At the end of my aisle, Reva clenches the back of a pew.

"Don't make the same mistake!" Art flips through several slides of drugs, beer, and people having sex. I glance at Maggie, who has narrowed her gaze at him. Her fists clench and nostrils flare from the force of her breath.

Art bows his head. "Lord and Master, we mourn Ben Wilhelm's tragic death, a seventeen-year-old child who followed the path of sin. We grieve his life, his very existence, and not helping him escape the wiles of alcohol."

And then, bluntly, we're dismissed.

Following chapel, I return to the bathroom for more cleaning, channeling my anger and fear through the scrub brush. Outside the doorway, Reva smacks something with her cane and complains about no-good lazy brats. There must be another new girl.

Every day, my heart tells me to take a stand against this, to turn Reva's cane on her and accept whatever consequence follows. But twice today, I've seen she's nothing more than a pawn. I think of another line from the book of James:

Be quick to listen, slow to speak, and slow to wrath, because human anger does not produce the righteousness that God desires.

I count to ten, then twenty, and then one hundred, until Reva's rant stops and her clunky footsteps fade.

Maggie's size-six loafers plant themselves in front of my brush. "Aren't you going to class?"

"Oh." I grin, bringing my hand up to cover my mouth. "Yeah, I guess so."

We rinse out the toothbrushes and bowl and return them to the closet. "I'm glad you cleaned this out." She points to the alphabetized shelf. "It's so much easier to find stuff now."

"Thanks."

We head to my room, and she helps me knot my hair into a tight braid, giving me pointers so I can do it myself next time.

"It's so dry here." Rubbing her arms, she sighs. "My skin is always chapped."

"Yeah."

"I wish they'd give us something for it."

A jar of salve is in the drawer next to my bed. It appeared out of nowhere a couple days ago. I consider giving Maggie some, but decide against it. I'm getting some kind of special treatment she isn't. But then again, Maggie gets a little snarky with Reva at times, whereas I obey. So, maybe that's my reward.

She finishes braiding. I admire the result, wincing from a pang of guilt. Amber always wanted to teach me how to braid and I never let her. Maybe Ethan's right. Maybe I did shut her out.

"Your hair is so soft, Callie. And I love that shade of brown. Wish mine was more like it."

"It's too wispy." I run my fingers through Maggie's dark, tight curls. "I've always wanted hair like yours."

"It's a pain." She laughs. "Come on, let's go."

The sirens sound. We finish, taking a moment to run by Maggie's room for her books. She grabs them, and a folded paper drops to the floor.

I bend to pick it up. Before I can see, she snatches the paper and tucks it under her mattress. Thank goodness there are no cameras in our rooms.

"If anyone asks, you've never seen that." Her eyes narrow. "It's a mess you don't want any part of."

"I don't understand. What is it?"

She grabs my arm and drags me into her closet, leaving a small crack so we can see. "Let me enlighten you." Her voice drops to a whisper. "Sometimes students disappear."

"What do you mean, disappear? Escape?"

"Officers come in and drag them away, one at a time. Rumor has it they go to some place for torture. And even worse, sometimes they come back…different."

Maggie whispers a name—Becky—a girl who never associates with anyone. One of the first to eat and shower, she heads straight to her chores after meals, and she locks herself in her room during free time.

"And the paper? What is it? How did you get it?"

"It passed through a few hands." Maggie averts her gaze. "It's a message from someone I thought could help me get out of here. They can't. But I keep it because I hope maybe someday..."

I hug her. "It's okay. I think about that, too. We're seventeen. Almost old enough to graduate. Maybe then we'll find a way back to the US."

"I hope so. I hope the US will still be standing by then."

I grab my left shoulder with my right hand, squeezing my uniform sleeve. Relaxing my hand, I hold it over my heart, remembering. I pledge allegiance. One nation, under God. "I hope so, too."

She sniffles, and blots her eyes with her sleeve.

"You know, there are verses missing from the Alliance Bible. My dad used to read this one to me all the time—I can do all things through Christ, who strengthens me."

"Christ?" Her brow scrunches tight.

"Jesus. Our Savior. Don't you know?"

"Oh, the Christmas story. Right."

I place a light hand on her shoulder. "More than just a story. His promise makes this all worthwhile. A place He's preparing for us. No sorrow. No tears. No abuse."

She pushes the closet door open and grabs her books. "We need to go."

We run through the door without incident, Reva nowhere in sight. Outside, we step in the path of a brunette, who runs toward the dorm, panting. I dodge her and start uphill to the church.

"More officers." Maggie points to the parking lot. "You've been lucky. They haven't been here in a while. But there are a lot of them today, so watch your step."

We separate, taking our places in the crowd and shuffling toward the classrooms. With best posture, I keep my face forward and expression blank, but make peripheral glances to the edge of the property, where a prison-style fence pokes out from the trees. Who could help us escape this? But the presence of Maggie's note gives me hope. Someone had to smuggle it in.

A white haired officer with a baby face steps in front of me and makes me stop. He presses his nose against my neck like he's trying to smell something.

I jump, and he backs up, laughing. Nice. I can't smile without consequence, but I guess he can do whatever he wants.

"We've got ourselves a newbie," he says to the officer next to him, then turns to me. "Sweetheart, this is just a routine inspection. Nothing to be scared of unless you have secrets."

I lower my eyes, and he lifts my chin. His cheeks stretch into such a wide grin that I almost smile back. I clench my teeth to keep my focus. Could this be a test?

"What's your name?" He pulls an electronic device from his pocket.

"Callie Lamb."

Perhaps I imagine it, but his eyes lose their twinkle. Was he hoping to catch me messing up and saying Noland? He pats my shoulder and moves to the girl behind me. I breathe a sigh.

A scream from my left cuts it short. Maggie. Two officers drag her to a dingy white van.

Chapter Seven

MAGGIE NEVER COMES BACK. With my one friend out of the picture, I focus on schoolwork in the daytime and pray instead of sleeping at night.

Now, I have two quarters under my belt, and I'm pulling straight A's in every class. I have to give the Alliance some credit. The methods employed by the school are heinous, but I feel more prepared to enter the real world than I did as a traditional high school student. I'm considering an engineering degree, something I would have sneezed at six months ago. Doesn't make me hate the Alliance any less.

We're breaking for Christmas, and some of the other students will leave for family visits. Will my supposed real dad come? I scrunch my nose. Doubtful, and even if he did, I don't want to see him.

I curl up in my bed and try to read ahead for next quarter. Tears keep spilling on my history book pages—for Ethan, for Maggie, and for Dad. Maybe even a small tear for Mom and Amber. I stare at a wet drop as it seeps into a heart shape. Did Ethan even notice I'm gone?

Footsteps from down the hall catch my attention. My heart skips a beat, and I dry my eyes on a pillow.

Reva marches in without her cane, dragging a wheeled-suitcase behind her. "Pack a bag. You're leaving."

I raise my eyebrows, but she doesn't elaborate.

"Yes, ma'am."

I scan the contents of my closet, wrinkling my forehead. What will I even need?

"Pack them all, Callie." Her voice is kinder than usual. "Wear the red one."

It reminds me of Dad's dress blues, crisp and stiff, in the back of Mom's closet. Every now and then, he'd wear it to a veterans' program at my school, patting his abs and teasing Mom about not losing his figure after years of her cooking. I grip my collar, my eyes moistening again.

Reva taps her foot. "Speed it up, girl."

She helps me fold my uniforms—gray for day-to-day, white for chapel, brown for outdoor activities, and blue for holidays. Inside the suitcase, I find new stockings and undergarments, as well as a pair of black leather heels.

"You're graduating. Moving up to the next level. Officer training. You'll be awarded more freedoms." Reva gestures to a cart in the hallway. "You can put your things there."

Adrenaline surges through my veins, and I can't hold back my smile. My hand flies to my face to cover it.

Reva laughs. "It's okay to smile, Callie. That rule is for the new recruits. This is a joyful occasion. You've done well."

She stuffs new textbooks into my satchel. "I'll take these back for you. I have to admit, I'm sad to see you go."

At first tentative, and then with confidence, I let a wide grin spread across my face and look up to the sky. Thank God. For the first time, everything makes sense. This place is a military school. Of course the first semester would require hard-core discipline and high, unbendable standards. Be tough as nails. Don't show emotion. It's boot camp. And I'm graduating.

I tuck the last uniform into the suitcase and fight the zipper to get it to close. Reva fixes it. "Stubborn old thing. You came empty-handed, so I brought this one. I'm more than happy to turn it over to you."

"Um... Reva?"

She sits on the bed next to me.

"Do you know what happened to my mom? They said she'd come for me. How could I find out?"

Shaking her head, Reva smoothes my blanket. "I thought you knew." Reva presses three fingers against her lips. "It's not my place to tell, but you'll find out soon enough."

She pushes off the bed and steps into the hallway, closing the door. Puffing my cheeks, I exhale, then run my fingers over the velvety red skirt. I trace the silver trim before shimmying out of my gray one. The jacket is like the ones the officers wear, with small round buttons and two pockets at the waistline. Come to think of it, Maggie didn't have one like it in her closet.

It's smaller, and more fitted than my other uniforms. My eyes widen as I catch my reflection. I was skinny before I got here. Though I've gained some muscle, I've lost a lot of weight. More than I needed to. In this uniform, I look like a heroin model.

I examine the dingy room one last time before stepping out to the hall, dragging the suitcase behind me. Reva waits, and I study her wrinkled face. "Can you tell me anything about my new school?"

"You won't go there at first. You'll have to do the graduation ceremony. But when you get there…"

She frowns, nodding to the camera. "You'll still be monitored, of course. You'll have more down time, and you'll be permitted to go a few more places with friends."

"That's good. Will the classes still be on the quarter system?"

"Yes, and you'll get to take some skill courses. Are you interested in archery? Or maybe shooting?"

I raise my eyebrows. Using weapons? "I guess so."

"Weightlifting, of course."

"Of course." Because all teenage girls should study weightlifting. "How far is the facility from here?"

"About ten miles." She escorts me to the end of the sidewalk where a black van waits. The other students trudge up and down the hill in their gray uniforms to lime green buses, dragging suitcases behind them.

I hesitate before the van. "Am I the only one graduating from here?"

Reva nods. "Callie, you're special. Don't let anyone ever tell you otherwise." She surprises me with a tight embrace, pressing her face close to my ear and whispering. "Please forgive me for being unkind. Here, we all play roles because we're powerless. But you—you have power. His power. Go, save your mom. Save us all. Make your dad proud."

Save mom? Disconnected, I feel like I'm watching someone else climb into the van and slide into the seat. What does she mean? I have no power.

Behind the wheel, a blurred hand waves and tells me to buckle up. The click of my seatbelt sounds far away. But wait… Reva knows Mom. And his power—whose power? Dad's? Does she mean my real dad or this new one?

The driver coughs, and I examine him out of the corner of my eye. He's stiff, just like the students were in the cafeteria. No chance of conversation. I keep my focus on the trees and pavement.

In less than ten minutes, we arrive at a facility identical to the one I just left, except the façade boasts decorative trim. Two boys in red uniforms usher a group of adults through the full parking lot and into the church.

When we stop, a young female officer escorts me into the church to a room on the right side of the pulpit. There, about ten girls sit while their mothers make them up and brush their hair.

"Are you excited?" A blonde girl smiles at me. "I've wanted to be baptized for two months now."

"Baptized?" I cock my head to the right. Two brunettes give me emphatic nods. "I've already been baptized."

One of the mothers stares at me, her lips pressed white.

"Me, too," says the taller brunette. "It's going to be a lot easier this time. They use confetti, so we don't even get wet."

A baptism without water? Does Mom approve of this?

The door flies open, and she bursts in, beaming.

My jaw drops. Guess she does approve.

"Callie!" Her face is lit up like I've never seen, and her long, wavy locks have been twisted into a regal braid. Porcelain skin shines beneath soft, creamy foundation, and high cheekbones frame her face behind a bronze-colored blush. The red suit she's wearing resembles mine, but with gold and purple adornment.

"How are you? Have you been well?" Her eyes are shiny, but glazed.

This is what I get? She's been missing for months, and she wants small talk? How could she think I've been well? Heat surges through my veins like acid. I rub my thumbs over my fingers like that would quell it.

Deep breaths. I can't afford to lose it here. "I've been… worried." Lie. Can she read it in my eyes? I've been furious, heartbroken, and torn.

Lifting her doe-eyed gaze, she reaches for my hand.

I jerk away. "Why did you leave us, Mom?"

She pulls a handkerchief from her inner jacket pocket and dabs at her eyes. "He said it was time."

"He who? And time for what?"

She reaches into her shoulder bag, releasing a whiff of strong, floral perfume. "I'm so sorry I couldn't tell you. But I had to go."

"Why? Did you leave us for money?" Though I'm whispering, the other girls cast curious glances. Mom takes my hand and leads me into an inner room, closing the door behind her. She sits me in a chair, spreads the contents of her bag on a counter, and begins dabbing my face with a makeup-covered sponge.

She swipes foundation across my forehead. "I need you to be patient, and I'll explain."

"You left Dad for another man." No way will I be patient. How long have I waited for these answers? I grip the chair arms tight then release them.

Looking at the floor, she lets out a slow breath. "I dated him a few weeks while Martin and I were separated."

"What?" Rubbing my hands over my velvet-covered arms, I search her face. "Why now? Why, after years of happiness with Dad, you go back to this man?"

She dips a blush brush into a copper powder matching her own cheeks and swirls it on my face, her eyes focused on the ceiling. "There was never happiness with Martin."

Never? My chest hardens, and a headache spreads across my temples. "Did you apologize to Dad?"

"No. Be still." She paints my lips a glossy red.

"Who is this other man? They said he was my real father. How? When?"

"Adrian Lamb." Her shoulders slump. "We had an affair. About eighteen years ago. The timing was right."

So matter-of-fact. Is she even sorry? "Dad is my father." I struggle to keep my face muscles from twisting into a scowl. Through clinched teeth, I press on. "Tell me why you sent me to that horrible school. Why are you making me do this?"

"To prove my loyalty. Callie, please don't let me down. The consequences..." She trembles as she paints shadow across my eyes.

I draw in a deep breath and hold it for a few seconds. "I don't understand this baptism. Doesn't it go against everything you've ever taught me?"

"Oh, sweetheart." She cups my cheek and kisses my forehead. "Please, trust me and in a few days you'll understand."

I fold my arms over my chest. "I want to understand now."

Mom sighs and fusses with my hair. "Well, you're now in what's called the Alliance of American States."

"Tell me something I don't know."

Her jaw sets. She gives me her I-mean-business look. "Your father is the front-runner for President. I'm going to be the First Lady. You'll be First Daughter. I need you on my side in this."

My face muscles go slack.

"Close your mouth. It's not ladylike."

I clutch the top buttons on my uniform, pulling the fabric tighter around my neck. "You want me to convert to a new religion so you can be a president's wife?"

"Let's just say I've been enlightened." She smiles, but it seems forced. "One day you will be, too."

"Do I get to meet Adrian? When will the election take place?"

This time, she makes a more deliberate motion with her eyes toward the ceiling. I look up at another ever-present camera.

Leaning even closer, she brushes her lips against my earlobes. "I can't tell you more, so please don't ask. I did this because I love you."

Another woman pokes her head into the room. "It's time, Ella."

"Soon, Callie. Soon you'll understand. Be patient." She leaves me.

I stagger out of the room. Was she talking in code? She's been enlightened? Or threatened into compliance like everyone else around here?

The mothers have left, so I join the other girls and fake a few giggles, though I can't understand their excitement. After a few more minutes of intolerable bursts, a bearded man shuffles us onto the stage with several boys. We form a semicircle around an imprint in the carpet where a pulpit once stood. I'm the only one dressed in red.

To either side of the stage, behind a curtain obscuring them from the audience, four men point military rifles at our heads. I glance at the girls, whose shoulders have tightened. Their faces are now somber. Are they scared? Were they just acting excited for the cameras?

The bearded man faces the crowd and grabs a microphone. "Ladies and gentlemen, we welcome you as witnesses to the Redemption of these wonderful young men and women. Have a look at them." He waves from one side of the stage to the other, like we're animals in a circus. I'm tempted to bow just for spite, but the other students remain still, so I do, too.

The crowd breaks into a roar, waving and jumping. Catcalls, shouts, and even bullhorns blare, just like high school graduations back home. Not appropriate behavior for a baptism.

The bearded man cuts them off with a wave of his hand.

"Children, raise your right hands."

We do.

"Repeat after me." A wide smile crosses his face. "I pledge allegiance…"

"I pledge allegiance," we repeat.

"To the flag of the Alliance of American States."

"To the flag of—"

A bullhorn drowns the rest of our chant. Officers swarm a pudgy man wearing a hooded sweatshirt. Three officers make a big show of dragging him out of the room.

"And to its alliance," the man continues, "for which we stand."

I snort. Could this government not even come up with an original pledge?

"From one nation was born two," the bearded man says.

I open my mouth to repeat, but clamp it shut as everyone else hushes.

"Our magnificent country suffered great contention, one our leadership ended by agreeing to divide to pursue our respective interests. Six states, bound as one, walking in unity toward a better America—an Allied America!"

Six states? Weren't there seven? Stifling a gasp, I raise my hands with the other students.

The crowd erupts in cheers.

The man pivots and points to us. He stops at me. "This group of students, our first Alliance graduating class, symbols of our new beginning. Their lives stretch out before them as…"

His words mean nothing, mere babble to placate the crowd. When he finishes, someone hands him a velvety black bag with gold trim like his robe. "Please, kneel."

We do.

He walks to the student at the far end of the stage. "State your name."

"Adam Shepherd."

The man reaches into the bag and pulls out a handful of confetti. Small pieces spill to the wood floor, glittering as they fall. He sprinkles them over the boy's head and bows with a princely flourish. "I declare you redeemed, through the power vested in me by these Allied States of America."

Adam stands. The crowd goes wild.

In the balcony, a tall, thin man with thick black curls watches me through binoculars. He wears a tooth-baring smile and a crisp white shirt. Mom stands next to him. His uniform matches hers. Adrian, no doubt.

Student by student, the bearded man leads us through the ceremony, and I fidget, waiting for him to get to me.

"Callie Rae Lamb, I declare you redeemed."

He didn't ask me to say my own name. Noland. My name is Noland. Like the other students, I rise, take a step back into the line. My heart pricks as I remember Matthew 10:33. Does this count as denying Christ before men?

A voice inside my head tells me it does. I consider taking back my words and screaming out what I know Dad would want me to say. I'm redeemed by the Blood of the Lamb. If I decry the Alliance, will I be committing suicide right here on stage? Is my soul ready?

My eyes travel again to the balcony, meeting the gaze of the man claiming to be my father. Beside him, guns are trained on a hooded figure, whose tawny hair and catlike face peek out. Amber.

Chapter Eight

THE MOMENT we leave the stage, I escape the other recruits to the lobby, making a frantic search for the balcony stairwell where Amber stood. A woman shouts for me to stop, but I run from the crowd, straight into the bulky chest of an officer.

"You can't be in this part of the building." He sweeps me over his shoulder with one arm and carries me back to the recruits, but not before I see my sister's handcuffed, hooded figure.

Pounding my fists against his back, I wriggle against him. "Amber!"

She turns, meeting my gaze with glistening eyes. The officer sets me down, blocking my vision with his bulky shoulders.

I try to look past him, but he moves with me. "I need to help her."

He puts his hands on my shoulder and forces me to face the recruits, who somehow remain expressionless. "You're not permitted to fraternize with prisoners."

"But she's my—"

"You're not permitted." He nudges me into the line of recruits.

They start walking down the long hall to the front of the building, and I fall into step. Officers herd us like cattle into a side room reeking of antiseptics. A long row of chairs, the kind you'd see in a hair salon, line the right wall. Next to each chair stands a small table, covered in an assortment of tubes, bottles, plastic gloves, and tissues.

"Sweet, we've earned our tattoos," says one of the boys. I think I heard someone call him Caleb. His voice shakes. Wonder if he really means it.

"Ugh," a girl answers. "Do we have to?"

"If you want to be redeemed." Caleb hops into a chair and takes off his uniform jacket.

I sigh. I'm not crazy about the idea of getting a tattoo, but who knows what could happen to Mom or Amber if I don't.

"Take your seats. Please. And remove your coats." A thin woman with burgundy hair links arms with a gangly boy and drags him to the far end of the room.

The other recruits rush to the reclining chairs. With drooping shoulders, I hover beside the closest one. As I slide across the leather, a bald guy with way too much facial hair kneels beside me. "My name is Levi. I've had the pleasure of doing most of your father's ink, and I'm honored to do yours."

I squint at him. He means Adrian. Not my father. No way. "So what do I have to do?"

"You get to choose one of three designs—the star, the heart, or the caterpillar."

"What do they mean?"

"Unlike fifty stars for fifty states, the single star represents the unity of the Alliance. The heart represents the blood shed for the cause."

Blood? Whose blood? Not choosing the heart, that's for sure. "And the caterpillar?"

"It represents metamorphosis and bravery. Being willing to do whatever is necessary to incite change."

The boy in the seat next to me winces as his artist inks the tattoo gun.

I pull my teeth over my lower lip, tugging away some of the skin. It smarts, but nowhere near as much as that needle will. "The caterpillar." The smallest one.

"It's going to go right here." He touches my neck a couple of inches above my right shoulder. Twisting my hair, he secures it into a tight bun. "Stay still, and this will all be over soon."

While he shaves invisible hair and disinfects my neck, I stare at the ceiling. *Lord, forgive me. I hate what I'm doing here, but I don't know what else I could do. I don't want Mom or Amber to get hurt. Or me. Please, help me find a way out of this mess.*

I repeat the prayer dozens of times, focusing on the swirly drywall pattern surrounding a large, white vent.

Levi presses a piece of paper against my skin, moistening and rubbing it.

My eyes drift to his. Blue. Warm. Twinkling like Ethan's. I imagine it's his lips instead of Levi's fingers, kissing me in that spot the way I'd seen him do to Amber so many times. Which is stupid. It's not like he ever loved me.

"There. I've made a faint mark. Would you like to see?"

Clutching the chair, I exhale. "No. Just get it over with."

Levi starts prepping the inks and needles and whistling a melancholy tune. Like a gospel song. "I'm ready now." He meets my gaze. "This is going to sting, but it won't take long."

As the needle penetrates my skin for the first time, I squeeze my fingernails into my palms and stretch out my toes. Tears spill. They run over my nose, wet my hair, and drip onto the leather. I close my eyes and take deliberate breaths.

The tattoo gun's constant vibration soon numbs me. Or, at least I don't feel the intense sting any more. True to his word, Levi finishes within a few minutes and rubs a bit of ointment over the skin. He applies a bandage and pats my shoulder. "All done."

Footsteps clack behind me, someone in heels. "Oh, Adrian, we're too late." Mom.

"Which design did she choose?" Adrian's voice, higher-pitched than I expected, drips with honey.

Levi holds up the card with the caterpillar. It quavers in his hand.

"Excellent." Adrian sucks in his breath, whistling as he exhales. "Exactly as I'd hoped."

More footsteps, and then Levi heaves a deep breath. They must be gone.

I wait on a velvety couch. Before me, the other recruits' faces twist in various stages of pain. The whirring guns rattle my nerves. Gradual conversation replaces the mechanical hums as we await the last recruit's tattoo. A freckled boy, he wails as the needle pierces his flesh for the first time. When he's finished, we move in stoic silence to the bus.

Twenty minutes later, the driver drops me off at a wrought-iron gate inside a chain-link fence topped with razor wire, identical to the one surrounding the school I just left. None of the other recruits are asked to leave the bus, so I drag my suitcase down the steps and bump it against the curb, making a yellow paint stain on the black plastic. The bus pulls away, and I puff my cheeks.

"Welcome, Ms. Lamb."

Ms. Noland.

An older man with kind eyes greets me, taking my suitcase. We walk toward the main entrance. He gestures to a small crowd of students standing in front of a dorm down the hill from a plain brick church, and I join them.

"Deja-vu." I shake my head. Even the parking lot is shaped the same.

"Different faith, same builder," says the girl next to me, following my gaze to the enormous steeple. She tucks her pixie-cut blonde hair behind delicate ears. Mom would call her cute-built and peppy.

"I'm Sara."

"Callie." I stifle a yawn and blink a few times. "Do we get free time soon?"

Sara chuckles. "We do. We get two hours here. The last school, we got thirty minutes."

"Let me guess. Monongahela."

"Oh, Callie. You poor thing. You don't know much about this place, do you? All the schools are part of the Monongahela Academy."

"How many schools?"

"Ten, as far as I know. Two for every high school grade, two middle grades. But there are probably more."

My neck itches, and I raise my hand to scratch it, forgetting the tattoo.

"I see you've been redeemed."

I cringe beneath her sarcastic tone.

"Yeah." Smoothing my skirt, I take a step toward the dorm, and she tags along. I follow her lead, forgoing my rigid posture and letting my shoulders slump. Questions form in my mind—what does she know about the Alliance? Does she know who Adrian is? Does she know who I am? Perhaps questions better kept unasked. "How long have you been here?"

"Two years. I'm a senior." Her chest puffs. "I've been here since the place started, and I've never worn a red uniform."

When we cross the threshold into the dorm lobby, an auburn-haired woman greets us, her face stoic. She extends a stiff hand, and I shake it, wincing as she squeezes the life out of me.

"Hannah."

My eyes flit between hers and Sara. Is she telling me her name? Does she think I'm Hannah? "Um... I'm Callie."

She gives me a curt nod. "Your belongings are in room 217. Melanie, your roommate, should be in soon."

Sara snorts. "Lucky draw."

"Sara. You may retire to the thinking room for the evening."

"But, Hannah…"

"Go!"

Sara skitters down the hall and ducks into an open doorway.

"You'd think she was six instead of seventeen." Hannah sighs. "She's friendly, but not a friend. You'd be well advised to not follow in her footsteps."

"Yes, ma'am."

"You'll be getting a schedule in the morning. For now, you'll need to change into your gray uniform and report to my office for your chore assignments." She points to a room at the end of the hall. "If you ever need me, I'm always there."

When I find room 217 and close the door, I sneak a smile. Hannah doesn't rule with a cane.

A few minutes later, a plain-looking girl appears wearing our standard-issued bathrobe, same as what we wore at the last school. Wet hair hangs past her hips, and she flips it around, slapping me with it.

"Ow!"

Her eyes widen. "Sorry, I was looking for my sash." Clutching her robe with one hand, she extends the other. "I'm Melanie."

"Callie."

"Welcome to paradise." She giggles. "They said you've just been redeemed."

My heart aches. "I didn't get a roommate at my last school."

Melanie dashes to the closet and shoves her uniforms to the right, leaving about eight inches of space on the rack. "You can hang your stuff here. I spread mine out since it was just me."

My suitcase is in the corner. I glance at it and shake my head. "Maybe tomorrow."

"Oh." She appraises me, wrinkling her nose. "You might want to at least change stockings before we eat."

I look down and lift my skirt. A snag runs from mid-thigh to the tip of my shoe. "Okay... Anything else I should know?"

"Ask for extra vegetables. Don't eat the chicken or pork chops. They're always either bone dry or halfway done."

She bounces out of the room before I can answer. At least the students seem a little more upbeat than my last school. I change, then dig through Reva's suitcase, looking for new stockings. In one of the pockets, I find a pamphlet.

The Last Edge of Freedom. Must be Reva's. I pick it up, planning to tuck it back into the suitcase pocket, when the author's name jumps out. *Published in 1995 by Martin Noland, Ph.D.*

Dad. The pamphlet falls to the floor.

A quick glimpse shows me it's a tract like the ones they used to display in our church. Why would Reva have something like this? And from Dad? Had he managed to contact her somehow?

When I bend to pick it up, I sneeze, rustling the floor dirt under the bed. Guess I know where I'll be cleaning first. As the warning bell rings, I stuff the brochure back into the suitcase and slide into the fresh stockings.

Supper and chore time pass like always, except we're released an hour early and given time to meet together in a game room. Sara sits in at a table with a big chessboard.

When I walk past, she grabs my arm. "Sit. Play with me."

"I don't know how."

Melanie tugs at my other sleeve. "Come on, roomie. Let's go see if they have any hot chocolate." She snickers. As if.

I meet both their eyes. Melanie's look earnest and Sara's hopeful. I hate to disappoint either of them, but I've got plans. "Maybe tomorrow. I'm still tired from the ceremony."

As soon as I get to my room, I sneak another look at the tract. Dad never told me he'd written anything like this.

He comments on Mark 12:17, suggesting there's a fine balance between giving back to Caesar and giving back to God, and the two are sometimes mutually exclusive. He concludes that we fight for freedom so we can maintain the right to worship according to God's will, and if we lose sight of the goal, we'll be forced back into persecution.

My mind goes to Reva with her cane. Isn't that what I just experienced? What would have happened if she'd caught me quoting those scriptures cut from our Alliance-issued Bibles? But at the same time, she seemed to be in her own battle for freedom. She asked for my forgiveness. Would she have maybe let it go?

In closing, Dad quotes the line that's haunted me since I left the Redemption ceremony. So simple and to the point—*As the great Apostle Peter said in Acts 5:29, we ought to obey God, rather than man.*

I hear the footsteps two seconds too late. A freckled hand snatches the tract from mine, and locks of auburn hair spill over my shoulder.

"Where did you get this?"

Turning, I meet Hannah's blazing green eyes. "I found it in my suitcase. I don't know where it came from."

She rips the tract to shreds, tearing my heart as she does it. I've waited so long to feel a connection with Dad again.

Her eyes narrow, and she scans the rest of my room. "I'll need you to come with me while we search your luggage."

My heart screams to refuse, but my lips just manage a quiet "Yes, ma'am." I follow her down the hall to a small, dark room.

"This is the thinking room." She holds open the heavy wood door, revealing nothing but a single wooden chair. "You'll have to stay here until tomorrow morning, then and you may resume your schedule."

"But I haven't received my—"

"You'll begin chores at five a.m. We've assigned you to the kitchen." She taps her fingers against her forearm. "Do you need the restroom?"

"Yeah."

She points across the hall to a tiny bathroom with scarcely enough room for a stall and sink, let alone a person. I squeeze in and try, but it's futile. I'm sure I'll need to go in about twenty minutes and I'll have to wait. I think I'd prefer the cane.

Taking a couple extra minutes washing my hands, I study my reflection. My tattoo has gone from itching to burning, a constant reminder of my spiritual weakness.

When I step out, I'm rubbing it, and Hannah pats my arm. "I can give you relief for that."

I jerk away, narrowing my eyes at her. Why the sudden kindness? How can she be so calm about assigning me hours of torture? I don't need her sympathy. "No, I'm fine."

She nudges me into the straight-backed wooden chair. "Suit yourself. Someone will be back in two hours to give you a five minute break." She shakes her head. "I told you not to follow in that girl's footsteps. She's going to pay for her bad influence."

When Hannah lets go, the massive door slams shut, engulfing the room in cave-like darkness.

Chapter Nine

MY STOMACH growls, and I cross my legs, wiggling with an intense need to use the restroom. Hours of darkness, tears, and prayer have passed. Dad's words have played over and over in my mind. Fight for freedom. But how? Taking even the smallest stand would lead to pain, torture, or death. But maybe that's the point. Accepting the pain, standing tall through the torture—these things I can do until I can take a bigger stand. I brush away tears and press my back deeper into the splintery chair. I've got this.

Hannah jerks the door open, flooding the room with light. "Come on. I forgot about you. It's almost lunchtime."

I blink, adjusting to the light. My fists clench and I stand. She forgot me? How dare she! Rushing past her, I dash to the bathroom. I don't care if it makes her mad.

When I come out, she hands me a gray uniform and sends me to the bathhouse to shower and change. I glance at the dismal tile. Could be worse. I might have been on my knees scrubbing all day.

After dressing, I hurry up the hill. Hope there's still food.

The all-seeing camera swings from one side of the cafeteria to the other, aiming at the entrance as I walk in. Its steady blinking light denotes the seconds as two officers move through the room, pausing every few moments. Bright sunlight streams through the tall glass windows, a stark contrast to the thinking room's utter darkness. I bathe in its warmth.

Sara waves from the back of a long line of students, and with an unsteady gait, I cross the room to join her. She's okay. *Thank you, God.*

One officer I recognize—the young, white-haired one who'd made fun of me at the first school. He's winking at me. Bet he's trying to get me to mess up and show emotion. Fat chance. I square my shoulders, aiming for surer steps, and the hairs on my arms stand on end.

When I reach Sara, I wrinkle my nose, trying not to smile. Still plenty of food. Blessed again.

The officers make a wide sweep of the room, and I hold my breath when they get closer. I grab a Styrofoam tray and a cup of peaches. My hands tremble so much the tray snaps in two and peaches spill on the dirty tile floor. Great.

I set the tray on the counter and grab a handful of napkins. Kneeling down, I clean my mess as fast as I can.

The cafeteria lady accepts my broken tray, tossing it in the trash behind her. She hands me a new one. "Would you like grapes? We have extra today."

"Sure."

She drops four plump ones on my new tray, and I point to the salad. "That, too, please, and the ham. No, wait. The fish."

Sara giggles, drawing a sharp glance from the cafeteria lady. "Stop," the lady whispers, serving a steaming fish fillet on my tray.

We head to the nearest table. After setting down our trays, we plant our feet, although my wavering skirt betrays wobbling knees. Splinters from the wooden table dig into my clammy fingers. I press harder.

The officers move so close I smell the blend of their colognes, one woodsy and the other sporty. When they pass, I read their badges—Officer Caudill, the white-haired one, and Officer Henry.

"You may sit," Henry says in a deep, booming voice, and everyone obeys.

As I lift the fork to my mouth, Sara draws in a sudden sharp breath. I glance at her from the corner of my eye.

A slight draft moves in behind me and the barrel of a military rifle presses hard against her long, thin neck. Static hairs cling to the black metal.

The cafeteria bustle dies. Students freeze in the aisle next to us. A boy sneezes and a grape slips off the edge of his tray. It rolls across several tiles and lands next to my shoe. I debate for a second and then pick it up and drop it on my napkin. Cleanliness is next to godliness, after all.

Henry, the taller officer, a bulky blond with a close-shaven beard, steps over to me. He squeezes my shoulder so hard tears well in my eyes.

I try to hold correct posture, scrunching my nose and pinching my lips to keep the tears from escaping.

He stiffens and then tugs my uniform collar. "Here she is. This is the one."

Caudill gives him a curt nod. "The other girl is right beside her. Our lucky day."

"You'll need to come with me," Henry says.

Why do they want us? My stomach gurgles and I cast a disdainful glance at the tiny fish fillet still steaming on my plate. As I scoot backward, I snag my stocking on the seat's rough edge. Awesome. Another reason for them to be upset with me.

Henry prods me and Sara out of the cafeteria. When we reach the hallway, he points to me. "The other girl is insignificant. But this one… Her father wanted me to be the one to question her."

"Sure, whatever." Caudill shrugs. "I've already done her paperwork."

Paperwork? Question me for what? The pamphlet?

An older man ushers me into a nearby classroom and I sit in one of the rickety wooden desks. The harder I try to be still, the more it squeaks, and the more he stares at me, saying nothing. Behind his head, an analog clock ticks agonizing seconds. After an eternity, he leaves.

My stomach growls and I can't stop yawning. I memorize every detail of the faded paisley wallpaper and count the thumbtacks in the corkboard. The inside of my cheeks become raw from chewing, and the taste of blood mixes with my saliva. What do they think I've done?

The two officers return, bumping shoulders at the door and drawing a snarl from the older man who trails in behind them. He grabs my chin and jerks it upward. "Yes. This is the one."

Glancing at Caudill, he gestures to the door. "James, go help. Hannah said she's a spitfire, and he might need an extra hand to restrain her."

A scowl flickers across Caudill's face before he walks away.

Henry pulls an electronic tablet from his pocket. "State your name."

Instead of responding, I glance at the door Caudill left ajar. I consider bolting. Pointless, I'm sure.

"State your name, young lady." The old man's voice is flat and robotic. Dark eyes peek out from under bushy gray brows.

I stretch to appear taller. "Callie Rae Noland."

"Try again." Henry types with one finger and then swipes across the screen.

Huffing, I shake my head. If he knew, why did he ask? "Callie Rae Lamb."

"Age."

"Seventeen." Like everyone else in this school. Duh.

"Status."

"Redeemed..." *by the blood of the Lamb.* Even though the words form in my mind, I can't make myself say them. Not yet.

"Status." The older man's voice raises a notch.

"Once Redeemed by the Alliance." What I was told to say. Lifting my hair to show them the tattoo, I squeeze my tongue with my teeth.

Henry leans in close. His breath reeks of coffee and I struggle to keep from gagging. "Well, well, Ms. Lamb. Your father must be proud of you."

I draw a deep breath. "I haven't heard from Dad in months, not since I was kidnaped. Does he know? Did someone tell him?"

Henry's face contorts into a deep snarl, and the older man digs his bony fingers into my wrist.

"Your real father." Henry brushes dust off his suit. "Communication with anyone from your past is forbidden." He pats his rifle.

I shudder.

He smirks. "Your father wishes you to join the Alliance Special Forces. You'll be attending the Second Redemption ceremony this afternoon. It's all been arranged."

"I… I just did the first ceremony a few days ago. Why so quickly?" Could joining give me more power to take a stand? Or would it mean selling out? What would Dad do?

"You have thirty seconds to choose." Henry points to the old analog clock. "It's Redemption or jail. If you choose Redemption, you'll be the First Daughter upon your father's election. If not, you'll be in exile like your sister."

"Jail?" I picture Amber, standing in the balcony with military rifles pointed at her head. Did she get this choice? Was she offered the chance to be First Daughter and chose jail instead? What if he's not elected?

"Twenty seconds…" The older man puffs his chest.

Henry removes handcuffs from his belt loop. If I go along with this, maybe I could save Mom and Amber, like Reva said.

The old man taps his fingers against his thigh. "Ten."

"Okay, fine." My chin quivers. "I'll do the Second Redemption."

"Excellent." The fingers still.

Henry drags me through the foyer, across the parking lot, and to an old rusty van bearing the official mark of the Alliance. Strange. You'd think they'd transport their intended First Daughter in a new vehicle.

A scuffle. Screams. Just like Maggie. I turn.

Two of the male dorm supervisors drag Sara out the door.

Caudill follows. He moves to the van and opens the sliding door. The men shove Sara forward, and Caudill averts his eyes.

My heart sinks, but I can't stop watching.

She bucks and kicks as they force her into the van and secure her to a steel bar with handcuffs, like Agent Wiseman did to me. When they start to shove me, Henry shakes his head. "Not this one. She agreed to the Redemption."

So Sara didn't? Was she offered?

Caudill's eyes widen, but he clinches his jaw. Maybe he is like Reva, a prisoner to the cause. He meets my curious gaze with a hard stare. Maybe not. "Her father will be pleased. Let's get on the road."

My stomach rumbles again. "Can I get something to eat before we go?"

Henry scowls. "You can eat later."

A maroon sedan with tinted windows pulls up behind the van. Three identical ones follow. Henry leads me to the third car and shoves me into the seat. A black plastic divider separates me from the front. The tinting is so dark I couldn't see out if I wanted to. It doesn't matter, anyway. The view is the back of Henry's head, rows of trees, and abandoned buildings. Blah. When the door closes, I rest my eyes and lean against the cold, leather seat.

This drive takes longer than the last one, and the silence is reminiscent of the thinking room, other than the engine's slight whir.

When we stop, Henry opens my door and I step into a frenzy of scuttling men and women wearing suits and dresses.

"Your First Daughter!" Henry shouts, and the bystanders applaud, waving election signs with Adrian's face. Henry clasps my left hand and lifts it high over my head, shielding the bright sun from beating down on us.

When he lowers it, four bulky men surround us on either side. Bodyguards? This is getting ridiculous. He drags me down the sidewalk, and I stalk every step, clanking my shoes against the city sidewalk.

Empty storefronts hint of life before the secession. Several in a row advertise going-out-of-business sales and complete liquidation. The Alliance insignia covers signs. Shadowed by the placards in one store, women sit at desks typing on computers.

A poster catches my eye, the same image in the newspaper at Michael's house—the woman with the babies. A chain has been drawn around her neck, attached to two humungous black spheres releasing smoke coils. On the ground, a third sphere, full of money, is engulfed in flames. Jagged letters scratch across the bottom of the picture. Five prophetic words: the Alliance will destroy everything.

They already have.

Henry snatches the poster from the window and dumps it into a nearby trashcan. "Don't stop moving. We'll be late."

Though the faded displays and broken windows tempt my gaze, I keep my focus on the sidewalk and follow Henry several blocks to an old brick church. Could things have changed so much in six months? I remember the mass exodus of West Virginians to Kentucky after the chemical spill. Who remained to fight for these people? Where was the US military? Michael mentioned people losing federal aid. Maybe Reva had no choice but to take a job where she had to abuse kids.

The arched facade boasts stained-glass windows. Large red banners bear white crosses and Icthys reading Worship The Lord.

Did they intend to keep the symbols? Do they even know what they mean?

As we walk up the steps, another officer holds the doors open and frowns. "She's not dressed."

"We'll get her dressed." Henry tugs me across the threshold, yanking me face to face with Adrian.

Chapter Ten

"HELLO, CALLIE."

The man who claims to be my father stands two feet in front of me, with a grin so wide it splits his face. This guy, with the gelled-up curls, is Mom's Prince Charming? At least he's dressed for the part—although his purple sash bulges out like a fanny pack.

Behind him, two officers hold military rifles at a diagonal across their chests, the tips of their guns coming even with thick, gold shoulder pads accentuating Adrian's ivory jacket. The statuesque officers watch my every step.

The mingling crowd stills, and Officer Henry pinches my arm. Guess I should speak.

"Adrian." My firm voice carries, drawing sharp glances from the people in the lobby.

He engulfs my stiff frame, squeezing my folded arms so hard my chest hurts. Weird. He appears much weaker. Through the sash, cylinders rub against my ribs. Pill bottles? Judging from his hazy eyes, yes. "My sweet daughter. Please, call me Dad." He squeezes again. "I have waited so long for this moment."

A murmur passes through the men and women. Dressed in their Sunday best, they lean to each other's ears and cast me smiles.

"She resembles him," a woman exclaims. "Such a beauty!"

Frowning, I free myself of his grasp. "I—"

"Don't be nervous, dear." He cups my chin with bony fingers, drags them to the tip, and pinches the tiny cleft matching his own. "Why don't we go somewhere more private?"

My brain recoils like he's wiped hot acid all over my chin. I jerk backward, catching the shoulder of my uniform on a protruding nail, loosening a piece of the faux-oak paneling.

As it clatters to the floor, Adrian pivots with a cheesy wave and starts upstairs. Henry pushes me forward, and I tumble a few paces. Gripping the old, wooden rail, I ascend slowly, nausea growing as the distance between Adrian closes again.

Teal carpet covers the small landing and continues into a long hallway. Adrian points to a room two doors down. "Let's join your mother, shall we?"

I shudder, but square my shoulders. "Where's Amber?"

"She couldn't make it." He draws in a deep breath. "Ella!"

Mom bursts into the hallway, a vision in an ivory silk dress covered in sheer layers of lace. Springy curls and small lavender flowers frame her face. Makeup blanches her skin, punctuated with rosy cheekbones. Her downward curling mahogany lips jut in a pout. A dress, identical to the one she's wearing, dangles over her thin, fragile arms. Bet it's my size.

Dashing to her side, Adrian squeezes her hand, his knuckles growing white from the pressure. "You were right, dear. She did come."

"Bow," Mom hisses, through clenched teeth. "Show your father respect."

I bend my knees and bow my head, and Adrian claps. "She's so polite."

Is this guy for real? Mom smiles and bats her eyes at him. She's never given Dad such adoration, at least not to my knowledge. Guess it makes sense she'd have an affair.

Mom shows me to a restroom, and I change. The gown drapes loose over my chest and stomach, but she twists and pins it into shape. She braids my hair and paints my face, and by the time she finishes, my reflection is more Amber's than my own. My heart stops. Amber has Adrian's cleft chin, too.

We emerge, and Adrian claps again. "Oh, beauty. Beauty!" He grips both our hands and leads us into a hospitality room, decked out with long tables of finger foods and appetizers, albeit the healthy kind the Alliance serves. "Maybe eating will ease your nerves." He points at a whole-grain cracker topped with light cream and a cucumber slice.

"No thanks. I'm not hungry." My stomach growls and I sigh. "Well, maybe a little."

"I hope you'll accept my deepest apologies, sweet daughter, for not making contact years ago." He fills a plate with vegetables and sits on one of the high-backed canvas chairs lining the room. "If I had known the truth..."

"Oh, Adrian, I'm such a thorn in your side." Mom twists the huge diamond on her ring finger, her lower lip protruding. For a moment, she stares as if waiting for him to validate her. When he doesn't, she turns to me. "I wasn't sure until we did the DNA test a year ago."

"I was sure." Adrian chuckles. "You had my nose."

This is Dad's nose. Isn't it? And Grandma Noland had a cleft in her chin. Maybe Dad even has one under that beard. I touch my face, tracing a finger between my eyes to my lips. Our profiles are similar. "Can you explain why Mom abandoned us?"

Mom grimaces.

"It's fine, Ella. The girl has questions. It's natural." He pats the couch beside him, and I sit as close to the opposite arm as I can.

"Your mother and I worked in the same law office." He punctuates each word with a snarl, as though it's a terrible memory.

Snapping my head toward Mom, I gasp. "When?"

"Not long. I was a secretary, and then I decided to go back to school. Your da—" Mom rubs her hand across her forehead, but straightens at Adrian's sharp glare. "Martin and I dated a few years before that, and then I met your father. Sadly, we split, and Martin and I reconnected. We married a few years later."

Adrian links arms with her and smiles. "And then we found each other eighteen years ago. Nine months before you arrived."

An older woman enters carrying a bucket with iced champagne. She pops the cork, sets it on the table, and nods to Adrian before backing out the door.

"Why did you disappear without telling us?" I pop a cucumber into my mouth and chomp it loudly.

"Callie!" Mom shakes her head. "I'm so sorry for her poor manners. I taught her better than this."

I swallow a scoff. She's made more outbursts in front of me than I've ever made.

"Ella, calm down." Adrian scoots closer and drapes his arm over my shoulder. I get a whiff of his cologne—a nice, oceanic scent. At least there's one thing to like about him.

"Callie's entire world has been disrupted. Cut the girl some slack." He releases me, approaches the table, and pours champagne into three fluted glasses. Smiling, he offers me one.

Is he trying to poison me like Ben? No thank you. I raise my eyebrows at Mom, but she averts her gaze.

"Please, drink," he says. "A toast."

"I thought alcohol was forbidden."

Mom pinches my arm. "Champagne is permitted on special occasions in small quantities."

"Is it poisoned?"

She glares, and a flicker of annoyance crosses Adrian's squirrelly face.

"Fine." My lead arm resists as I reach for the glass, imagining Dad's disapproving eyes. Maybe I can get by with a tiny sip.

Mom accepts her champagne, and the three of us stand together in a triangle, though it's clear who is at the head.

"To my beautiful girls." Adrian touches his glass to ours, a serene smile crossing his face. "May you always be mine."

Shivering, I lift the glass to my lips and take a small sip. Wonderful and curious. Tiny bubbles dance through my nose and throat, and though it's sour and bitter, a bit of sweet lingers.

No. How easy would it be to slip into this world? I set the glass on the table next to me.

Adrian shakes his head. "Oh, come on. Drink up. Calm your nerves."

"I…" Amber advised me to do the same. "Um… "

He hands me my glass. The corners of his lips upturn into a slight smirk. "A few small sips won't hurt you."

Adrian guides the glass to my mouth, and I part my lips. When the bubbles hit my tongue, I close my eyes. Though the first sip has yet to hit my stomach, the room starts spinning. Is it tainted?

"That's my girl."

Mom clears her throat. "We'd better hurry. It's time for the ceremony to start."

We return downstairs where Henry waits, stoic, except for his flinching jaw.

"You are my daughter's sponsor?" Clasping his fingers behind his back, Adrian puffs his chest and examines Henry's rigid face. "I trust you've prepared her."

"Yes, Lord."

I gasp so loud people on the other side of the lobby turn their heads. Lord? Is he kidding?

A tall, thin Abraham Lincoln-type man approaches and grasps Adrian's hand with both of his. "Congratulations on your victory. We will all be blessed under your service."

Adrian nods. "Go ahead. Get her inside."

Honest Abe shows me to a cushy pew in the crowded auditorium

Henry slides in beside me. "The ceremony will be quick." He hands me a plastic card on a lanyard, and I slip it around my neck. "You'll make your oath, pledge your loyalty to the Alliance, and then go to training school for a few weeks."

"And then?"

"Most recruits go back to their schools. When the Alliance needs you, they'll call for you."

"To do what?"

He points to two young boys wearing uniforms like his, except blue. "Spy. Punish. Proselytize."

A portly man in a green velvet robe approaches the pulpit and waves us all to silence. Guess he hasn't been on the Alliance diet.

"Welcome to the Second Redemption," he says. "Welcome officers, families, and new recruits. We have gathered this day for these young men and women to dedicate themselves to serve our great new world. If the recruits will come forward, please."

Henry nudges me. "Go on."

I ease out of the pew, smoothing my skirt. Wayward wisps of hair tickle my cheeks as I advance toward the pulpit.

We gather on steps at the front of the stage, a group of lanky, awkward teens with sweaty brows and trembling knees. They're wearing velvet; I'm wearing silk. Reva was right. I'm different.

The robed man opens a leather book and turns over the first page. "Repeat after me. I, state your name…"

The boy next to me takes a deep breath. "I, Lucas Evan Sparks…"

"I, Callie Rae No…" Biting my lip, I scan the crowd for Adrian. He gives me a curt nod. "Callie Rae Lamb…"

The girl to my right speaks, and I allow myself a deep breath. Once we've all stated our names, the robed man lifts the book again.

"Now this part you'll all repeat together, like your recruiter coached you."

Henry gives me a smug wink. Jerk. He never even considered coaching me.

"I do solemnly swear I will uphold the ideals purported by the Alliance of United States."

We repeat, although my voice is strained.

"I pledge my allegiance and loyalty to their cause and vow to obey the laws and officers who guide me."

I meet Mom's eyes as I stumble over the words.

"I accept the Alliance Creed as the true word of our Lord and Master, and vow to honor the words therein."

Lord and Master? Swallowing, I bite my lip. I can't do this. Mouthing the words, I pray they can't tell I'm not saying them.

Military guns point at us from all angles. There are truths in the Alliance Bible. At least I'm not swearing it to be the complete Word of God. I swallow and repeat. It's better than getting shot.

"I will not add to these words or take away from them, and I will defend them at all cost."

My eyes burn. When we finish our oaths, a large screen lowers from the ceiling. Adrian's image appears, his dark curls contrasting his pallid face. His cold, hard eyes pierce mine and his clenched fists seem to be coming off the screen at me. How did I sell out to this man?

Another recruit reaches for my hand, and we raise our arms above our heads, forming an intertwined circle. According to the robed man, we're showing our unity to each other and the Alliance. Wonder if I'm the only one who's in it for survival.

Following the ceremony, Henry disappears before I can ask him what to do next. The other recruits say goodbyes to their families. I hover at the edge of the stage and examine a fraying electrical cord. The robed man starts walking in my direction.

My chest tightens. I rush down the stairs where the two young ushers are waiting.

"Your father sends his regards," says one. "He was called away."

"Would you like to go on out to the convoy?" the other asks, revealing a dimple with his smile.

No. I do not want to go on the convoy. I want to go home to my dad.

The usher's brown hair is soft and wavy like Ethan's. My cheeks grow warm as I imagine my fingers tangled in it. "Yes."

"Come on." He escorts me outside to a sparkling white limousine, parked before a green bus. "Did you bring any luggage?"

"I wasn't permitted to." I'm sure they'll redistribute my belongings and trade them for contraband since I'm so important.

Amber would laugh at me calling myself important. Where I felt terror, she would have felt excitement. Even with her flaws, I'm sure she refused to publicly embrace Adrian's doctrine. I haven't stood up for anything.

I settle in the back of the limousine, and we arrive at the training facility within minutes. Faded orange brick covers an old emergency room drop off. The hospital sign still hangs over the door.

The recruit bus pulls behind us as I'm getting out. Women escort us into the facility this time, which is unusual for the Alliance. Like the officers, they wear red suits with gold trim, although they are in skirts instead of pants.

The unadorned women have twisted their hair into loose braids. My hand flies to the gold chain I've worn since my fourteenth birthday, a gift from my grandmother. So far, no one has asked me to remove it, but I slip it free from my neck and tuck it into my pocket. Tonight, I'll hide it somewhere. I grimace. I thought I'd die before giving up my faith, too.

One of the women steps away from the rest. "Do not speak unless spoken to. Girls to the left, boys to the right." She points to a table where more women sit. "Register, gather your toiletries and uniforms. Shower and go to bed. Be up by four."

After my turn at the table, I'm directed to a college-aged girl who holds a card bearing my name. She's tawny like Amber, freckled with a missing front tooth and a faded bruise on her forehead.

"This will be a great experience," she says. "Life changing."

Doubtful. I eye her injuries. "When did you first get here?"

"Six weeks ago."

She opens the door to my room, which is much larger than I'd expected. Several pieces of dormant monitoring equipment surround a hospital bed. A couch, dresser, desk, and bookshelf cozy up the remaining space.

The girl pats my arm. "The first week is worst. Don't fight the leaders and try your hardest at everything. You'll be fine."

Down the hall, I hear a scream. Same old story. Different setting.

Chapter Eleven

SQUEAKS FROM my brand new sneakers echo down the long hallway, drawing the other recruits from their rooms. Their faces bear furrowed brows, twisted snarls, and slivered eyes. I hate the attention, but Adrian has insisted I wear the shoes.

When Amber started dating Ethan, I felt invisible and loathed it. I'd give anything to feel invisible again.

Numbers on the digital clock above my doorway flash. Still twenty minutes until chapel and I've already finished my chores, so I sit on the bed and wiggle my toes against the stiff leather.

"Callie Lamb?"

Noland.

A raven-haired man walks through my door. Adrian? No, can't be. He's identical down to their too-narrow eyebrows, tight curls, and wispy beards, but this man has a smooth, narrow nose. Closer examination reveals other slight differences—a shorter chin and a rounder face. Is this a purposed look? So weird.

I lean against the stiff plastic headboard. What now?

"Callie?"

"Yes."

"Your mother is downstairs. I've come for your things."

Stealing a glance at the calendar, I frown. "Thought I had to stay three more weeks..."

The man shakes his head. "Not anymore. Your father won the election."

Another dark-haired man, also with a strong resemblance to Adrian, pokes his head in the doorway. "We've got the boxes. You go on and take her downstairs."

The pile of gifts from Adrian teeters in the corner. Poor guy, he'll be moving my stuff all afternoon.

My forehead, bruised from a training accident, aches as I squeeze it. "What's going on? The election wasn't supposed to happen for three more weeks."

"Circumstances changed." They both say it at the same time.

"The other candidate withdrew," the first one finishes. "And the interim leader is stepping down for health reasons."

"Oh." I chew on my pointer finger. Did Adrian cause the health reasons? "Well, I'll go find Mom."

She's waiting in the lobby with a red velvet dress draped over her arm that matches her own. Guess Adrian wants to make us twinzies again. Behind her, an army of men and women wield makeup brushes and salon equipment.

I retreat a step, almost preferring the riflemen.

They shove me into a side room, coming at me from all angles to change my clothes, tug and pull on my hair, and scrub my face and nails until they deem me perfect. When they finish, Mom drags me to a limousine, and we climb into the back, alone at last.

Mom presses the button to close the window between us and the driver. "You're beautiful." She sits across from me. "Like me when I was a teenager."

"Thanks. Where are we going?"

"Adrian's Inauguration. They're swearing him in as President." She smiles. Is it forced? "You'll become First Daughter today."

Swell. "Isn't there supposed to be time between an election and an inauguration?" Tires squeal as the car moves forward, and I brace myself on the door handle, pressing my back into the slick leather seat. "Are we in a hurry?"

"We need to make an hour drive in forty-five minutes. They took too long getting you ready." She twists a gold band around her left ring finger. "Adrian will be furious."

"Are you married to him? Did you ever even divorce Dad?" The pitch of my voice raises enough to shatter windows. Clearing my throat, I lean toward her, my lips pinched together so hard it hurts. "What about me? Are you worried about me being furious? Because I am."

"Callie, I…" She reaches for my arm, missing it as I jerk away from her. A tear rolls down her cheek, carrying a black streak of mascara. "The last thing I ever wanted to do was hurt you. Or Martin."

Yeah, right. I slide a few inches closer to the door. "Did you ever even love him? You said you were never happy with him."

"I had to say those things. Adrian was listening. And I didn't lie. I loved Martin then, and I still love him." Mom dabs her eyes with a tissue.

"Martin and I dated when we were younger. I went out with Adrian a few months after that." She folds the tissue and pats her cheeks. "In college, I rekindled with Martin. Then..."

My gaze darts around the limo ceiling, where the thick foam cushion could obscure a small microphone. I shiver, and mom places a light hand on my wrist. "No surveillance here. Adrian is adamant about his privacy. We can talk."

"Tell me why you didn't tell us you were leaving."

She taps pointy red toes together as if counting off seconds. Or perhaps excuses. "Because I'm a fool. Adrian has this strange power over me. I keep trying to end our affair, and he's… persistent."

"And?"

"He met me after work; he often did. He'd slip into the van, hide in the back, and wait with chocolates or roses. Always the gifts, and

I always struggled to explain to your dad where they came from. I looked irresponsible, as if I'd spent the money on myself when we didn't have it. I think he suspected, but he never questioned." Another tear spills and she sniffs, long and hard before heaving a labored breath. "I've hated what I've done to him, but I didn't know how to stop."

"So Adrian kidnaped you?"

She shakes her head. "I chose to go. I sent a message to Martin, but it must have never been delivered." Sighing, she wipes a tear from her cheek. "Running away sounded exotic."

She buries her face in a fresh tissue, soaking it with tears and mascara.

I hand her another. She waves it away, reaches into her purse, and pulls out her familiar paisley makeup bag.

"What about Amber?"

Mom straightens her shoulders and a tube of mascara rolls off her lap. It drops to the limo floor and rocks between her pumps. "She's in a rehab facility where she needs to be. They caught her stealing Adrian's medicine and trying to sell it."

"She's Adrian's daughter, too?"

"So the DNA says."

I glance at my reflection in the window. It's like meeting Amber's eyes, so it makes sense we should have the same father. "But Amber favors Dad."

"I know. For so many years I was relieved. I thought things worked out because you both share so many features with Martin. But I guess it was coincidence. Adrian looks a lot like your father." She digs in her purse and retrieves a Ziploc bag with an ivory lace scarf. "Here. This was your grandmother's. I want you to wear something today to remind you of who you are, to make you feel protected."

"Wow." Thinking of Grandma's necklace, hidden in the toe of my shoe, I slip the scarf out of the plastic bag and drape it over my shoulders. "Did you divorce Dad? I can't believe he'd agree to it."

Mom sighs. "I did. I served him the papers, and when he didn't respond, the judge granted a default judgment. He didn't have to agree."

"I miss him." Folding my arms across my chest, I send Mom the stern look she used to give me when I misbehaved. "Do you know he sobbed when you left? He cried until he was hollow. You destroyed him and took away everything he loved."

"Adrian did that."

"You chose to go. You did it."

She bows her head, bending almost double. Her shoulders shake and the bag clatters to the floor, spilling colorful pencils and powders onto the pristine beige carpet. "I did.choose."

"Leave Adrian. Apologize to Dad." I rest my hands on my lap, interlocking my fingers. "Explain everything. He'll take you back."

She lifts her head and locks her gaze on mine, her eyes growing wide, wild. "Don't ever talk like that again. Adrian would kill us both."

She's right. Part of me wants to scream at her, but it would be like screaming at a small child. How do I discern the victim side of her from the irresponsible side? I rub her shoulders until jagged breaths turn into even ones. At the end of the day, she's still Mom.

When she's calm, she picks up the spilled cosmetics and retrieves a pack of facial tissues. Wiping away the makeup removes all traces of her youth, exposing wrinkle lines around her tight-lipped mouth and swollen, red eyes.

"Oh, Mom. You're a mess."

Laughing, she reaches below the seat and grabs ice from a small freezer. "Let me show you a few tricks, sweetheart. If you're going to be in Adrian's world, this is a survival skill."

She clutches the ice in her fist for a minute and then brings cold fingers to the outer corners of her eyes. Moving to the inner corner, she dabs them with a tissue and holds the ice another minute before doing it again. After several times, the puffiness diminishes and the red blotches fade. A mirror drops down from the ceiling when she presses a lever, and her breath condenses when her reflection meets my eyes.

"Now, concealer…" A twist of a brown tube reveals a yellowish liquid. Mom dabs it over her entire face and smooths it with a wedge sponge. "Hides everything."

I snort.

"I know. Ridiculous now, but wait." She twists cap after cap, pours liquid from bottle after bottle, dabs powder after powder. It's like she's trying to cover years of pain instead of ten minutes of tears.

And it works. Her reflection transforms from a tired, blotchy middle aged-woman to the princess Adrian desires. Remarkable, but then Mom has always been able to make beautiful things from nothing. I smile, and she does, too.

"You're thinking of your Winter Fling dress."

"Yeah, I still can't believe you made it from a curtain—like Scarlet O'Hara." I reach for her hands. "Before today, I wasn't sure if we were on the same side or not. But I'm with you, Mom. We will find a way out of this."

"We will." She squeezes my palms. "And we'll free Amber and get you back to your dad."

"Can we pray about it?"

Mom bites her lip and turns her face from me. "Pray to yourself. I don't think I can pray anymore. God wouldn't listen if I did. I've made so many mistakes."

"We both have."

We're quiet the rest of the trip. She touches up my makeup and brushes out a couple of imperfections in my hair. By the time we arrive, my stomach has settled, and my resolve has tempered to steel. Adrian will pay for destroying my family.

We step out of the limo onto a tarmac runway, where men in dark suits lead us to a waiting plane. A thin, peppy woman glides forward, her waist-length braids bouncing with every step as she ushers Mom to the front area. "Ella, you're going to have to change again. Adrian wants you in dark olive."

An older woman whisks me to an ivory couch. Across from it, a tray of fresh broccoli and an Italian-style dip await. "Eat," she says. "You might not get another chance for a while."

An hour after we finish, the plane lands, and we approach a dark sedan. The ever-present suited men keep a close distance. "What about Mom?"

"She'll meet you there. We're crossing to the hotel."

In the distance, Mom stands on the tarmac, her shoulders slumped. Her white gloves cover her face. The peppy woman offers another dress, this one a brighter shade of green.

Mom shakes her head, and they shout for a few minutes before the peppy woman strikes Mom's cheek. Armored men move in on her, and she accepts the dress.

I'm nudged into the sedan, and as I slide into the seat, the driver turns to wink at me—the same white-haired officer who'd been at my school.

"Hi, Callie." He faces forward and presses a button. A glass panel begins rising, separating the front seat from the back.

I meet his eyes in the rearview mirror before the glass closes.

"Martin says be patient and have faith."

Chapter Twelve

"CALLIE, MY DEAR!"

Adrian runs toward me, knocking me backward with his enthusiastic, almost childlike embrace. Not very fitting for someone about to rule our little nation.

Four stone-faced men in dark suits follow.

"There's so much to tell you." Adrian clasps my white gloves and drags me past several double doors to a spiral staircase leading to the second floor. People lean on the railing, crowded so thick they're almost tripping over each other, and he casts them a disdainful look. "We don't have any time."

"I've been told." Shivering, I tuck my hands under my grandmother's lace shawl and rub both arms. I should acknowledge his victory. "Um... congratulations on the election."

My voice sounds flat, and I'm sure Adrian knows I don't mean it. I miss Dad. He'd be so disappointed. He might not even recognize me. My once-scrawny arms are now muscular, and my dull brown hair reaches my waist. Brushed to a shine, it scarcely resembles the tangled mess I used to wear. Thick makeup obscures the fading bruise on my cheek, and fake curves fill out my red velvet dress.

When I was young, I used to daydream about being a princess, hoping Mom and Dad would buy a big palace. Adrian's ritzy hotel is a poor substitute.

He points to a stage jutting from the second floor between the stairs, supported by six thin cables. Glass surrounds it on all sides, bulletproof, I'm sure. Three high-backed chairs form a row behind a large podium. "We're going to walk the entire circuit," he says. "I want you to shake as many hands as you can. When we come full circle, we'll move to the stage and give our speeches." He smacks his lips. "I trust you're prepared?"

"Yes." All three lies of it. "They've already walked me through a practice run."

"Oh. Of course." He gives a dismissive wave, and two of our bodyguards back away a few steps.

Across the room, Mom waits, also surrounded by several stone-faced men. She's breathtaking in her silky green gown and shimmering tulle lace. Adrian's face lights up and she beams.

"I'm proud of you." Adrian slaps my shoulder, knocking me a couple steps forward. I wobble on my three-inch heels and touch his arm to steady myself. His smile widens. Guess he thought I was being affectionate. Sorry, dude.

"Thanks." I lock eyes with a dark-haired boy about my age. His appraising gaze darts between me and Adrian before he turns away.

"They said you passed every test with flying colors." Adrian chuckles. "Did you know that phrase relates to ships and their flags? To show your colors is to show your true allegiance. I'm pleased you've placed your allegiance with me."

Sure, I did. My nose itches, and I'm dying to scratch it, but the makeup would ruin my pristine white glove. Instead, I draw a few calculated breaths, as if I can ease the tickle with the air.

Adrian reaches for my hand, and I let him take it, though bile floods my throat. He pulls my arm close to his chest, again making me wobble on my heels.

Releasing my arm, Adrian draws back as if he's holding a military rifle and pretends to fire. "I heard you beat everyone in sharpshooting. Elliott says you're the best semi-auto shooter he's ever taught."

"I was okay, I guess." I suppress a scoff. I was terrible. Missed every target, got a million bruises from the recoil… I did kind of redeem myself by the end, but I didn't beat out everyone else. Did Elliott say that? Or is Adrian making things up?

He grins. "You scaled the wall in less than thirty seconds with no grips."

Now that, I did. My little fingers fit in the mortar grooves, where others might have struggled to find a grip. And I had motivation. I was tired of being the worst student there, tired of the abuse.

The room erupts in applause, and a tall, thin man in a white suit approaches the podium.

Adrian nods. "It's time."

We step forward, and the cheering intensifies.

"Ladies and Gentlemen," says the man in white. "We are gathered today to celebrate a monumental moment for our great nation. We've done the impossible, accomplished the unthinkable, and today, we move forward, setting ourselves apart from our American friends."

The crowd roars, and he pauses. "Today I introduce you to our leader. A man, who has served in secret for twenty years—from the conception of this great nation to its fulfillment."

Okay, we get it. It's a great nation. I search the people's faces, expecting stark-raving lunatics, but finding businesswomen and construction workers, professionals in suits and college-aged kids in jeans.

"I introduce you…" The man sweeps his hands across the room, gesturing to me and Adrian. "…to Lord Adrian Lamb, his beautiful daughter Callie, and his graceful wife, Ella."

Please, feet, don't fail me. I accept Adrian's arm and approach the spiral staircase. I'd give anything for my squeaky new sneakers, or even those heavy combat boots. On the first thin step, my pump sinks into cushy burgundy carpet, and I exhale, almost smiling. It's not slick at all. Confidence bathes me with each defeated step, or perhaps I'm encouraged by the cheers. When I reach the top, Adrian moves forward first, and the crowd swarms him, leaving me alone for a brief second before fingers begin clasping me from all directions.

I inhale their perfume and breathe out fear. They touch my dress and hair, and a child even slips under the hem and kisses my knee. His mother chuckles and pulls him away, while several hands brush the backside of the fabric.

I glance at the stone-faced men, hoping they'll send the people back to the railing, but they stare straight ahead as if they don't notice. Pressing forward, I inch closer to Adrian, escaping one group to find another.

The women gush and the men leer, their touches approaching parts of me I consider off limits. Some have rancid breath and lean close to my face. Trembling, I swallow, suppressing the persistent bile. I struggle to keep my footing and maintain my posture.

Adrian meets my eyes and claps. "They love you!"

How can he be so calm?

At the top of the other staircase, Mom receives the same treatment, inching through the circle in the opposite direction. She can't like this at all. Every time Dad as much as draped his arm over her shoulder, she'd protest. "I can't stand it when people touch me," she'd say, and he'd back away, wounded. But if she doesn't like it, you'd never know from her glowing face.

Hours seem to pass before we make our way through the crowd and step into the glass box surrounding the podium. My entire body tremors, and Mom has to steady me.

"They had their hands all over me," I whisper.

"It's a small sacrifice for what Adrian has done for us," she hisses back, though her eyes are soft with tears.

The man in white holds the door open and locks it behind us. Several people press their faces to the glass.

Once in, I can tell it's not a full enclosure, only the sides. For a brief moment, I consider shoving Adrian over the edge. I gasp. Doing so would be suicide, of course, because two sharpshooters have their rifles trained on my forehead, but even worse, it would be spiritual suicide. My heart is hardening, and I don't like it.

Men on hydraulic lifts come at us from every angle, wielding monstrous cameras. If the sharpshooters were to take me out, it would be broadcast on TV, maybe even as far as Dad.

I can hear him now, pleading with me to take a different stand—not a stand of murder, but rather a verbal decrying of the Alliance and their denouncement of certain scriptures. Either way, the shooters are ready, but right now I'd be dying unprepared. My breath catches. Faith has been the last thing on my mind during training. I worked hard to remember scriptures, but stopped praying when I understood God was not going to take away the abuse.

My eyes sting with tears I cannot permit to fall. Branching from my aching chest, tingles of pain span my entire body—arms, legs, even toes. I force air in and out of my lungs, clutching the side of the chair.

Adrian steps up to the podium and waves the raging crowd to calm. "It is my pleasure to address you. I will borrow words from the great George Washington, who stood before his country for the first time, as I come before you today.

"Washington said, 'I was summoned by my country, whose voice I can never hear but with veneration and love, from a retreat which I had chosen with the fondest predilection,' and I feel the same."

Adrian waves his hand again, pausing until everyone has settled. "We have chosen a different path from presidency, establishing a system of Lords, much like those of our forefathers, whose dream was to establish a nation on Biblical principles. May we ever have the freedom to pursue our religious desires without fear of repression."

Yes. Let me have that freedom. Racking my brain, I think of every repentance passage I can recall, which turns out to be a mere couple. But I remember King David's words, begging God to forgive him of his sin to Bathsheba.

Have mercy upon me, O God, according to Your loving kindness; According to the multitude of Your tender mercies, Blot out my transgressions. Wash me thoroughly from my iniquity, And cleanse me from my sin. For I acknowledge my transgressions, and my sin is always before me.

Dare I ask forgiveness, when I'm getting ready to stand in front of this crowd and pledge my allegiance to the very evil that's pulled me into my sin? It's too late to back down now. I've already chosen this path, and at this moment, I can only follow through with it.

Adrian grips the podium and rocks on his feet. "I have chosen the title of Lord and Master because we are a nation of service. As I serve you, so shall you serve me. We are all master and slave to each other, for the like purpose of furthering God's will for our great nation. As they did in Bible days, let us have all things in common, giving without inhibition."

He points to the ceiling, where a net contains clear, sparkling balloons with money inside. At his signal, the net drops. As the balloons glide downward, the crowd dives for them, shoving each other out of the way.

Adrian watches with a bemused smile as one balloon drifts over the railing. A lanky boy lunges for it, toppling over the rail and crumpling in a heap on the first floor. The crowd stills in a sudden, eerie silence.

The boy's neck is twisted at an angle. Instant death. Turning my head away, I puff my cheeks and exhale.

Adrian gazes down at the boy's body and blows him a kiss. "This one, so sweet, such a young, gentle soul, and so willing to die for his country."

"He died for a hundred dollars!" A bulky white-haired man raises his fist, shaking it over the balcony from where the boy fell. "He didn't die for you!"

A collective gasp moves through the crowd as the man touches his shoulder, pulling his hand away to reveal a trail of blood, pooling to the burgundy carpet. Stone-faced men cart him away.

Adrian turns to me. "Callie, it's time. You're on."

Now? I glance at Mom, who gives me a nod. Her eyes are blank, like she doesn't understand what's happened. Like Amber. She's high. How? When?

When I reach the podium, I peer through tears to faces now paralyzed with fear. The sharpshooters are everywhere now.

"My name is Callie Rae Lamb." First line, first lie. "I pledge my full support to my father, Adrian Lamb, and my full allegiance to the Alliance of American States." Second and third. I draw in a deep breath. "May we ever live to serve each other, in the full accordance of Allied Law."

Stone silence meets my speech, rather than applause. I spin and return to my seat, biting my lip and gripping the metal support.

Adrian rushes back to the podium and claps his hands. "My beautiful daughter!" As his gaze moves across the crowd, the audience lets out muted cheers.

He finishes his speech, uttering words that never reach my ears. Then he summons me and Mom, and we stand on either side of him, our hands raised as if in triumph. But it feels nothing like triumph.

This time, when we walk among the crowd, the stone-faced men prepare a clear path. Ten of them, each carrying a military rifle, surround us.

During our descent, I stumble. Adrian catches me, his grip on my arm bringing tears to my eyes. We leave the hotel lobby, walk through the long hall, and out a side door to his waiting limo.

"Take her away," he says, pointing at me. "I can't stand the sight of her."

My eyes widen and my jaw drops. "I did what you asked."

"You're weak." He slaps my face, and I almost laugh. It tingles more than stings. He's the weak one.

"No emotion, Callie. You can never, ever let them believe you are sympathetic to their side. You hear me?"

I lick my lower lip and rub my hands on my velvet skirt. "Yes, sir."

"Take her to the thinking room. Ten days."

Chapter Thirteen

THE HILLSIDE of the school is clear. Chapel time. No one to hear me scream.

Adrian arrives soon after the officers drive me through the gate. Possessed by an unknown force, I take a swing at him.

The officers attack in a swarm. Seconds later, my right eye oozes, and my busted lower lip aches. I can't help but smirk anyway.

Hannah greets us, her stern face flushed. "Go to the bathroom and change." She hands me a gray uniform.

When I emerge, she escorts me to the thinking room.

"You're calm." Her hand trembles. She glances down the hallway where Adrian is yelling at an officer. Does he blame her for my behavior?

I remain silent, my gaze fixed on the wall.

Instead of a painful squeeze, her fingers brush against my shoulder. "You little wretch." She leans closer. "Be patient," she whispers. "A few days."

Sympathy? Hope? When I gape, she snarls. "Don't you realize how many things your father has done for this country?"

Maybe I imagined her kind words. "He's not my father."

"What?" Her eyes widen, perhaps in fear.

"I have two fathers. Martin Noland and God." Footsteps approach. Someone strikes me, but I'm numb to it. A wet drop slides down my neck, maybe blood, sweat, or a tear.

"You pitiful princess. Spoiled, pampered, pathetic. Like your pothead sister." Adrian's voice sounds like Joker from the Batman movies. Wish Batman would come save me.

"Where is my sister?"

"Jail." Adrian coughs.

"I hate you." My fists hurt from clenching.

"Make her miserable," he tells Hannah. "Break her will. But no more visible marks." He sighs. "I'll be back in two weeks to inspect your progress. Perhaps she'll be ready by then."

Ready for what?

Hannah frowns. "Should I send the camera feed?"

Adrian shrugs. "I won't have time to watch it. Keep a close eye on her and report anything strange to me."

They slam the door, leaving me in the pitch-black room with my thoughts. I try to conjure happy ones. A youth rally from years ago comes to mind, the first time Mom and Dad let me ride in Ethan's Mustang. I wore my favorite pair of capris. Ethan put the top down, and a bird dropped on my knee. He thought it was the funniest thing ever. Me, not so much, but I loved his deep, throaty laugh.

I remember another time, when Dad drove the youth group out to the lake for a camping trip and taught them how to pitch a tent. One of the tent pegs popped loose, slamming Ethan in the forehead, which prompted Dad to tell us the story of Jael, the Kenite woman who killed the Canaanite king.

We passed that peg around the whole weekend, dropping it in people's knapsacks and slipping it into their shoes. Whoever got "pegged" had to be last in line for the next activity. The final night, Ethan snuck in the girl's tent to peg me.

He lifted my sleeping bag to tuck it inside, and jumped about four feet when he saw the plastic snake I was holding.

Giggles spread through the tent, and we all leaped from our sleeping bags, whacking him with our pillows.

"Callie Rae Noland! I'm going to pin you down and tickle you!" He chased me out of the tent.

I ran, but squishy mud caught in my bare toes, slowing me down. He wrapped his strong arms around my waist, and pulled me to the ground.

We landed hard, our faces less than an inch apart. I could feel his breath on my lips and closed my eyes. Two seconds later, a huge flashlight shone in our faces. Dad dragged me back to the tent, muttering about how he'd tried so hard to teach me right. A week later, Ethan met Amber.

Dad did teach me right. I know what I have to do. Repent and be faithful. I have to trust God.

I spend hours praying for forgiveness. A few times, I even venture to pray out loud and turn to singing. Hannah pops in at times to bring me food or drink, which I decline, but she never attempts to break my will. By day three, I've decided to ask her about the comments flat out.

When the door opens, Adrian waits on the other side.

He clamps a hand over my mouth and drags me three doors down to a conference room. There, two men sit at a long table with a tattoo gun and several different kinds of paint. They force me into a straitjacket and secure my feet in heavy wooden shoes. Two men in red uniforms stand on either side of the room, military rifles pointed at my head.

I keep silent. It's not time to take my stand.

Adrian retrieves a shiny page from his pocket and shows them an image, a red and white butterfly outlined with thin black lines. "This one." He traces the caterpillar on my neck, making me shudder. "Her metamorphosis will be complete."

I hate that caterpillar tattoo anyway.

While the artist preps his gun, I grit my teeth, keeping my eyes trained on Adrian. He's not dressed in uniform, but rather a plain black t-shirt so tight you can count his abs. Scrawny but fit. Tattoos cover his arms to where his shirt sleeves would end.

Vines snake up his left arm, culminating in an arrow-pierced heart bearing my mother's name. An inked angel covers his right forearm, reaching for a butterfly matching the image on the page.

I stare straight forward until they force me onto a leather table and prop my head at a thirty-degree angle. Then I close my eyes and try to think happy thoughts.

Something brushes my uniform skirt, and then I feel a sharp prick. The now-familiar haze blurs my vision, and my tensed muscles go limp.

My bandaged neck aches when I wake, a throbbing pain pulsing through my veins. I try to raise my hand to touch it, but I'm still restrained.

Adrian leaves, and Hannah frees me.

I sit up, wincing as I twist my sore neck.

"Follow me." Hannah's voice is flat and not quivering.

I trudge to her office. Her wooden desk calendar reminds me it's been ten weeks since I left for the redemption.

She sits across from her computer screen and pulls a chair next to hers. I collapse, catching a glimpse of her monitor, where a long list detailing my Alliance history fills the page.

She scrolls to the bottom of the file. Words form, first the date, next her name. And then, a few spaces.

Sorry for what I said before, Hannah types. *Please forgive me.*

What? Drawing in a deep breath, I resist the urge to crease my brow.

She deletes the words, and her fingers fly with rapid pecks. *I will help you. At midnight tonight, the camera outside your room will be disabled. You'll find a dark t-shirt and jeans under your bed. Put them on.* After deleting once more, she leans over and inspects my tattoo. Then she adds more. *Run to the woods, as fast as you*

can. Leave everything behind. Everything. Someone will be waiting.
Another erasure, and she begins describing my tattoo.

I scrape my teeth over my lower lip. Is this a test? Dare I trust
her?

"This cream will help you heal faster. You can put it on three
times every day." She reaches into her medicine drawer and retrieves
a small white bottle and a package of bandages. She doesn't release
the items, and her gaze locks with mine. I think I understand her
meaning. I need to leave this behind, too. She wants to throw
suspicion off herself.

I take it and twist the cap off. When I lift it to my nose, the
pungent odor brings more tears to my already misty eyes. "Thanks."

"Let's cover your bruise."

After about twenty minutes of her patting makeup and
powdering my face, she settles in her chair and appraises me.
"That'll do. Now, go eat."

When I leave the dorm, the outside air has a slight chill, although
summer is right around the corner. I button my uniform up to the
neck, ignoring its painful rub against my tattoo. Part of me wants it
to hurt, to remind me this is all real and not a bad dream. I have to be
careful every moment, every day. But maybe not after today.

Melanie waves at me from across the hill. Smiling, she rushes to
my side. "They sent you back."

"I know. I can't believe it either." I lean forward making sure my
hair covers the bandage, and drop my voice to a whisper. "You're
brave, smiling."

She smirks and gestures to the other students meandering about
the hill. Instead of somber whispers, they're engaged in lively
chatter. "We've decided we don't care. One, the cameras don't reach
the hill; two, the supervisors are too busy managing other things.
Three, even if they did watch us, they don't have the manpower to
punish us all at the same time."

"Still…" I point to my face. Even with the makeup, I know the bruise is visible. I mean it covers my whole cheek.

Several emotions move through her eyes—fear, jealousy, anger? But she gives a dismissive wave. "Four, they tote those guns around like soldiers, but our parents would wreak havoc if they shot anyone. The Alliance needs them on their side."

I think of the boy who fell over the railing—his empty stare, his twisted neck, and his mother's wail. "I wouldn't be so sure."

Melanie reaches for my trembling hand and steadies it. "Where did they send you?"

"Another facility."

"Was it bad there?"

"I was treated well." Adrian told me to say so.

"Sure, you were." She links her arm in mine and tugs me to the cafeteria. "Let's eat." We reach the threshold, one of the camera blind spots, and she checks both directions. "Was Sara there?"

I give her a sad shake of my head, and we fall into line with the other students.

Melanie and I carry our plates to an empty table, and a hush falls over the crowd. My heart falters, and I scan the room for officers. I blush. All the students have stopped to gawk at me. The bandage has peeled away from my neck, and the tattoo is showing. I tear a small piece of tape from the secured side and reapply the gauze.

"It's chicken day." Melanie forks a bland tender and dips it into a vinegary sauce. "Yippee."

"Right. Chicken day…" I skewer a few kernels of corn. "This is Wednesday, right?"

Melanie nods. "Chapel at eight and then free time."

"Awesome."

As I bite into the corn, she laughs. "I thought you'd be changed. Though… your appearance is different." Her eyes are trained on my bandage.

The crowd quiets. The officers are here. Melanie straightens and slips into her forward stare.

I focus on a scratch in the table, going through the ritual I started at the Redemption facility. *This is the covenant that I will make for them after those days, says the Lord.* Sixteen words. Seventeen chews. Seventeen like me. *I will put My Laws into their hearts, and in their minds I will write them... their sin and lawless deeds, I will remember them no more.*

Swallowing the pureed corn, I cast a cold stare into the camera. Hope Adrian is watching.

The baby-faced officer is back. He resembles a CNN anchor Mom used to have a crush on. Wonder if she's met him.

He moves in front of me and makes notes on a clipboard, meeting my eyes. Whatever they are planning, he's involved. But other officers are crawling all over the place. Could Hannah intend me to run when there is such scrutiny?

I can't afford even a hint of recognition, but my thumping heart betrays me. I clasp my hands in my lap and glance down. Baby Face's pen scratches across the clipboard, and then he marches away.

After eating, we go to our chores, and Baby Face approaches me as I walk down the hill. He follows me to the dorm and pats my shoulder as I reach to open the door. "Your father sends his regards."

As he says it, a supervisor steps out, and I jump. "Adrian? Tell him I send my apologies and beg for his forgiveness." My inner voice drips with cynicism, but my outward voice sounds sincere.

The supervisor frowns at Baby Face. "Is there a problem?"

"A quick inspection." Baby Face nods to me. "Extra security and all."

"We've handled it." Spinning, the supervisor opens the dorm door and lets us inside. He brings us to the room assigned to me and shows us each point of security. When he finishes, he smiles, revealing eerily white teeth. "You'll be safe, Ms. Lamb."

Baby Face coughs.

"Is there something else?" The supervisor glances at his watch. "I have to meet with the academy board in ten minutes."

"No, thank you." Baby Face pulls a sheet from his clipboard. "I need to finish this report. You're dismissed."

He scrawls a few lines on the page and steps toward my door. With his back to me, he whispers, "Sara says hello and to tell you she's safe. She says not to be afraid."

I stumble back onto the bed. Did I hear him right? Sara is okay?

Hannah comes in before I can process what he means. "You forgot your salve."

"Sorry."

"No chores or chapel tonight. I told them you'd need time to heal. Perhaps do some reading."

"Okay, thanks."

An Alliance bible is propped open on the pillow. I read for a while, filling in mental blanks, but cannot stop fidgeting. After five chapters, I decide to start going through my closet and drawers.

Under the bed, as Hannah promised, I find a black t-shirt, an old pair of black sneakers, and a pair of dark jeans. Wonder how Hannah got them past the camera. But then again, they could have been in the room a while. Even the dust is undisturbed.

I flip out the lights and crawl under the sheets, watching minutes change on the digital clock above the door. My body is restless until 11:45, when I ease out of the covers and reach beneath the bed for the clothes.

It takes less than a minute to change. I move to the window where a thin, glowing wire reminds me of the dangerous voltage entrapping us. At 11:47, I hang my gray uniform in the closet and twist my hair into a braid. By 11:53, I'm pacing. I should have gone to the restroom first.

Hurrying, I change back into pajamas, loosen my braid, and run across the empty hall.

At 11:57, I'm sliding into bed as the night supervisor peeks into the room. She nods and closes the door. I wait agonizing seconds while her footsteps retreat, and then change again. 11:59.

Exactly midnight, the digital clock numbers fade to black, and the glowing wire darkens. I open the window, wincing as it creaks. When the space is wide enough, I drop to the ground, about three feet below.

After a brief struggle to close the window from the outside, I race across the dark field, straight into an officer.

My stomach sinks as he hoists me over his shoulders, pinning both my arms.

Chapter Fourteen

"PUT ME DOWN!" I squirm as the officer carries me deeper into the woods. Hold on. Where's he taking me? Not back to the dorm. I stop fighting.

He waits a minute, lifting his finger. "Be quiet. Do you want to get out of here or not?"

I straighten. "How do I know I can trust you? Is this some kind of test? Is Adrian trying to trick me?"

"You don't know." He sets me on the ground. "But you have two choices. Come with me or get caught."

"I thought I was caught."

He snorts. "Martin said you were complicated. A good girl, but complicated."

Dad. My heart flutters. "Where are we going?"

"Just follow me."

We move through a thick patch of forest. He keeps his flashlight trained close to the ground and stops every few minutes for who knows what. After a good bit of hiking, he kneels and brushes a pile of leaves away from the base of a monstrous oak.

Hidden between the roots, a small door promises an escape. He lifts the hatch and shines the light. A set of wooden steps lead underground.

"Go." He points.

"You want me to go first?" I gingerly place my foot on the top step. "It's dark in there."

Baby Face emerges from the shadows. "It's dark out here. Hurry."

"It's surreal to see people helping you who've put a gun to your…"

He clenches his jaw.

"Okay. I will. I will." Pulse racing, I descend, gripping the stone wall.

Baby Face shines the light at my feet. The hole only goes down a few more inches and then opens into a tunnel. "See? It's not so bad."

When he begins to lower the door, I yelp and look up at him. "I have to go alone?"

"We need to be at our posts. Follow the light." The door closes between us.

Light? I don't see any… After blinking a few times, my eyes adjust. It's barely enough to see. But the tunnel seems fairly, straight so I continue with careful steps.

I finally reach a small lantern, which rests on a stone shelf opposite a corner. Turning, I forge on, to the second lantern and the third, until I lose count. The tunnel stops at a rusty door, slightly ajar.

I feel like Alice, opening the door and peeking into a rabbit hole. The dim room on the other side is some kind of warehouse, full of boxes, desks, chairs, and equipment. Maybe storage for the school. In the middle of the room, Hannah waits.

"I see you made it." She smiles, moves to me in three long strides, and takes my hand. "This is going to be a little uncomfortable, but it's the easiest way to get you off the grounds. You'll climb in one of these boxes, and the forklift will load you on the truck. Once you're inside the trailer, someone will help you out of the box, and you'll ride with the merchandise until you reach the safe house."

"Will I be able to breathe?"

"The box is ventilated."

A man I've never seen before approaches and brushes my shoulder. "Hang in there, Callie. This will all be over soon, and you can return to your dad."

He disappears into a nearby aisle, and Hannah leads me to a corner. "The cameras have been disabled for about twenty minutes. If you need to use the restroom or anything, go ahead, but hurry. It's going to be a pretty long ride." She frowns. "One more time in the thinking room…"

"It's okay if you get me to Dad." Hope that's really where I'm going. I step into the restroom and close the door.

When I come out, she hands me a small jar of cream and a pack of bandages. "For your tattoo."

"Thanks." I nod to a large cardboard box a few inches away from several identical ones. A forklift idles next to it. "This?"

"Yes." She runs her fingers down the box's upper left corner. A catch trips, and she swings the top open. Inside, it's not cardboard at all, but like the cedar chest in Michael's basement where Angela stored her ribbon. There's a thick cushion, a flashlight, and two bottles of water. Hannah laughs. "Hope you're not claustrophobic. Good thing you're small."

I eye the space, about eighteen inches wide and maybe five feet long. "Won't it be suspicious to take out such a big box? Why can't I just climb into the back of the truck?"

"We can't turn off the cameras in the loading dock." Hannah brushes a bit of dust off the cushion. "We move boxes this size out all the time. Most of the time, they hold pieces of the pews from the churches the Alliance has taken over. They'll sell anything to make an extra buck."

The man pops back around the corner. "Eight more minutes. You need to get out of here. Let's do this."

He helps me into the box, and they close and latch it. Within seconds, my knees ache from the cramped position. Through a small hole, I see Hannah running toward the red door and disappearing into the tunnel. The men pace the room for several minutes, stopping occasionally to write on clipboards. One of them makes a low whistle, and they all glance at each other. "Live in thirty seconds," he says, and they return to their menial tasks.

A motor roars, something beeps, and then the box jolts. The warehouse floor drops as the forklift raises me closer to the ceiling. My stomach churns as I lurch forward, and then hit a bump as the forklift starts moving up an incline. It lowers, and one more bump jostles me.

Men's voices carry from a few feet away. "Two minutes until departure."

"We're loaded up," another answers. I hear shuffling and more bumps.

After what seems like forever, something clicks, and a sliver of dim light streams into my chamber. "Quietly," a voice hisses. The lid lifts, and a muscular man extends his hand to me.

My knees wobble. I grip the box to keep steady and plant ginger feet against rubber and a gritty layer of dirt covering the floor.

The man hands me the cushion, water, and flashlight and gestures to a space big enough for me to sit in the corner. Then he checks a set of bungee cables securing the other boxes to the truck wall. He hurries down the ramp, grabs a handle, and pulls the sliding door down.

Once again, utter darkness engulfs me.

As I lean against the cool steel wall, my pulse resonates through the metal. The whir of the wheels lulls me to sleep. When I wake, something whimpers on the other side of the truck. Did we stop for someone else? Am I not alone?

I shine the flashlight, seeing nothing but boxes a few inches from the opposite wall. Crawling closer, I reach into the space. My hands brush against straw, then a tiny fur-covered paw and soft, droopy ears. A sandpaper tongue licks my fingers, and I hear the whimper again.

The little pup sniffs all around me, poking its inquisitive head against the hem of my shirt, and licking at the trim. I pick it up, and its tiny body quivers.

"There, there, little fellow." Cradling the pup against my neck, I try to stand. A mistake. My equilibrium thrown, I tumble to the gritty floor. The pup lets out a sharp yelp and backs away from me. Poor thing. So scared. How did it get here?

"Come on, buddy. It's okay."

The pup sniffs my outstretched palm and gives me another chance. Its little tail slams up against my leg, over and over, although when I hold it, I can feel its shivers.

"We've got to calm you down." I stroke its ears and nuzzle its nose against my own, but the poor thing still whimpers. Then I have an idea. I'll sing.

The first song I recall is the last one my mother and I sang together before the Alliance took me away. "Mine eyes have seen the glory of the coming of the Lo—" My breath catches. I clamp my jaw shut.

I can do this. I can sing these words again. "He is trampling out the vintage where the grapes of wrath are stored." My voice shakes, but the pup stops whimpering and pokes me with his nose.

"He has loosed the fateful lightning of his terrible, swift Sword." I sit up straighter. "His Truth is marching on."

His Truth. I rub the bandage covering my butterfly. The Truth I turned my back on.

Truth I've been reciting in my head for months, the Truth the Alliance couldn't take away with their brainwashing and incomplete Bibles. I remember my grandmother's words. "A Christian doesn't need a printed Bible."

She's right. The Bible clearly instructs us to write its words on our heart, and I've done that. I've not been brave in other ways, but maybe remembering scripture counts for something.

I sing on with a stronger, surer voice.

By the time I finish the song, the pup is snoring in my lap. I rub my fingers along its collar and the letters engraved on its tag. "Wish I could read your name," I whisper. "Who do you belong to?"

On the one hand, these people are helping me escape. On the other, what kind of people would lock a puppy in a dark truck? Maybe they left it to keep me company. Otherwise... I shudder.

My mind drifts to the movies I used to watch with Dad when I was younger. Men in army fatigues, trapped in a foxhole, marking days with notches and tapping out seconds to measure time. I crawl around the floor, feeling for anything I might use as a weapon. Nothing. Just more grit and small rocks.

The truck jerks to a halt, and the pup slips out of my lap. It yelps again and head butts my feet.

"Aren't you the little tough guy?" I smile. "If they try anything, you'll bite them, won't you?"

I wait, expecting someone to check on me, but they don't. A few minutes later, the truck starts moving again, and I settle on the floor with the pup, leaning against a crate and falling asleep.

Daylight floods my prison chamber, and Baby Face greets me with a smile. "I see you met Barkley, our little stowaway." He kneels and scratches the dog under its ears. "We found him in the woods, and he wouldn't leave our side." He laughs. "We were afraid he'd get us caught, so we brought him along."

I chuckle as Barkley wags his tail so hard he tips over. "What time is it?"

"I'm not sure. Seven thirty, I think. I slept most of the way here." He huffs. "I have to work another shift at midnight."

A car squeals up behind the truck, and Baby Face turns to look out. An officer slams the door and climbs up the ramp to join us.

"Friend of yours?" He points to me. "Something you're not telling me, Caudill?"

The taser is out of Baby Face/Caudill's pocket before I can blink, and in seconds, the officer is laying face-down on the floor with plastic ties securing his hands and feet.

Caudill's expression remains bland, malice-free. If anything, his sharp blue eyes reflect worry. He's still wearing the red and gold coat signifying his loyalty to the Alliance, but it's the only sign of his allegiance.

I follow him to the ramp and climb out. "Who is he? Is he going to be okay?"

"Officer Kendrick. He's a loose cannon." Caudill nods to three approaching men. "He'll recover. They'll take him to a safe place."

"Who's 'they'?"

"A few others who help with extractions." His eyes dart in all directions. "I hope he was alone."

Another man, also dressed in officer attire, emerges from the front of the truck, dragging an officer with his head covered by a burlap sack and hands cuffed behind his back. They sit him on a large stump.

The man wipes a bead of sweat from his forehead. "Just one more, far as I can tell. This one tried to tell me he's on our side."

Muffled words come from the burlap sack, and the officer lunges.

"How did they find us, Dave?" Caudill's jaw tenses. "That's impossible. We covered every angle. No mistakes."

"I don't think they followed the truck. Logan said he thought Kendrick drove behind him the whole way. Same taillights. But he didn't think anything of it because he didn't notice the lights until he hit the Interstate." Dave shakes his head. "They've given him a sleeping pill for now. Maybe we can hold him, and they'll suspect him of the kidnaping."

I put my hands on my hips. "That's just as bad as what they did to me."

Caudill sighs. "It's complicated, Callie. We can't let them go, because they will turn us in to the Alliance. Plus, Kendrick just saw you."

I kick a stone down the dirt road. Trees hover over us from every angle making it seem darker than it really is, but it's familiar terrain. "Where are we?"

"Jonesville, Virginia. We're close to Cumberland Gap. Hoping to get you across the border there and turn you over to your dad."

My stomach lurches as I recall a family vacation from years ago. Dad drove us to the top of a mountain, where the parking lot was barely two cars wide. We walked about a half mile to see this monstrous boulder chained to the side of the mountain, looming dangerously over the city. I'm sure it's close to here.

A car speeds by, stirring up dust, and pulls over in front of the truck. Two men drag a bound Kendrick to the car and load him into the backseat.

I shiver. "What if he called someone and told them where we are?"

"He can't. There's no phone service in the Alliance right now. Not in any of the seceded states."

"Really? How?"

"Have you heard of the FCC? The Federal Communications Commission? Turns out, Adrian and his cronies had enacted a plan to phase out landline phone service in most of the Alliance states before all this happened. And they cut off their wireless service because it's regulated by the federal government."

"So…" I wrinkle my forehead. "So no one can make any calls? That's insane."

"Sometimes you can get service by the border. In their infinite wisdom, the Alliance leadership didn't think about needing federal money or support to keep up certain necessities. They're actually using telegraph in some places and broadcasting old-school TV." He scowls. "I think Adrian likes it that way. It helps him keep people under his thumb because they can't communicate like they used to."

Kendrick secured, the two men join Dave, who preps a hypodermic needle with a clear liquid and heads back to the stump. "Let's see who else we have here." He lifts the burlap sack from the second officer's head.

I gaze directly into Ethan's baby blues.

Chapter Fifteen

HOT BLOOD pulses through my veins, into my icy heart. In spite of my anger, it warms my soul. No matter how much I want to keep hating Ethan for choosing Amber, I can't. But knowing he followed me from the facility—how can I trust him? I brace myself against a nearby sycamore and steady my wobbling knees.

His dark brown hair, longer now, tumbles over his forehead. Piercing blue eyes peer out from under thick, wayward curls.

When Dave removes the cuffs, Ethan reaches for me with arms far more muscular than the lanky ones I saw last.

I force a few deep breaths and move closer. "Hello, Ethan."

Dave raises his eyebrows and steps back.

"Callie." A mixture of emotions cross Ethan's chiseled face— relief, fear, maybe sadness. "I was so worried Kendrick would get to you."

Some of the men move between us, but James puts his hands out to stop them. "He's on our side."

"Is he?" When did he leave Kentucky? Why? Did he go after Amber? Does he still love her? I cross my arms and stare straight into his eyes. "You have some explaining to do."

"After we fought that last day, I had to find you." He brushes hair away from his forehead. "I confronted Amber about what you said."

My cheeks warm. He did hear me.

"She admitted she knew you loved me and went after me anyway. Then she rubbed it in your face. No wonder you hated us." He looks away. "I should have known."

"Yeah, you should have." Though my words are firm, my lips quiver.

"They came for her a couple weeks later." He reaches into his pockets and rocks on his heels. "She was strung out, higher than I've ever seen her, and I knew then I'd picked the wrong sister."

He's earnest. I'll give him that. While he speaks, his eyes darken several shades. But I scoff. I know why he picked Amber—she was pretty and adventurous; I was plain and boring.

"I had to find you. To tell you…" He scuffs his shoe through the gravel shoulder, making a wide arc. "I hope I'm not too late."

"Tell me what?" I lurch closer, grab his shoulders, and force him to look at me.

His gaze falls to his shirt. "I love you. I just didn't know it at the time."

How many times have I dreamed of those words? I palm my face and shake my head. "Seriously?"

Dave coughs like he's suppressing a laugh, and I pinch my lips together, glaring with narrowed eyes. Wish I could make him disappear.

Ethan frowns at him, and then turns back to me. "So, am I?"

I kick at a tuft of grass. A plump earthworm pokes its head out of the earth, and I cover it with the loose turf. "Are you what?"

"Too late." Ethan reaches for my hand, but stops short. "Do you even care anymore?"

"You know what? I made it through some of my darkest moments thinking about good times with you." Did I just say that? It feels like someone else is talking, as if I'm watching our conversation play out on television. "But this... it's a lot to forgive."

He flashes a bitter smile, and my heart melts.

For a split second, I want to embrace him. But I can't bring myself to touch the gold trim on his jacket or the embroidery lining his collar. "You're one of them now."

"Yes. When I need to be. I was forced to join when Kentucky seceded, but after we recommitted to the US, the Alliance let some of us freelance. Pockets of Alliance supporters still remain back home."

My saliva tastes like venom. "You're hypocrites. You guys go into these schools and rough people up and then—"

"It's not like that." James puts a hand on my shoulder. "We play roles to save people."

Ethan laughs. "Let he who has no sin…" He picks up a small stone and throws it into the trees. "Maybe we are hypocrites. Nice tattoo, by the way. You might want to put something on it."

I touch my forgotten bandage, which is hanging loose from my neck, and try to make it stick again. "That's my business."

James gestures to Dave, and they head toward the front of the truck. "You go on and make the deliveries."

"What about the dog? If they do an inspection..." Dave's face pales.

"Take him." James holds his hand out and accepts Kendrick's keys. "You'll have a reason to have been acting suspicious. They'll give you a citation for the dog and move on to the next truck. But you need to hurry so you'll make the deliveries on time."

"What if Kendrick told someone else?"

"Kendrick won't be available for comment. They'll suspect he's covering his own tracks. I'll drive his car somewhere north and hitch a ride back to the school."

Dave climbs up in the cab and speeds away. The other men follow, leaving me, Ethan, and James standing in the middle of the dirt road with Kendrick's car.

"I'll give you a minute," James hops into the driver's seat.

Ethan walks me through a small gap between the trees, and we sit on an old fallen log. He puts his arm around me, but drops it when I shoot him a stern look.

"Relax, Callie. I dress as an officer when we go on extraction runs and work freelance security jobs. Last night, Kendrick confided that he knew something was up and he was going to stop it. I convinced him to let me ride along." He tears a blade of grass into tiny slivers. "I thought I could protect you."

"James held a gun to my head. More than once."

"He's really a good guy. Believe us or not." Ethan shrugs. "Heard you met Sara."

He knows Sara? Cute, perky Sara? Does he like her? "So what if I did?"

"Sara gets reckless sometimes. She's a spy wannabe, and she volunteered to enroll in the school so we could get an insider perspective. She made Kendrick suspicious, and he started following people around. Especially James."

"So, have you been home? Are things there as bad as they are here?"

"I don't think so. After you left, everything settled."

"Didn't the state fall under chaos?" I frown. Like Mr. Sanders told me.

Ethan shakes his head. "You've missed so much. Kentucky's secession didn't pass. It might have, until they tried to take the guns out of the hollars. A lot of people didn't want to give up their federal aid, and they didn't want to leave the homes they've been in for years. We had to declare martial law for a while to restore order. You can't secede from a government that's helping you out."

"You'd think West Virginia would be the same way. And Virginia—there's so much US heritage here. All probably destroyed by the Alliance."

"It all started with those chemical spills, though. People couldn't stay if they wanted to live. The companies gave out settlements like candy, bought up the land, and everyone moved out." He leans closer. "You know what's weird? As soon as they abandoned the properties, Alliance families moved in. They built a purification plant and claimed to have discovered a new chemical process to clean up the water and leach it from the soil. But it's suspicious. It happened so quickly."

"Where did the families come from? I mean, really? Who'd want to move to a wasteland?"

"They were all part of this Redemption Party movement. They had something like 1.8 million members in a Facebook group. We studied them in college—they were an extreme branch of the libertarians, and President Roberts was a secret member, even though his official affiliation was Republican. When he was elected, somebody leaked it, and they assassinated him. I guess that stirred them all to action."

James bursts through the trees. "We have to move. Now. I just saw officers combing the trees beyond the clearing where we've parked."

"Guess we can't take the car, then." Ethan's gaze darts from tree to tree. "Can we hide somewhere?"

"Hope so." James sprints deeper into the trees. "If we can find someone sympathetic to the rebel cause, they might help us get to the farm. It's about twenty miles from here."

Ethan and I struggle to keep up, ducking under low-lying branches and almost sliding down a grassy hill. We reach a clearing behind a church and a modern-looking bank, and James surveys the forsaken landscape. A number of the buildings have burned, leaving charred brick walls and gaping roofs.

"Okay. If I remember right, that was a middle school, and the Alliance uses it as a training facility." James points to a crumbling marquee. "Bad idea to go that way. Officers'll definitely be around."

Ethan nods to the church. "Chances are it's been converted, too."

"Well, at least it's early and not many people are out." I edge closer. "Could we walk at the tree line for a while and find a neighborhood? Maybe there's an abandoned house somewhere."

"Not many neighborhoods left around here." James ducks into the trees anyway, and we move between them, stopping every few feet to reevaluate our situation.

After a half-hour of walking, we stop. Dave's truck is pulled over in the middle of an abandoned gas station's parking lot. He's about150-feet from the edge of the trees, maybe a half-mile from where we're standing. Swarming officers gesture toward the cab and shout.

"Let's move closer." James presses forward, but Ethan and I stay frozen. He stops, turns to us, and frowns. "Come on. We need to find out what's going on."

"You'll get us caught." Ethan grits his teeth. "You go first, and we'll follow."

James crosses his arms. "I think we need to stay together."

"He's right." I move to the next tree, touching something sticky on the bark. Wrinkling my nose, I try to brush it off on my pants.

Ethan's shoulders remain taut as he stalks forward, taking calculated steps between the trunks. "Wish these stupid uniforms weren't bright red."

A few minutes later, James and Ethan have positioned themselves behind thick trees at the clearing's edge. I hang back.

Dave leans against what used to be a gas pump, his back to us.

"We still aren't close enough." James eyes an empty building next to the gas station, perhaps what used to be an apartment complex. One of the doors is ajar, and the windows have all been broken out. A line of tall bushes leads down to it, and James stares a few seconds before dropping to his knees.

"Are you crazy?" Ethan falls to his knees as well. "Do you really think we can go right up to them without being caught?"

"It's our best chance. We know the officers behind us will eventually catch up. If these guys leave Dave with a citation, maybe we can get back in the truck with him and he can drop us at the observatory. If not, I have some friends and family close by who might be able to help."

Ethan and I stay frozen.

"Fine. I'll go first." James scoots down the hill, stopping beside a huge trash bin. He disappears behind it and emerges on the other side, about three feet from the gas station. Grinning, he points to a short fence blocking the rear of the building from the officer's view, and gives us a thumbs-up.

Ethan follows, and when he reaches James, he motions for me to join them. I crawl to the bottom of the hill, but when I near the end of the lot, I come to a small gap. They could see me. Paralyzed, I peek out from behind a bush, ignoring Ethan's waves for me to come on.

"Go ahead and search every box," Dave says. "I have nothing to hide. Do you have that much time to waste?"

One of the officers sneers. "You'd better be careful with that attitude."

"Found something!" A man shouts from inside the truck. He emerges a moment later with a tail-wagging Barkley.

"Well, well." The sneering officer pats Barkley on the head. "Isn't this our lucky day? Wonder if he'd recognize her scent."

I stifle a gasp as Barkley's tail moves so fast he almost falls out of the officer's hand.

"Okay, little buddy," the officer says, holding a gray uniform to the pup's nose. "Go get her."

Chapter Sixteen

BARKLEY RUNS around the gas station parking lot, his little nose working overtime. He nuzzles a tuft of grass that's broken through the concrete and growls at it before flattening it with his paw.

"Come on, you good-for-nothing mutt." The officer closest to Barkley scans the woods we just left.

After intensive sniffing, Barkley moves to a mound of dirt, farther from where we're standing, and starts digging. The officers follow him, their backs to me.

Ethan motions for me to crawl to the gas station. Heart pounding, I do, and we duck inside the dilapidated building, keeping low to the floor.

Cobwebs cover the counter and stretch to the ceiling, where an old, rusty frame barely holds a plastic panel in the light fixture. Toppled shelving units and a few stray wrappers offer the only evidence of the food mart advertised on the faded sign. I wrinkle my nose, resisting a sneeze.

Outside the gas station window, the corner of an officer's sleeves slips into view. I clench my hands. *Please, God, don't let him turn this way.*

The other officers gather around the rear of Dave's truck and climb inside the trailer. They toss out the pillow I'd sat on, which Barkley promptly devours. Every few seconds, a piece of cardboard or packing material sails out to the parking lot.

"We can't hide here for long." My whisper comes out as more of a nervous squeak. Glass windows surround the officer's side of the building, giving us little protection.

"Restrooms." James heads down a narrow hallway and tries the three doors. He shakes his head. No luck. But we crowd into the hall anyway and wait.

Dave's truck roars, and James sneaks a look. "They're letting him leave. I guess there goes our ride." He rests against the men's room door, closing his eyes.

His lips move, slowly at first with no sound, and then faster. "Dear Lord, we thank you for providing this shelter. Please help us remain hidden until we can find a way to safety."

My eyes widen. James is a Christian, too. Then again, I should have known. If Dad trusts him…

Ethan points above us at a gaping hole where a couple of the foam ceiling tiles are missing.

James climbs on the counter, risking exposure for a few seconds while he hoists himself to the steel support beams. Must be nice to be tall.

"It's an attic," he whispers. "Secure. Come on up. Hurry. Quietly."

Spry as gymnast, Ethan grabs James's arms, lifts himself into the void, and then leans over the side to bring me up.

I start to stand but duck again as two officers approach the food mart entrance. Now what?

There. A small cabinet below a short Formica counter forms an L-shape with a longer one. I crawl inside and close the door to a sliver as Ethan disappears into the ceiling.

I examine the officers through the crack. One is short and stumpy with a long, red beard. The other dwarfs him by about two feet, taller than even James.

The tall officer leans against the counter, his pant legs brushing the edge of my cabinet door. "No evidence of anyone here."

"She's in Jonesville. I know she is." Stumpy kicks an empty soda can in my direction. "Kendrick and I've worked together before. He's solid."

"Where is he, then?" Tall guy stops the can with the tip of his boot. "Maybe he led us across the country on a wild goose chase. After all, he hasn't answered your contact in over an hour."

"You heard him this morning. There's good evidence they came this way. Just think of the reward."

I tremble, cover my face with my palm, and peek out through my fingers.

Leaning into my line of sight, Stumpy bends to pick up a quarter off the concrete floor. His eyes meet mine—dark and dull under thick, bushy brows. My breath catches, but surely it's too dark inside the cabinet for him to see me.

"Come on, Chris. Kendrick was a member of the Redemption Party from its inception." Stumpy stands and pockets the quarter. "He worked toward this goal for years. Why would he sabotage his own nation by kidnaping the First Daughter?"

"Why would Adrian Lamb arrange the assassination of his own President?" Chris reaches into his pocket and pulls out a smart phone. "Have you read the latest CNN blogs?"

"Do you really believe that nonsense?" Stumpy shakes his head. "No Internet here, remember?"

Chris pockets the phone, traces his fingers along the cabinet door, and presses it closed. It bounces back open, and he catches it with his knee before it swings wide enough to reveal me.

"Right. One of the benefits of living in a non-Allied state."

Something strikes the counter above me. "You're out of your mind. If anyone else hears you talking like this, they'll—"

"They'll what?" Chris backs from the counter out of my view. "Banish me from the country I don't live in? Deny me the bonus they never delivered?"

"Or worse."

Something crawls across my arm, moving up my shoulder and onto my neck. Probably a spider. I shiver. Tears well in my eyes.

"What now?" Chris's voice travels in a different direction from Stumpy.

I make a slow, silent pivot toward a small crack in the counter and try to scoot closer to it. Feet. Two more pairs, first outside the entrance glass, and then inside. "Any evidence?"

Chris clears his throat. "Looks like a couple of teens broke curfew. Somebody call the local office and tell them to ramp up their night watch."

A slight movement catches my eye, but before I can gasp, a shot rings out and a bullet ricochets between the wall behind the feet and a toppled shelf.

"Don't move, fellas." Chris laughs as a three-foot black snake skitters across the room. Both pairs of feet hurry backward. "Let's get out of here. We're not getting any closer to finding her by hanging out in Loserville."

"Jonesville." Spit sprays from Stumpy's gritted teeth.

An eternity of silence follows. Though I've yet to see Chris's face, I imagine them locked in a dreadful faceoff.

"Let's go," another officer finally says. "You're right. We're just wasting time here." Footsteps grow distant. A few minutes later, engines roar and tires squeal.

A thud thumps the counter, then another, and two more. Feet shuffle above me and then comes an outrageous clang. Metal scrapes the concrete, shattering glass. A door slams. Nothing drowns my rampant pulse.

"You can come out now, Callie." Ethan opens the cabinet door. "Bad guys are gone. Snake and all."

"But not Dave. Praise the Lord." James points out the window, where the old truck driver grins, waving for us to join him.

Dave lifts the cargo door, and Barkley races to the edge, his little tail swishing so fast it cracks the air like a whip.

We rush from the food mart and jump into the truck, and Dave grabs the handle to lower the door. "I can't believe you guys made it all the way here."

James shrugs. "We were motivated. Officers all over the hill."

"And they didn't see you."

"They were idiots. Probably still looking over Kendrick's car."

Dave grins. "That, they were." He lowers the door and encloses us in darkness.

We move to the rear of the truck, stepping over pillow remnants and shredded cardboard boxes. Ethan and I stretch on the gritty aisle floor, back to back.

Barkley licks my fingers, and I help him into my lap. "What if somebody saw us?"

James pats the box next to me a couple of times before finding my shoulder. "Don't worry. Dave watched them all leave."

"But what if officers were driving by? Or across the street?"

Ethan arches so his cheek touches mine. "We've prayed about it. Things are going to be fine. The observatory isn't far, maybe twenty minutes, and…"

His breath warms my neck. If I made just a slight turn... I grit my teeth and pull my face away from him. Even if he did kiss me, memories of him making out with Amber would ruin the moment. "Isn't an observatory like an astronomy thing? I don't see how a telescope is going to help us out of the state."

James laughs. "You're right. The pews are for the observatory. That's our delivery. The place we're going is actually US territory, not Alliance. It's closed, except for science research to protect certain cave species in the area. The Alliance fought hard to keep it, but lost."

"Fought? Like a war?" Barkley butts my hand, and I stroke his ears. "I didn't know there were wars. Does Adrian have an army?"

"Yes, Adrian has an army. All officers are part of his army. It's a good-sized one, too. He recruited them to the Redemption Party through social media before the petitions went live. Then, once the first state split from the US, he started training them and promising them wealth and rewards in exchange for their loyalty. They're ruthless hunters." He swallows. "In fact, half of them are combing the Alliance countryside for you right now."

"So did a lot of people die?"

"It was more of a diplomatic standoff than a full-out war. The man who owns the property is financially powerful and the US backed him. Also, the US fought to keep some of the national park land. Adrian had to pick his battles."

Barkley bounces from my lap and runs to Ethan. Ethan laughs, but sobers within seconds. "What's the plan once we arrive?"

"Hide until we come up with a way across the border." James's voice deepens, with a hint of a quiver. "No one anticipated trouble. Extractions have always gone smoothly."

"I know." Ethan sits straighter. "But we've never extracted a First Daughter before."

The truck moves on, thirty minutes longer than they said it would take to reach the observatory. Ethan's back muscles grow tense behind me, James breathes harder, and we lurch to a stop.

Seconds later the cargo door rises. Dave greets us, clutching his chest and gasping for air. "Just picked up officers on the CB. They're headed to the observatory. You guys need to get out. I'm going to circle back, like I was lost."

We scramble from the truck, and Ethan whips his head left then right, hair falling into his widened eyes. "Where can we go?"

Dave points to a road sign across the street, almost obscured by overgrown maples.

James grins. "Genius, Dave. Exactly where we dropped Sara. A few feet from here, Callie, and you'll be in Tennessee. The USA. Just go that way and keep straight." He scans the countryside. "There might be a fence, maybe a few cameras, but I don't think you'll encounter any border guards because this is private property. I've heard there's a strong pocket of rebels there, men who conduct their own extractions."

"You're not coming with us?" Ethan clenches his jaw.

"Think I'm going to ride with Dave and make sure his drop-off goes smoothly. You can handle this, and I'll catch up later."

A sedan whizzes by, and we duck behind the trailer.

James pulls out his wallet and offers me couple hundred-dollar US bills. "Callie, if you can cross the gap, your dad is waiting on the other side. That's all you need to do. This should help if you need anything."

Before I take it, he turns to Ethan. "We're close to Sara's family. Maybe less than a mile. Scope out the area. Look at mailboxes. Her last name is Childers. They can help you cross the border." He clasps my hands in his, transferring the money. "Good luck."

"Right. Childers." Ethan peeks out from behind the truck. "The coast is clear. Let's jet."

We cross the street and run into the woods, leaping over tree roots and darting between thick trunks. After about a mile, I have to stop.

Ethan glances toward the road and narrows his eyes.

"What? Am I not going fast enough?"

"It's not that." He snaps a hanging branch from a monstrous sycamore. "I can't believe he left us. Your dad will be furious."

"Maybe so, but we have a bigger problem." I look at my feet. Heat singes my cheeks. "I have got to find a bathroom. Like now."

Ethan relaxes his scowl and chuckles. "At least you aren't dehydrated." He points to a patch of forest, thinner than the rest. "You may be in luck."

No way I'm going to pee in the forest. But maybe I won't have to. I follow Ethan's gaze just past the trees, to a log cabin.

Jagged glass covers half a window, and thick branches surround the foundation, twisted in kudzu. "Maybe so." I grin. "Finally, some good news. Let's check it out."

We aim for a quieter gait, circling through trees and creeping up to the cabin from the rear.

Thick mud covers parts of the porch and exterior walls, almost as though someone sprayed it there. It's spotted with prints from something definitely not human and spattered with shredded trash.

"Bear." Ethan takes a deep breath.

"Should we try the door?"

"No, we'll leave prints, too. Let's stick with the tree cover for now and try to step on roots. And we'll get some leaves or something to use to open the door." He scans the cabin roof. "Weird. There's even mud on the gutter."

"Tornado. Now, what are you doing on my property?" A click behind us accompanies a man's voice. Ethan stills, and I turn to face the muzzle of a rifle.

Chapter Seventeen

"LET'S GO INSIDE so we can talk." The man with the rifle laughs, a deep, throaty sound like Ethan's. "I always wanted to catch me an officer."

He's younger than I expected, maybe in his early forties. Muscles bulge from his olive Army tee. US Military, not Alliance.

"We don't mean any harm." Ethan drops his arms to the side, and I do the same.

"You sure are a young pup. Why aren't you carrying? Don't you know how to use a gun?" The man cocks his and prods Ethan's stomach.

"She needs to use the restroom." Ethan nods to me. "That's all we want. Then we'll leave, and you'll never know we were here."

The man lowers the gun and slaps Ethan's shoulder. "I'm guessing you might want a bite to eat, too. And maybe a place to stay for a while."

My jaw drops. "Are you serious? You're going to help us?"

"Maybe."

"Who are you?"

"Isaac Banks." He slings the gun over his shoulder and extends his hand to Ethan. "Son, do you read the Bible?"

"Yes."

"Prove it."

Ethan lets out that triumphant grin he's given me so many times. "Neither have I gone back from the commandment of His lips; I have esteemed the words of His mouth more than my necessary food."

Isaac's eyes widen. He gives Ethan another slap. "Book of Job. Huh."

"Yep."

"The whole book? Not an Alliance copy? What else you got?"

I clear my throat. "The restroom?"

Isaac bolts to the door, mud squishing beneath his feet. He digs in his pocket and retrieves a ring full of keys. As I wiggle and wait, he tries several, and Ethan mimes a dripping faucet.

"Stop," I mouth.

When Isaac swings the door open, it catches on broken glass. He kneels and picks up the pieces, his lips pinched.

Mud cakes the cabin's interior walls. Blotches of it pepper the floor. I take cautious steps, following Isaac into a short hallway.

He whirls around, and his eyes brighten. "My wife and I are going to start cleaning this mess on Monday. Maybe the two of you could help."

"I don't know." Ethan draws in a long, deep breath. It comes out in a stifled yawn. "We would, but we need to get to Tennessee. Her dad is waiting for her there."

"Oh. A runaway." Isaac brushes Ethan's sleeve. "Borrowed?"

"The uniform? No, I'm really an officer." Ethan grimaces as Isaac's eyebrows rise. "But not at heart. Rebellion men helped us escape. The same men who helped Sara Childers. Do you know her?"

Isaac blinks. "Are you looking for Sara?"

I bite my lip and stand straighter. "We're trying to cross the border. Officers are looking everywhere for me right now. I just need a place to hide."

Isaac shrugs. "Wouldn't be the first time I've helped a runaway." He nods to his gun. "Might be the first time I shoot an officer if you aren't telling me the truth."

Veins swell as Isaac flexes his muscles. It's doubtful he'd need the gun if Ethan tried to challenge him. He'd probably just squish us like bugs.

"I'm sort of a bigger deal than your average runaway." I huff as Ethan scoffs. It did sound kinda arrogant. "No, really. They might look harder to find me."

"If by 'they', you're talking about that nincompoop who runs the country and his trophy wife, then I'm definitely not worried," Isaac leans closer, "Callie."

My eyes widen.

"The restroom is right here." He opens a door and flips on a light.

I step inside a pristine room lined with marble tile accentuating the granite sink. The toilet is nicer than any residential one I've seen, with a modern digital gadget that knows when to flush. If not for the stagnant air and the dirt on my clothes, I'd feel like a celebrity. After I've done my business, I wash my hands and return to the living area where Ethan and Isaac are looking over a busted curio cabinet.

"This place is beautiful." Under the mud splatters, broad cedar trim encircles the walls at chair rail height and lines the ceiling. Broken picture frames and knickknacks litter the floor, likely thousands of dollars of destruction. Michael Harding might have built a place like this for Angela.

Wonder if his house is still standing, or my house. Or the church…

Isaac seizes a fist-sized stone from the Berber carpet. He tosses it out the broken window, and it strikes an uprooted tree. "It used to be."

"It will be again." I cross the carpet to linoleum and rub dirt from a kitchen chair with my thumb. "When did this happen?"

"Two weeks ago. We've lost a ton of crops and a few nearby families were displaced." More sweat beads cover Isaac's forehead and he dabs at them with a towel. "The insurance company has been in to take pictures, so I guess now we just clean up and move on."

I set a frame on the counter. Sara smiles at us from the center of a group picture, surrounded by a man and woman who bear a strong resemblance to her.

"Is this the Childers family? Do they live close to here?"

"A bit south, but not too far. Walking distance." Isaac opens a cedar door, revealing a dark staircase. "Their property is fine. But we'll probably see them in a few minutes, and you can ask about it yourself. You guys ready?"

He motions for us to follow and begins a slow descent, the rifle bouncing against his shoulder blade.

"Ready for what?" I glance at Ethan, who holds out his palms and shrugs.

Shivering, I imagine Isaac's muscular arm pinning us down while he forces us into shackles. "Can we trust you? You're not going to lock us down here or something, right?"

"Never put your trust in man." Isaac points to a splintered coffee table slammed against the living room wall. A large-print study Bible rests on top of it, completely untouched except for a few drops of mud on the cover. "Trust in the Lord with all your heart and lean not on your own understanding. You know that one?"

Ethan grins and steps toward the staircase. "In all your ways acknowledge Him, and He will direct your path. Providence, Callie. It's not Isaac you don't trust."

He's right. It's hard to trust God when so many things have fallen apart, but I know I have to.

A flip of a switch illuminates windowless concrete walls. There's no evidence of a basement outside of the cabin. If he locks us down there, no one will ever know. I take several deep breaths. Trust God.

A steel door looms across the room, taller than the standard doors I'm used to. Isaac sifts through his keys.

I tap nervous toes as he struggles to pry the heavy door away from the jamb, even with his strength. Ethan helps, and together they slide it far enough to activate the prop hardware.

Isaac removes headlamps from a knapsack and passes one to me and Ethan. He lifts the thick carpet from the closet floor, revealing a rusty metal trapdoor. "Have you guys ever been spelunking?"

"Yeah." Ethan shines the light in my eyes. "We used to go through the caves in the Red River Gorge, at least until they closed them due to endangered bats."

Coils of rope, harnesses, and carabiners dangle on hooks encircling the closet wall. Isaac hands me a harness.

"You, too." He passes a harness to Ethan and puts one on himself, demonstrating how to attach a double lanyard on the front. "You'll find anchors along the walls and places where the floor drops off, leaving only inches to pass through."

My stomach churns but flutters when Ethan takes my hand and squeezes. If he's afraid, I can't tell.

The trapdoor squeaks when Isaac lifts it, and chunks of dirt tumble to the cave floor, maybe thirty feet below us. "You'll go first." He lowers me into a tight chamber of slimy, wet rock. The clammy air smells like pond-trodden socks.

Crickets chirp, and I hesitate. What else could be down there?

"Take about fifteen steps forward, and it will open up a little wider. You'll be descending, but there are no drops in this part, only walls."

I give a shaky laugh. "I've never met anyone with a cave in their basement before."

Isaac's laugh rumbles like an avalanche. "They call me Cave Man around here. I own seventeen properties with chambers like this. My great-grandfather willed them to me."

My elbow brushes against the cool mucus covering the walls. Chills blast from my fingertips to the base of my spine. "Why would someone want to own a bunch of places like this?" I wince. If Mom were here, she'd pinch me for being so rude.

"Well, most were part of the Underground Railroad. Some are more modern."

Ethan's feet bump mine when he drops beside me, and I stumble forward. He grabs my waist, hooking his fingers around the belt loops on my pants.

Gritting my teeth, I loosen his grip and move forward. It would be so easy to let him charm me into the kind of relationship he had with Amber. Not happening.

More dirt falls from the ceiling as Isaac lands beside us. The walls taper from where we stand, and Isaac moves to the front, helping us inch through the narrowing passage.

A drop of water strikes my nose and rolls onto my lips. Before I can stop myself, I lick them, gagging on the bitter, metallic taste. It's probably arsenic. I make it all this way, and I'm going to die from cave water.

Trust. I close my eyes, letting Isaac and Ethan guide me. Occasional jagged rocks jut from the wall, scraping my elbows and arms. "Hey, Isaac. Does this cave pass into Tennessee? Can you get me there without being seen?"

"It doesn't, but I've got others that do. If we can get you there, I'll sure try to help you across the border." He clears his throat. "Stop a second. It's going to get a little tricky here."

My harness tightens as Isaac holds up a weird bracket, kind of shaped like a U, and slides its parallel plates over a cable running waist high along the rock wall. I try to follow—a brake mechanism, a pulley—wish I'd paid more attention when we'd hiked back in Kentucky.

Isaac checks to make sure my lanyard is snug, watches Ethan secure his, and then attaches his own. "Okay, now I'm going to teach you how to move past a fixed anchor point. After you've shown me you can do it, we'll move on."

Ethan shrugs. "I've done this before."

I mimic his moves with surprising success.

"Good." Isaac checks my lanyard one more time. "We're good to go. Now, about eating. Hope you don't mind a potluck. We're having a special meal today to honor our Sunday school teachers. There will be more than enough to share."

We're going to a church meal? In a cave? I chew on my lower lip and sigh. I didn't even know it was Sunday.

Isaac makes a small leap to a lower part of the cave, letting a downward trending cable be his guide. "We'll take a break here in a second. Soon as we get through this rough part."

Ethan helps me through the leap and then clasps my hand. We ease forward, guided by our dim helmet lights. I count steps, thirteen, fourteen, fifteen, and sure enough we turn a corner and the space opens to a wider chamber.

"Turn off your headlamps. We don't need them for a while." Isaac reaches over my shoulder and strikes a match against the wall. He touches the flame to a torch, which, in a rush, brightens the whole room—a wide chamber with crudely carved benches surrounding the walls.

"Wow." Ethan's eyes sparkle, rivaling the flickering torch. "I guess the slaves gathered here?"

"It was a depot of sorts. A resting place. My great-grandfather rebuilt the cabin years ago when the original one burned to the ground. I remodeled recently." He grimaces. "And I'll have to remodel again."

Ethan releases my hand and scratches his chin. "Hmm... You'd think the state would have tried to buy it. You know, to preserve it."

"Well, for one thing, this place isn't one of the tourist sites. It's always been on private property." Isaac chuckles. "And my great-grandfather was a stubborn man. It's in his will to never, ever sell. No matter what."

We walk on. The chamber narrows again, and this time, Isaac stops to shine his light over the entire space.

"There's a big gully here." He points to a shadowy area opposite a murky light fixed somehow to the wall of the drop. "To the right of it, we'll follow a trail, about six inches wide in some places. We're going to stay hooked on this cable and take slow, steady steps to the bottom. Then we'll be past the worst part."

"The narrow way." I smile, reach over, and squeeze Ethan's hand. The first of the scriptures we memorized together. "Remember that one? Because narrow is the gate and difficult is the way that leads to life…"

"And there are few who find it," Ethan finishes, flashing me a wide smile. "You remember."

My cheeks grow warm. Thankfully, he can't see my face. But the dim glow below us is eerie, and I tremble with each small step.

A few more crude stairs lead us to a corner. Light fills a huge chamber on the other side of the wall, revealing an interior covered in drywall, not stone. Colorful paintings hang every few feet. Some of the pictures I recognize—Jesus between two thieves on the cross, Peter denying he knew the Christ. That's me. Ethan's not the one needing forgiveness. I am. I look down at my muddy tennis shoes just as the rock beneath me crumbles.

Chapter Eighteen

I FLAIL as the harness catches and jerks me to a sudden stop. My hands grip a jagged rock as I dangle there, bouncing a little but not falling further. The lanyard holds. I relax my arms, loosen my death grip, and admire the network of spacers and beams transforming the chamber into a church. "Wow."

Isaac swoops from the ledge and lands below me. He looks up at Ethan. "Are you a decent climber? There are several deep pockets along this wall, and you can always reach around and grab a support beam. You should be able to get a good grip."

Avoiding the place where I slipped, Ethan grabs a jutting rock. He turns to face the wall instead of the drop and then taps his toes until they catch in a groove. Another rock, another groove, he scales the wall as if he's climbed one like it every day.

Ethan lands a couple feet from where I'm hanging. "You scared me."

I manage a shaky laugh. "I scared *me.*"

"No more drops." Isaac releases my harness and lowers me to the floor. "Well, what do you think?"

"It's beyond incredible." As I round the corner, I brush the back of a cushioned pew. "How did you get these in here? And when was it built?"

Isaac points to an opening across the chamber. "The other entrance is much wider." He leads us to the pulpit, flips a trigger, and lifts the top. "When the Alliance took over the church I attended, they gave us a couple hours to move out all our belongings. The elders needed a place to store them, and the few remaining members needed a safe place to meet."

Inside the pulpit, a worn leather Bible bears the name Isaiah Banks. "My great- grandfather preached for decades. He knew this book cover-to-cover and could quote just about any verse on demand. I'm not there yet, but someday…" His eyes darken. "It's one of the last remaining complete versions in the state, as far as I know."

When he places the Bible in my hands, I shiver. This book alone could take Adrian down, if people would have the nerve to read it. Or the motivation.

I hand the Bible back to Isaac and sit, swinging my feet under the seat. Just like home, my feet don't touch the ground.

Ethan grins.

"Don't you dare call me Shorty." I fold my arms and slap them against my chest.

"I'd never." Ethan slides in beside me and lifts his gaze to the ceiling. "I bet the acoustics are fantastic."

"Unbelievable." Isaac closes the pulpit and moves toward the other opening. "You can hear them for yourself in a few minutes."

Ethan and I follow Isaac into a passage built to imitate a traditional church hallway. It even boasts a plastic water tank and a pamphlet rack. After several feet, we come to another passage and then another chamber. This place must go on forever.

White plastic tables topped with faux floral arrangements fill the room—bright stems in mason jars, supported by the same limestone lining the cave walls. I smile. Mrs. Whitman decorated our church bathroom with fresh flowers every week. Mom always said church ladies could turn a worn cardboard box into a beautiful centerpiece if given enough time. She'd like it here.

A sudden flux of conversation fills the chamber. Above the hum wafts the pungent scent of barbecue sauce and buttered cracker crusts. The women follow, holding food carriers. Then come a few young children, men, and teenagers toting Alliance Bibles and songbooks.

A petite blonde woman squeals, "An officer?"

All eyes turn to us, and Ethan ducks his head.

Isaac steps in. "He's with me. Nothing to fear. This boy knows the true Bible, and he does not serve the Alliance in heart." He gives Ethan an apologetic shrug. "My wife, Lisa. Lisa, meet Ethan and Callie. Callie Lamb."

"Callie Noland." My name echoes, hanging in the air. Stares bore into me as the weight of my presence hovers over the room.

"I know them, too," says someone from the crowd, one of the men who took Kendrick away. "They're not a threat."

The women return to their chatter, though they cast me the occasional wary glance, and the men continue making trips to carry items into the chapel area.

A younger boy drops a couple of the Alliance Bibles, spilling out photocopied papers. Ethan retrieves them. "What kind of church is this? I don't see any distinct denominational markers."

"You won't find any." A passing man sets his books on one of the tables and offers a handshake, his mustache twitching when he smiles. "When we planted this church, neighbors all came from different backgrounds—Methodist, Baptist, Independent Christian. And at first, no one could agree on anything."

A little brown-headed girl pokes my leg. "You're dirty."

I smile, patting her curly head. "I am." I turn back to the man, who's grinning. "So, what did you do? Everyone seems to get along now."

He hefts one of the Bibles. "We decided to let the Good Book tell us. We made a commitment to each other that, before we made any decisions regarding our worship, we'd meet and have a study, adding in the missing pieces. Turns out we needed about ten studies before we could find common ground."

A bearded man joins us, placing his books next to a covered casserole dish. One of the women gives him a pointed look and moves them to a different table. "We had many doctrinal differences, so as you can imagine, intense discussion dominated the first month or so of our meetings. We had to find ways to compromise, and no one could go back on their beliefs."

Isaac nods. "So, we created a worship service just like they did it in the New Testament."

"We call ourselves New Testament Believers." The bearded man takes my hand and squeezes. "It's a pleasure to have you join us today. We've been praying for you since Sara returned."

A teenage boy walks by and gawks at me, and Ethan drapes his arm over my shoulder. "It's like the Restoration Movement. Do you remember when we went to Cane Ridge and toured the old church? What was it Mr. Whitman kept telling us? 'Speak where the Bible speaks, and remain silent where the Bible is silent?'"

"Right." Isaac takes a Crock-pot from an elderly woman and carries it to a table. As she shuffles after him, the girl behind her looks up, a wide smile covering her face.

"Sara?" She looks nothing like I remember. Her hair is now deep auburn, and her little pixie cut now feathers down her shoulders.

She engulfs me in a hug strong enough to rival a python's grip. "Callie. You got out. We've prayed so hard."

Her once-green eyes have deepened, contacts, maybe. Her caterpillar tattoo is gone.

I touch the bandage covering my butterfly. It's lost almost all the sticky. "How…?"

A woman who shares Sara's profile wraps her arm around my waist. "We have something to remove it. Ordered it straight from Hollywood and had it shipped to Tennessee, then snuck it across the border. There's plenty left if you want to try."

Before I can answer, another woman tugs at my arm, and I'm swarmed in a flurry of hugs and shoulder pats. Then I'm ushered back into the chapel. One of the older men goes to the pulpit, and everyone else files into the pews, about forty people all together.

"Good morning." The older man leans on the pulpit while his echo responds. "Welcome, all. By way of announcements, we have several. Please pray for Nancy's mother…"

While he speaks, I examine the crowd. Ethan seems to be doing the same at first, but his eyes keep trailing to the back of Sara's head. I knew it. As soon as there's another girl in the room…

The older man finishes, and a younger one takes his place, a skinny guy with dark hair and glasses. "We will be singing number four hundred and fifty-one. Four fifty-one. Let us be standing."

As the crowd obliges, he raises his hand and moves it in a four beat motion. "Sing the wondrous love of Jesus…"

They all join, including Ethan. I try. My chest constricts, and I struggle to form the words. Do I even count as a Christian anymore? The notes are amplified as though a hundred people are singing, so other than Ethan, I don't think anyone will notice my silence.

I peer at him through the corner of my eye. He's looking at Sara again. Doubtful he notices, either.

They pass around the communion trays, and I partake. The bread sits heavy on the back of my tongue, and the grape juice leaves a bitter taste. Salty tears drip down my cheeks and hang on my lips.

Here am I, a traitor, sharing in these emblems with others who have risked their lives to meet here today, and I've put them in even more jeopardy by showing up. I feel as though a neon sign hangs above my head, deeming me the weakling that I am. But what could I have done? Adrian would have had me killed.

A portly gray-haired man steps behind the podium and lifts a clear plastic bag, filled with tiny round beads. He pours them into a small bowl and passes it around the crowd. "Mustard seeds. Take one." Raising his Bible high, he sweeps it from left to right in one great arc. "What is the measure of your faith? Who is there among you of whom it can be said, 'ye of little faith'?"

Vigorous nods from the crowd convict me. I have no faith.

"In the book of Luke, chapter seventeen and verse five, the disciples pose a simple request to Christ: Increase our faith. You'll have to read that one from the insert." The preacher lowers his Bible to the podium and steps in front of it. "Our Lord had a simple answer—we do not need faith the size of a mountain to choose to serve our God. If we have faith the size of one of these tiny seeds, according to Scripture, we can tell the mulberry tree to pull itself up by the roots and be planted in the sea, and it will obey."

More vigorous nods. Isaac, too. "Amen!"

"It's interesting..." The preacher looks straight at me. "It's interesting how the Lord chose a seed for this illustration. Faith, my friends, is something that should be planted, cultivated... grown."

His last word echoes and I squeeze the pew seat in front of me. I did try to cultivate my faith. I read and memorized Scripture and attended youth activities. Why wasn't that enough?

"In Second Thessalonians, the first chapter, and verse three, where Paul, Silvanus, and Timothy address the church in Thessalonica, they say, 'We are bound to thank God always for you, brethren, as it is fitting, because your faith grows exceedingly.' Here, we have evidence of a church cultivating their faith. And how? They worked to spread the Gospel, they brought others to Christ, and they abounded in love."

I force myself to exhale. I did none of that before the Alliance, although I could have. There were kids at school, friends at church who weren't faithful. I even turned a blind eye to Amber's blatant disregard for Truth.

Ethan glances at me, his lips pressed tight into a frown. He must be worried.

Sitting straighter, I focus my gaze on the engraved cross spanning the pulpit's front panel.

"The early Christians were martyrs." The preacher points at several people in the audience. "Should the Alliance storm this cave today, would you deny your God to uphold their creed? Would you be willing to face death to defend true life through Him?"

My head drops to my chest, and tears flow. Ethan scoots closer, and I rest my wet cheek against the red wool covering his shoulder.

The rest of the service is a blur. I manage to pull myself together by the end and follow the other members back into the fellowship room. Ethan mingles, shaking hands and running for mayor, as Dad used to say. I slink into a chair at the edge of the chamber and watch the women bustling to get the food ready.

Sara joins me, rattling off words I don't hear.

A few more pats and sympathetic hugs, and I clutch my collar. They're smothering me.

"Here, sweetheart, let me fix that bandage." An older lady stoops and digs in her monstrous purse. "Ah, here we go. Now hold still, while I doctor you up." She retrieves a first-aid kit and washes her hands with a medical wipe.

"Thanks. It was really bothering me." I glance at Ethan, who has the preacher cornered by the entrance. Sara walks up, and he places his hand on the small of her back.

My teeth clench, and I set my face to glare.

A loud, human growl startles me. Did it come from my mouth? Shaking my head, I hold my breath as it sounds again. My eyes fix on a point just past Ethan and Sara, where a wild-haired man stumbles into the room, with hands cuffed behind his back. He meets my gaze and lunges toward me. Kendrick.

Chapter Nineteen

KENDRICK PLOWS headfirst, knocking my chair to the cave floor. He scowls, blowing hot, rank breath in my face. "I knew it."

The men surround us, pin his arms, and drag him to a corner.

"Dare you bring this violence into God's house?" The preacher wags his finger in Kendrick's face. "You chose to ally yourself with Adrian Lamb; my allegiance is to the God of Abraham. Have you read the Bible? Don't you know the fate of those who rebelled against His will?"

Kendrick charges, though he's unable to escape the men's grasp. "When I get out of here…" He bumps his shoulder against Isaac, who twists his arm tighter. Gnashing his teeth, Kendrick tilts his head. "I'll have you all killed. Every last one of you."

A young woman covers a small boy's ears.

"Let's get him out of here." Isaac nods toward the entrance. "How'd he get here in the first place?"

"It's my fault." The man who drove Kendrick away from Dave's truck steps forward. "I take full responsibility. I left him in a side chamber and thought he'd stay passed out until after church. Truth is, we're not really sure what to do with him."

An older woman slides a serving spoon into a pan of green beans. "We should at least feed him."

"Linda's right. We should." Isaac grabs Kendrick's collar. "Let me explain something to you. There's no way out of this cave other than my way. Right now, seven miles of path surround us. Seven miles to get lost in. Do you have a family? Would you like to see them again?"

Kendrick averts his gaze.

"I can offer them protection. Freedom. Just tell me where they are, and I'll make it happen."

"I don't want your protection." Kendrick clamps his jaw and turns away from Isaac. "The Alliance has offered me plenty of protection. They're probably out looking for me right now."

Ethan moves to Kendrick's side. "You're right. They are looking for you right now." He places a light hand on Kendrick's shoulder. "Think about it. One, you drive off in an Alliance-issued car the same night Callie disappears. Everyone else is accounted for—everyone except you. Two," he counts off with his fingers, "your car turns up in the middle of nowhere, and you're not in it. No sign of you, no sign of Callie. Three, you were on guard duty when she disappeared. I don't think Adrian Lamb is going to offer you any kind of protection."

Kendrick spits at Ethan's feet. "What do you know? Traitor."

"Nice. Real mature, man." Ethan rubs saliva off his ring finger. "Four, you have no idea where you are. You don't even know what state you're in—if it's Alliance territory or not. For all you know, we've smuggled you into the US, and believe me, it's going to be real suspicious if you have to come back across the border after disappearing."

"Everything's ready." Sara's mother glares at Ethan and Kendrick, hands on her hips. "If you boys want to calm yourselves, we'll eat."

Isaac drags Kendrick to a table, shoves him into a chair, and retrieves a semiautomatic pistol from behind the wall.

A couple women gasp.

"Uncuff him." Isaac points the gun at Kendrick's chest. "Let him eat until he has his fill, and then we'll cuff him back."

"I'll make him a plate." Linda spoons a heap of mashed potatoes on a Styrofoam tray. She goes down the line, adding baked beans, pasta salad—several things I haven't seen since being in the Alliance. When she fills it to the point that it bends, she plops the tray in front of him and pats his back. "Enjoy."

"But not before we pray." The preacher instructs everyone to bow their heads and close their eyes, but I can't take mine off Kendrick.

Throughout the prayer, he stares me down, his iciness giving me shivers. Still, I keep a steady gaze, and I'm pretty sure Isaac does, too. When the preacher finishes, the other members go through the line. The man with the key removes the cuffs, and Kendrick shovels food in his mouth like he's never eaten before.

I fill my plate with small portions. Ethan sits next to Sara, so I choose an empty seat beside her mother.

When his plate is empty, Kendrick allows them to cuff him without complaint. He glares at me as they escort him out of the chamber, and the crowd settles into normal chatter.

"Come on." Mr. Childers points to the cave entrance. "Let's get you guys out of here so you can relax."

Sara and her mother join us as we follow him along a straight, flat path lit by candles.

Mr. Childers nudges Ethan. "Have they managed to convert any more of the teachers?"

"From what I suspect, none of them are truly loyal to the Alliance, but they're all afraid to rebel." Ethan's hand brushes Sara's, and I press my lips together.

Enough. I'm not going to let myself be jealous. If he wants to be with her, that's fine. It's not like he's made a commitment to me, anyway.

His words in the woods come to mind. He said he loved me. Is that not a commitment?

Tears sting my already burning eyes, and I bite my lip.

"You poor thing. You've had a rough go of it, haven't you?" Sara's mother reaches in her purse and pulls out a pack of tissues. "Those schools..." She grabs a tissue for herself and hands me one. "If we'd have known, we'd never have let her go."

The path forks. and we walk to the right. A few feet ahead, a ladder drops from the ceiling. Mr. Childers climbs and opens a door, letting bright light flood the cave.

Isaac catches up to us and taps my shoulder. "The men want to meet with you a few minutes, Callie." He points to where Mr. Childers is waiting. "Micah, go to the conference room. We'll all be there in a minute."

As we ascend, Ethan meets my eyes and frowns. Is he worried?

Shelves of canned foods and three huge freezers fill the unfinished basement. A restaurant-style kitchen occupies one whole side of the room, and a series of couches and armchairs fill the other side. Wall-to-wall bookshelves stand opposite the kitchen, full of Bible class teaching materials and coloring books. All contraband, I'm sure.

Catching mine and Sara's reflection in a brushed nickel mirror, I rub my neck, which has grown sore since I've stopped to think about it. "Mrs. Childers, you said you could help me remove the tattoo. Could we do it soon, even though it hasn't completely healed?"

"You can call me Rita, sugar." She tucks the tissue pack into the side pocket of her purse. "We'll try to bring it next time we come. It's not always easy for us to get to church. Depends on whether or not the officers are feeling lenient."

"Right now they're all looking for you." Mr. Childers closes the door behind us and leads us through the basement to a set of stairs. "Which means we might not even get to go home for a few days. We have to be careful not to draw attention, and if too many people leave at once... "

"Oh." They can't go home and it's my fault. I inspect my shoes, finding one of the laces loose. As I kneel to tie it, Sara leans to Ethan's ear and whispers. I clench and unclench my fists. Why am I so jealous? But then again, it feels like the sting of Amber's betrayal all over again.

We follow Mr. Childers down a long hallway to a room lined with floor-to-ceiling oak shelves boasting hundreds of books. Leather office chairs surround a large conference table in the center.

Ethan and I sit in the ribbed-back chairs, but Sara's dad makes her leave the room.

Isaac joins us. He slips on a pair of reading glasses and takes the seat at the head of the table. He points to a picture hanging in the center of the only open wall. "My grandfather. The ever-jolly Isaiah Banks."

A toothless old man grins from the frame. His three-piece suit starkly contrasts his salt-and-pepper beard and scraggly mustache. Isaac's large nose and cleft jaw perfectly match.

Isaac smiles when my gaze flickers between him and the picture. "My great-grandfather, Isaiah Banks, was one of the wealthiest men who ever lived in the area, and no one knew it but him."

"Some of us suspected." The older men guffaw as they filter into the room. I can't help but laugh with them.

A familiar sparkle ignites Ethan's eyes. He used to love playing cards with the older men at church. I bet he'd be happy just to stay here instead of going to find Dad. With Sara.

A mustached man calls to him from the hallway, and Ethan leaves the room. I catch my dopey, wistful grin and shake my head.

Isaac coughs, bringing my attention back to the conference table.

I run my fingers along the smooth table edge. Beautiful craftsmanship. "Tell me more about your grandfather. He sounds so cool."

A wide grin stretches Isaac's stubbly face. "He was cool. Papaw Isaiah worked on the railroad. He inherited a bunch of money from a long-lost uncle and just kept on working and saving." Isaac grabs a thick photo album from the shelf behind him and slaps it on the table, sliding it toward me. "You'll find all kinds of pictures of the men who built this place. It's really neat how they smuggled the materials and workers in on the trains."

Leaning forward, I slide the book closer and flip through the pages, finding photo after photo of men using cell phones, hydraulic lifts, and Craftsman tools. No trains. I can imagine myself in the picture, with my engineering degree and hardhat, building something awesome like Isaac's bunker. Still, his words didn't mesh. "I thought you were going to say he built it decades ago. These pictures are recent."

Mr. Childers flips a few pages to older pictures with rounded edges and monochromatic brown hues. Bulky men in hard hats lift huge boulders on makeshift cranes and smile from pickaxe poses. And so many of them—amazing. "Most of it was built decades ago. You're right. Isaiah died in the 1970s. But Isaac's done a lot of work on it in the last five years as the government grew more unstable. And more importantly, he lets us use it. They converted the bunker into our office space."

I close the book and examine their faces. They seem nice enough, maybe trustworthy. But smuggling stuff is not Christ-like. What's that verse? Render unto Caesar? "Aren't we in a church? What is it you do exactly? Why do you need to meet underground?"

Isaac sneezes, and the man next to him, a raven-haired fifty-something, hands him a handkerchief. Rubbing the cotton in his fingers, Isaac stares into the fold before looking up at me. "I guess you could think of us as freedom fighters, in a way. We smuggle people out of the Alliance's hold."

Freedom fighters. It makes sense. But like Dad always taught me, you can't make things right by doing the wrong thing. "I don't understand. You kidnap people and bring them back here? Like Kendrick."

Mr. Childers clenches his teeth.

I draw in a few deep breaths and try for a calmer tone. "How is that any better than pulling all the orphaned kids out of the neutral states and throwing them into prisons disguised as schools? How can a Christian justify kidnaping and drugging people?"

Someone knocks on the doorframe, and I sit back in the chair, forcing even breaths. James. He crosses the room and rests his hand on my arm. "We're rescuing them, Callie. Returning them to their families. Giving them a chance at a happy life. Isn't that what you wanted? Didn't you want to be rescued?"

"I did. But the students are in the custody of the Alliance. Couldn't you go to jail?" I chew my lower lip.

"Didn't early Christian families hide in the Catacombs? Isn't the book of Revelation full of their secret communications?"

I press my lips and nod. "Well, yeah, I guess so."

Isaac grabs a legal pad from the center of the table and flips to a clean page. He writes a few lines and then meets my gaze. "These families have custody of their children, so it's not illegal."

Did he write things about me? Maybe I need to temper things a bit. I soften my tone. "What about me? Dad isn't my real father."

Isaac shrugs. "You'll be eighteen in a few days, and it won't matter."

"Actually…" James scans the room. "Your father did his own paternity test and passed. We believe Adrian's is a fake."

Chapter Twenty

FOLLOWING MY DISAPPEARANCE, officers have set up checkpoints on all the main roads, so the church members leave a few at a time. Isaac has planned for this, providing rooms and food for them. Apparently, it's not the first time they've had to execute caution after a service.

I picture Stumpy driving back and forth through Jonesville, a scowl on his face. He'd harass these families just for the sake of doing it.

Sara's family seems particularly nervous. Mr. Childers paces the halls, Rita obsessively cooks, and Ethan stays by Sara's side, comforting her. I've spent three days holed up in a sitting room, avoiding them, reading C.S. Lewis, and chewing my nails to the quick. Bits of dust dance in the soft incandescent light, giving the room a mystical feel, and I imagine myself home with Dad, far from any of this chaos.

Yawning, I stretch my arms over my head and cross my legs the other way. Wonder how much longer I'll have to wait.

Ethan pushes the door open with his elbow, carrying two big chocolate milkshakes. "Want company?" He offers me a tall, thick glass.

"Meh." I turn the next page, and he sets the shakes on the coffee table.

"Callie, talk to me."

Slamming the book shut, I straighten. "You want to talk? Okay, let's talk." I wave my pointer finger toward him and narrow my eyes. "One, I loved you. You chose my sister."

"I—"

"Two, you guys flaunted your relationship and talked about me behind my back. Don't think I don't know."

He clamps his mouth shut.

"Three, you think since Amber's gone, I should act like nothing was ever wrong."

"I told you. I didn't know. I've felt terrible since you left."

"*You* felt terrible? I had to watch you guys make out on the porch, pretending like I didn't exist. You did things for her that I wished you were doing for me. Torture."

"We were friends before Amber. Why can't we start over and at least try to be friends again?"

"You're doing the same thing with Sara. It's painful, and I don't want any part of it."

"Sara? But she's—"

"I. Don't. Care." I toss the book on the couch and storm out, running into Isaac as I step into the hall.

He catches me in his strong arms. "I have news. Your father will be here in an hour."

The anger seeps from my heart like someone pulled the plug on a drain. "Seriously? How did you find him so fast?" I embrace Isaac then pull away.

He chuckles. "I have ways. We believe he can get you into Tennessee, to the US. The officers suspect me, and he doesn't want you here if they come to search." He winks. "I'll let you two resume your argument. You might want to hurry and make up before your dad gets here, since he's planning on taking Ethan with him."

I huff and return to the sitting room. Ethan props his feet on the coffee table. He's holding an open book, lips curving into a smirk.

"You knew."

Isaac's laughter echoes down the long hall.

Ethan picks up a milkshake and swirls the straw. "We used to be so close. Please forgive me for messing up."

I join him on the couch, taking a long, slow sip of my shake before setting it on the table. "I wasn't perfect. I've been a jerk about things. I need to get over it."

"Don't worry about Sara. She's got a boyfriend." His intense eyes focus on mine.

A shiver courses over me. Everything I love about him comes rushing to mind. I blink, squeezing my eyes as though I could hold back the floodgate of memories. My smile betrays me.

He cracks up. "You're thinking about the time we put police tape across Mary Whitman's front yard."

Snorting, I spray milkshake all over my shirt. "Am not."

He leans across the couch, pinning and tickling me, my shake sloshing dangerously close to the edge. "I'm not stopping until you forgive me."

I gasp and giggle until I'm breathless.

"Okay, fine." He scoots away and waves his hand. "Don't forgive me. But you're going to be stuck with me for a while, so you might as well play nice."

I stand and point my finger at him, pausing for another sip. "Listen. I'm already carrying a ton of guilt for denying my faith. I'm not falling in love with a party boy."

"I haven't been to a single party since Amber left."

"You're saying it was her fault?"

He moves my shake to the table and places his hands on my shoulders.

I try to step away, resisting his gentle tug. "And I'm not interested in making out or—"

"You want to be friends. Right." He silences me with his lips, entwining his fingers in my hair and closing the divide between us.

The ice in my heart cracks against the heat of his chest. When he rests his palm along my spine, I reach behind me, lowering to the couch and steadying myself with a shaky hand. As he drops with me, I lock my arms around his neck and stare into his smoldering eyes before he kisses me again.

"Wait." He grins instead, grabbing his shake and taking a long sip. "No way I'm letting Rita's masterpiece go to waste. So, about not making out, you were saying...?"

He dabs cold chocolate crystals on my nose before kissing it, then finds his way to my lips.

I scoot away, my heart plummeting as hurt fills his eyes. "Don't get me wrong. The kiss—amazing. A moment I've dreamed about for two years. But I can't."

"You can. You did."

Rubbing my temples, I give him a rueful smile. "Ethan, I'm not your type." Tears build on my eyelids. "I'm the girl you have access to right now, nothing more. It's a matter of time before you realize it."

"Callie—"

I shake my head. "We can't be more than friends. I don't even know if we can be friends."

He reaches for my hands, and I snatch them free. "The first time I saw you kiss Amber, it felt like I'd been stabbed. Not because you kissed her, but because you gave me a look like you'd won something. And I realized you weren't who I thought you were."

"I'm sorry."

"I found a message you sent her—you called me a baby. A baby. I felt like such a fool."

"And I'm sorry for that."

The buttons at my collar choke me, and I pull them away from my neck. "I don't want you to come with us. Why can't you go home to your parents?"

Sudden tears fill his eyes. "There was an accident. Amber was driving, and...she hit their car..." He punches the wall behind the couch, wincing as he draws his fist away.

"Oh, Ethan." I don't need him to finish. His parents are dead. Amber's fault. I melt into another kiss, and we cling to each other.

He withdraws, his eyes still trained on my lips. "I don't have a home to go back to. And after the accident, Adrian sent for her. Claimed he was her father, too. She volunteered to go, hoping she could save you."

For the first time since the thinking room, I cry without inhibition, soaking his sleeve.

When we part, our once-solid shakes are icy milk. I grab mine and grin, hoping to lighten the moment. "You're right, too good to waste."

"We're too good to waste."

My heart flutters. He's got charm, for sure. I down my shake with one long drink—brain freeze—but it clears my mind. I shouldn't have kissed him, but I need to forgive him. "I'm willing to try to be friends. So, tell me how you found me."

He wipes a sticky drop off the edge of his glass and licks his finger. "We've been searching for months and rescued several other kids from the Alliance's clasp in the process. More needs to be done, but I'm leaving it to the others since I've found you."

Ethan finishes his shake and places the empty glass on the table. It clinks, nudging mine to the edge. As the glass teeters, we both reach for it, and our hands brush. This time, when he interlocks his with mine, I don't pull away. But I should.

I slip under his arm, resting my head on his shoulder. "How did they get there? Did the Alliance kidnap all of them, like me?"

"It doesn't work that way. Parents send their kids to Alliance schools for academic and behavior adjustments. And the free scholarships—some poorer eastern Kentucky towns sent fifty kids in the first year."

"Do the parents still have custody?"

"It gets tricky. They sign clever waivers giving the school certain rights. The parents have permission to withdraw their kids at any time, but the Alliance stalls them with red tape and elusive details. The US government is working on enforcing full disclosure and immediate transfer, but guys like Isaac and James intervene their own way."

Ethan squeezes, pulling me closer. His fingers drum against my upper arm—one, two, three, four. One, two, three, four... What's he trying to tell me?

"It's more retrieval than kidnaping, I guess."

Everything makes sense, other than how things came to this in the first place. Some Kentuckians resisted, and the Alliance didn't win our state. Why didn't other states resist? Or did they, and the resistance paid some kind of cost? I shudder, thinking of what might happen if he doesn't come with us. Still... can I handle being near him all day, every day?

He stands and grabs the milkshake glasses. "We'd better go get ready. Your dad isn't going to want to hang around."

"I don't understand why he's taking you. I mean... I'm glad, but can't you just cross on your own?"

Ethan takes a tissue from a box beside the couch and wipes the rings our shakes left. "Well, first, I want to stay with you. And second, besides the rebellion, your dad is all I have left. My brothers and sisters won't talk to me since I became an officer." He starts toward the kitchen, but I stand still in the hallway.

Officer. My pulse races. "What if the officers spot me when we're running? They'll catch you."

"We hope not." Rita hurries toward me. A pencil-thin woman follows, carrying a bag of makeup and a black leather apron draped over her arm. Rita gestures toward her. "This is my sister, Emily, and she's a fantastic stylist. We're going to change your appearance so it will be harder for them to recognize you."

My arm hair stands on end. Residual excitement of Isaac's news or dread from being fussed over? "What about the kidnaping charges? Dad can't go to court without coming out of hiding, and Adrian will punish you guys if he does."

"No, he can't. But you're going to be eighteen in a few weeks, and it won't matter then. We have to keep you off the radar until your birthday, and after that you are free to choose." Ethan's eyes darken, and he turns to Emily. "Keep her beautiful for me."

Beautiful? My heart thunders as he retreats.

As Emily works, she whistles hymns. I hum along in my mind, envious of her relaxed state.

She pauses to open a box of hair dye, and I gnaw on a torn nail. "Do you think I can still be a Christian after those Alliance ceremonies?"

"Quit that." She gently smacks my hand from my mouth. "Don't you think Saul might have thought the same thing on the road to Damascus? Did you persecute Christians?"

"Well… no." I rub my tattoo bandage. "But I stood in public and denounced my faith. I denied God."

"As did Peter."

She's right. How many Bible characters had moments of weak faith? Dad would chide me for forgetting. My sins are covered by Christ's blood. I draw in a deep breath, and let His comfort wash over me. "When you put it that way, it does sound like I have hope." I smile. "After my baptism, I came out of the water sure I could conquer anything… pure, clean, and spotless. Now, I feel tainted and spoiled, like I can never be clean again."

"God doesn't rank order sins." Emily covers my shoulders with a leather apron and a towel, secures them with a clip, and then holds her hand in front of me, fingers outstretched. "It's like these fancy nails. I paid a lot of money to smuggle supplies over. Told my husband I spent less than I did. In God's eyes, my sin is no better than any of the ones you've committed."

I crinkle the leather apron hem, pressing the rough thread into my thumb. "What would you have done if they'd pointed a gun at you?"

"Maybe the same thing. It's hard to say." She slips on a pair of gloves and mixes hair dye in a bowl.

"It's been a few months. I still remember all the Bible verses I had memorized. I've recited them in my head every night since I left Kentucky."

"See? You didn't give up everything." While Emily finishes mixing the dye, Rita removes my tattoo bandage and covers my neck and forehead in Vaseline. "Before we get started with your hair, I'm going to take care of this tattoo. " She pats my shoulder. "Good thing it's a small one. Shouldn't hurt much."

She opens a plastic bottle and squirts several creamy drops on a cotton swab. "This will sting a bit."

"What is it?" I examine the label.

"A special formula we ordered from Hollywood. It was expensive, though."

"Oh… I—" Holding my right hand over my neck, I press my lips together.

Rita tugs my arm lower. "No worries. Isaac bought it so we could use it on all the recruits we free."

"I know I told you…" I shake my head. "Call me crazy, but I think I'd like to keep it. It would be a constant reminder to never go down this path again."

Emily taps her right cheek. "Hmm. Guess I'm going to have to rethink the hairstyle if we're hiding a tattoo."

Two hours later, I'm staring through the mirror at a chic, raven-haired diva with smoldering eyes and deep plum lipstick. A silky black tank complements her stiff denim jacket, and a sterling silver choker cuffs her neck. Her hair tumbles in soft, feathery waves. When I smile, she smiles …surreal.

Emily stands behind me, nodding. "You're going to love this cut."

I hope so. I tug at the wispy layers spilling around my shoulders. At least it's not a complete loss of length. The choker irritates my bandaged tattoo, but it's tolerable.

Rita points to a suitcase in the corner. "I packed you a few changes of clothes and some books. Ethan said you loved to read."

"Wow. Thanks." I hug her, rubbing against her moist cheek. When I pull back, a black smudge streaks down her face. "You're crying."

Laughing, she tweaks my eye makeup with her pinky. "I like helping people. It makes me feel good. And, Callie, I've prayed for you for a while. We all have."

"Thanks."

With Rita and Emily in tow, I roll the suitcase through Isaac's monstrous house, admiring the marble tile and six-inch mahogany chair rails for the last time. We pass rows of immaculate bedrooms and a ballroom with a vaulted ceiling—much different from the run-down churches where I've spent the last few months. All this luxury, and yet he's humble, devoting his life to risky service.

Spotless white linen sofas surround a huge Queen Anne table centered in his great room. I opt to stand as several men funnel in. Sunlight streams through stained glass windows in the lofty entrance, crawling over the threshold and across the great room floor. Ethan gapes by the door.

172

Chapter Twenty-One

I TWIST a lock of hair around my fingers, holding my breath as Ethan inspects my transformation.

His expression is more than a guilty, you're-the-only-girl-in-the-room kind of look. It's the same one he gave Amber the first time they met. I've wanted him to notice me like this for years, but this isn't the real me. Why did I let him kiss me?

He's wearing a tight white t-shirt and boot-cut jeans, and a shorter cut and bangs replace his tousled waves.

The men laugh, and Isaac stands to slap him on the shoulder. "You look like Julius Caesar."

"Melvin said he used to be a barber." Ethan nods to the bearded man who strolls in behind him. "I trusted him." He winks. "You'll do Isaac's next, won't you, Mel? Cut some figures in the middle of his buzz?"

"Anything for the Cave Man." Melvin takes one of my hands in both of his. "You look beautiful, Callie."

"Thanks."

Ethan crosses to me and drapes his arm over my shoulders. "Are you okay?"

"I'm fine. Nervous." Heat covers my cheeks, but I slide deeper into his grasp.

The two men across from us chuckle.

"What?" He follows their gaze, lowering his head and patting his muscular chest, well defined in the tight t-shirt. "Oh, come on. It's sporty. There weren't many choices close to my size." Nudging me, he smirks. "What do you think?"

"You look like one of those fashion magazine models." I shake my head. "All muscles and no brain."

He gives my arm a playful punch. "Be nice. Some of those guys are college educated."

I snicker, but the light moment fades. I'd have been filling out applications and making my final decision if not for the Alliance. Would they even accept me now? I'm sure my transcript is a mess, and to get a copy sent to a college…

Someone offers to find Ethan a few bigger shirts. Someone else passes around small bottles of spring water. Maybe Melvin. I take one, twist the cap, and lift it to the light, wondering if it came from a tainted source. Knowing Isaac, he had it imported. Unscrewing the cap, I give him a hopeful smile. "So, Isaac, at lunch I overheard someone say you heard from James. No one at the school has been in trouble on my behalf, right?"

"Not yet, at least we don't think so. It appears the focus is on Kendrick as we'd hoped."

I drop the bottle to my side, pressing the rough denim fabric against my callused fingers. "Are you guys going to hold him forever? Will he ever get back to his family?"

One of the men laughs. "She worries and thinks too much."

"We'll reunite them as soon as possible." Isaac reaches into a leather briefcase and retrieves a manila folder. He hands it to me. "We found a new rebel stronghold three miles from your old school. Discovered them by pure accident and saved them from discovery during the search. Our numbers have grown in the northeast. I think Virginia is about ready to renounce their secession and merge their split so they can be a part of the United States again. He's losing his grip here."

I open the folder and remove a map of North America, dotted with black circles. Most of the dots are concentrated in the southeast, along the Bible Belt. A dashed outline moves along the Kentucky-

West Virginia border and snakes through several other states, splitting them in two. "So all of this is the Alliance? It's bigger than I thought."

Isaac nods. "Sixteen states filed for secession when it was all said and done. But not all of them joined the Alliance. The border changes constantly, so this line here is no more." He points to the dashed line splitting North Carolina. "Two are now neutral states, soon to rejoin the US. Four are split between the Alliance and the US. And an additional four, including Kentucky, withdrew their petitions before their secession passed. They're still US states."

"And six remain completely Alliance." I trace the outline of the split Virginia Commonwealth and frown. How can I leave without doing something to help?

"You'll notice the darker shaded areas—Adrian's strongholds. Very few pockets of rebellion there. Mostly cities where the citizens can't grow their own food and find clean spring water sources. With restricted travel and lack of communications, he's isolated the rebellion members to a point where they can't unite against him. If I wasn't wealthy enough to bribe people, we'd never have the success we've achieved. But it makes me a target."

"Callie." The booming voice cracks.

My body quivers. I turn.

Dad stands in Isaac's entry, holding two long-stemmed roses— one yellow and one crimson, like he's bought me for my birthday every year since I was a little girl.

Burying my face in my hands, I peek between tears and fingers. Can it really be him? Why didn't he wait for me to cross the border?

He opens his arms, and I run to him, leaping into his fierce embrace. Thorns from the roses scratch my elbow. I smell the pine needles caught in his hair and sweat pouring from his brow. I kiss his cheek and taste his wet tears. He's really here. This isn't a dream.

He squeezes and then pulls away, his wide smile changing to a frown. Wrapping his thumb and forefinger around my wrist, he moves his hand back and forth. "You've lost... You're... so thin. Didn't they feed you?"

"Not much. I—" My breath catches when I meet his gaze. His salt and pepper beard has turned completely gray, and his hair has thinned. It's odd to see him dressed in camouflage instead of a suit and tie.

"I've missed you so much." He wraps me in his arms again, lifting me from the ground, spinning me, and kissing my forehead.

"Me, too." My body spasms as we slide together to sit on an ottoman. Dad keeps one arm wrapped tight around me and removes his glasses with his free hand, exposing much more pronounced wrinkles than he had before.

He glances around the room, and his eyes moisten again. "Thank you. Thank you all for taking care of my daughter."

"It's nothing." Isaac's voice catches as he hugs Dad.

All the men and women surround Dad, shaking his hand and offering embraces. A few of the women hug me, but my attention is drawn to the armchair where Ethan sits, his chin resting on folded hands, his jaw clenched. Dad is right to insist he come with us. He needs family.

When we settle, Isaac hands Dad a map. "Here's the plan. Callie will trade places with Kristie, Melvin's daughter, who is in her twenties. There's a slight resemblance."

Kristie, a raven-haired beauty, waves from the door. I'm supposed to take *her* place? Impossible. I smooth my new hair over my shoulders. I look nothing like her, but if they think it will work…

Isaac draws a few lines on the map. "Kristie will stay here a couple days, and Callie will leave with Melvin. They're going down this road, stopping here," he taps the site, "at Melvin's farm, which connects to one of my properties, where you guys will meet up."

Dad scratches his chin. "Why is she riding with Melvin and not me?"

"The Alliance is focusing all their efforts on finding Callie. We believe by staying separated, you have a better shot of traveling unnoticed. Here, we're mostly hiding from loyalist neighbors."

Isaac points to the man next to him. "Larry agreed to take Ethan. His land adjoins mine on the opposite side, accessed by a different road. He has four sons, so we figure one more boy in their van won't attract much attention."

Dad stares at the map and gives a slow nod. "And me?"

Isaac straightens. "I'll drive you myself and pummel anyone who tries to stop us."

He folds the map and points to the right of the crease. "You'll converge tonight at this cabin on the edge of my farm. And I'll let you guys stay there a couple days, maybe three. Lay low. Then we'll move you farther, to another property. It's close to the border." Isaac makes a circle on the map. "We'll move you one more time, and cross the border through a short cave. You're lucky. This is good terrain for hiding." He looks sideways at me. "Callie should leave right away. Sometimes the middle of the day is the best time to not draw attention."

I'm trembling to the point I stumble with every step. Ethan and Dad both give me strained, lingering goodbyes, and I follow Melvin and his wife, Sheila, to their car.

"It's so nice of you to do this for me."

"Our pleasure."

I crawl into the back seat of their sedan while Melvin loads my suitcase in the trunk. Sheila leans over the passenger seat and flashes a toothy smile. She's an animal print woman, with long, tawny hair like Amber's, an unusual match to Melvin's thin tufts of white-blond hair poking out in all directions. We make quite the motley crew heading down the winding country road to their home.

Surprisingly steady traffic moves along the forest-lined road. Through the tinted window, I see officers in every car, though most are just normal families. I think I'm losing my mind. "I haven't seen much outside of the Academy. Except trees."

"Yep. Lots of trees in Alliance country." Melvin, who donned a fedora and sunglasses, whistles off-key jazz while Sheila files her nails. Does he think he's a Blues Brother? He'd get along great with Dad—that's his favorite movie. If we go crashing into a mall, I'm bailing. Not that the Alliance has malls anymore. Wonder if people looted like they did back home.

We drive thirty minutes, farther than it looked as the crow flies. Melvin turns onto a gravel road and stops the car to open a rusty farm gate. He pulls through and stops again to close the gate behind us, then spins up gravel as we race down the road to a huge white farmhouse.

"We always sit on the front porch in the afternoons," Melvin says. "We'll stay out here a few minutes and watch the road to make sure the officers don't suspect anything. You can go through the house and sit out back. Watch for Isaac to wave to you from across the field." He unlocks the door and holds it open for me, leading me into the stuffy house. "You're lucky. Here, you don't have to worry about the neighbors. Larry's property is riskier. His neighbors opposite Isaac would turn you into the Alliance in a heartbeat."

My heart sinks. Right where Ethan's headed.

Sheila opens the drapes, letting light into the dim room. "Melvin, you shouldn't have told her. Isaac said to let her believe there was little danger."

"Don't you have electricity?"

"We do, but it's so expensive we rarely use it. Isaac is going to teach us how to make our own the way he does."

I follow Sheila into the house, hit the restroom, and hurry outside to a fancy cherry deck showing wear from months of neglect. Plopping down on a plump striped cushion, I rest my elbows on the patio table and scan the horizon.

"They'll make their move at dark." Melvin joins me and points to a clearing between two thick patches of trees. "The officers drive through about nine thirty to see we've all made curfew. Larry is going to send one of his boys out around nine, needing to have a flat tire fixed. The officers will help him. It'll keep them occupied long enough for Ethan to cross to Isaac's farm."

"And Dad?"

"He'll ride in the bed of Isaac's truck. They'll set him down in a burlap sack and pack several corn-filled sacks around him. So unless the officers do a thorough inspection, they'll never notice. If he gets stopped, Isaac will give the officers a bag of corn. They won't ask what's in the others."

"At least Isaac hopes." I resume my vigil, transfixed as the tree line darkens and wisps of red and purple stream across the Virginia sky.

Seconds later, Melvin nudges my shoulder, and I rise, knocking a wool blanket to the deck floor. Or, maybe not seconds later. "Oh. I…"

He chuckles. "You fell asleep, and we let you rest." Passing me a pair of binoculars, he points with them. "Look over there. Your Dad and Ethan are waiting."

The short run across Melvin's field feels like miles with me dragging my suitcase along behind. I meet up with Dad, Isaac, and Ethan, rush between the trees, and come to a cabin not quite as fancy as the tornado-damaged one.

A small porch surrounds the perimeter, and Isaac leads us to the rear. "There, the Smoky Mountains." He waves his arm over a field of tiny blue wildflowers tracing the top of the monstrous peak. "Tennessee. Not Alliance."

I outstretch my arms as if I could jump and fly there. "The view is incredible."

Ethan leans over the rail, peering down to the baseball-sized gravels below. "So, we'll spend three days here, right?"

Isaac nods. "Three days will give me time to mill about town and overhear the officers. Maybe get in touch with James again and ask if he's got any news." He grins. "The best part about this place is you can pick up a couple Tennessee television and radio stations. And…"

Reaching in his pocket, he bobs his head toward a distant tower. "We still have cell phone service since we're so close. Although I wouldn't get too excited. The signal isn't strong. Be careful what you say. You never know who might be listening. But it will connect you to me."

He leaves, and I follow Ethan and Dad into the cabin.

I'd hoped to have a long talk with Dad, but his eyes are droopy. He mumbles a couple of sentences about Ethan not being allowed in my bedroom and disappears into one of the other rooms to rest.

Ethan settles on the couch and picks up an old, worn car magazine. It's doubtful he's reading anything because the pages turn fast, and I keep meeting his sideways glances.

I examine the kitchen. A layer of grease covers the counters, and mold blackens the grout in the floor. The table sports remnants of a takeout dinner—a petrified quarter of a fast food burger and a handful of wooden French fries. "Wonder who stayed here last."

Ethan sets the magazine down and joins me, gathering up trash. "Isaac said it was a couple in their twenties he helped escape a few days ago. They had to leave on short notice because of a family illness. He apologized for not having the cabin cleaned. At least he had groceries brought in."

Dad returns to the living area and flips channels to the local news. A reporter sits at a desk in front of my giant-sized face, captioned Where is Callie Lamb?

The reporter clears her throat. "Knoxville police are stepping up patrols this evening as reports have come in regarding possible sightings of Callie Rae Lamb, the seventeen-year-old daughter of Adrian and Ella Lamb, First Lord and Lady of the Allied States. She is thought to be armed and dangerous. Authorities believed she crossed near Cumberland Gap and headed to Knoxville to meet up with this man, Martin Noland, who claims to be her father."

Chapter Twenty-Two

DAD PACES the cabin, tossing random items into a trash bag. He's even picking up things like hair. I'm too shocked to be scared at this point. We were so careful.

I flip the television channel and drop into an armchair. "What will we do?"

"What Isaac said. Wait here. Lay low." Ethan meets Dad's gaze, and they both crack up.

"What's funny about me being in danger?"

"Comic relief." Ethan points to the screen. "The last time I saw your dad, he watched every single episode of an *I Love Lucy* marathon, and I begged him to turn it off."

Dad tries to make a straight face and bursts out in laughter again. I can't help but join him. Who knows when I last had a real laugh? Who knows when I'll get to laugh again?

My mind drifts to a Christmas from years ago, long before Ethan. Dad stayed up way into the night wrapping presents, hoping I wouldn't figure out he was Santa.

I caught him racing into the living room and jumped into his lap. We both laughed so hard we woke Amber and Mom.

Mom, of course, had a snide comment. Thinking about it now, even then signs of trouble crossed Dad's deflated face.

Sighing, I squeeze between him and Ethan on the couch and pull the thick wool afghan off the back cushion and around my shoulders. We watch rerun after rerun, relishing in the laughter. Somehow I end up holding both Dad's and Ethan's hands, and when I look at Dad, his eyes are misty.

"Well, cupcake, we're not out of the rough waters yet, but I think you can rest easy tonight." He stands and stretches. "And maybe we should get a head start on resting in case we have to run tomorrow."

I do rest, a deep, dreamless sleep. For a few hours.

By morning, I'm going over a waterfall in Dad's car and Adrian laughs at the top of it. Then I'm trapped in a fiery prison, and at last shot from several angles in front of a mob. Faces pop out of the crowd—Sara, Maggie, Ben—and they all shake their fists at me. This is my fault.

My eyelids pop open. I draw in a deep breath and grin, smelling thick maple bacon like Dad used to fix for me when I was a girl.

I poke my head into the hallway and look both directions. Ethan's room is dark, so I'm guessing he's still asleep. Good. I can shower before he comes out of his room.

When I slip across the hall, Dad catches my eye from the kitchen. He's beaming, with a beardless face.

"Morning," he says in a low voice.

I smile. "Morning. Where did you get bacon?"

"Isaac. He grew the pig." Dad saunters to the stove, and I duck into the bathroom with my wadded fresh clothes. I lock the door and shower, letting hot water spill over my shoulders and drip onto my feet.

Twenty minutes later, I emerge, wearing a shoddy attempt at styling my hair the way Emily did. Dad is still alone in the kitchen, flipping hash browns.

"I talked to James. He said they found Kendrick's car—that's what this is all about. James didn't have time to clean it and make sure there wasn't any evidence. Kendrick kept a notebook. Several entries in it make him a good suspect—departure times, mileage, etc."

"Did he say anything about Ethan?"

"I don't know."

Bacon sizzles, the fan above the stove whirs. Still a slight haze drifts from the pan while Dad mills about the kitchen.

"Smells good in here." I lean against the counter. "Do you want help?"

"You want to scramble some eggs? Everything else is done."

"Sure."

He's already cracked the eggs into the pan, so I add salt and pepper and swirl the yolk around in the whites until there's one big yellow glob, then chop it into smaller pieces as it cooks. "I remember you making breakfast for us when I was little. Before you had to work so much."

His smile reveals dimples I never knew he had. Dimples that remind me of Adrian. I shiver, but settle when he hands me a piece of the crisp bacon "Every morning. You used to eat your weight in bacon. Can you still eat that much?"

"I think so." I glance toward Ethan's bedroom and frown. What will Dad think if he finds out we've kissed? "Why do you feel this obligation to take care of Ethan?"

Dad grabs a plate and covers it with a paper towel. He scoops the hash browns on it and sets it on the table. "His dad and I were good friends in college, before I met your mother. He's the one who got me into church."

"Oh."

"So, when Roger and Brenda died, I couldn't imagine leaving their son to fend for himself, not after I'd lost you girls."

He doesn't say it, but "and your mom" weighs heavy in the air.

"You've always had a thing for him." The bacon pops, and he jumps.

I switch off the burner and carry the eggs to the table. "He broke my heart when he chose Amber over me. I'm trying to forgive him."

Dad's face scrunches up like I pinched him. I'm sure he'd rather not talk about my love life. He coughs and turns the bacon with a fork. "Well, he's been a big help to me and Isaac. We wouldn't have found you if not for his persistence. Michael knew you were going to West Virginia, but until Ethan met James, we didn't know where to look. When all this is over, I'll set him up in an apartment, and he can finish college."

A sinking sensation swirls in the pit of my stomach. "I should be in school right now. There's no way I'm going to graduate on time."

"Don't worry."

It becomes Dad's mantra as our time in the cabin is extended. Isaac stops by a couple of times to give us updates. The same old-same old—officers comb the area, and it's not safe to move. But don't worry. I ran out of things to read, and there's nothing else to do in the cabin. But don't worry.

Wish I could stop.

All I can do is wait three days until I turn eighteen, and I'm no longer required to be under anyone's custody.

I spend the first day in excruciating boredom, playing around with the makeup Emily gave me and trying to master different faces. I'm unable to accomplish more than looking like a clown. After a while, they start feeling sorry for me and try to help, which turns out even worse.

The second day is a Sunday, and Isaac drops by some groceries, including Matzo crackers and grape juice so we can have communion. We worship, singing devotional songs for hours, and end up working out a decent harmony.

On the third day, the cell Isaac gave us rings somewhere around lunchtime. Dad listens. His hands grip the table tight enough to chip the trim. When he ends the call, he slams his clasped fingers on the table.

"They attempted another extraction, and Alliance officers stopped them before they made it out of West Virginia. The woman could have spilled a lot of info about Isaac's operation to save her own family. Thankfully, she didn't. But Adrian had her husband and children thrown in prison."

"What?" My breath becomes jagged, and I tip my face toward the ceiling, closing my eyes.

Ethan clears his throat. "Is the phone secure?"

Dad spreads a packet of mayonnaise on his sandwich. "Isaac has a contingency plan for everything. This is an untraceable line."

My skin tingles all over, and I feel like my heart might explode. "Why? How?" I pick at my plateful of contraband potato chips, finding a small triangular one, and press its center, breaking it into several pieces. "What did she tell them?"

"She refused to talk, so they released her into Isaac's custody and took her family." He lifts the bread to his mouth and pauses. "It's a tricky situation, Callie, because we're Christians and we can't lie. What we're doing is illegal, even if you were in an unjust situation. That's always been part of the deal. If we're caught, we have to pay the consequences."

Ethan brushes crumbs from the table into his hand and drops them in his plate. "This hasn't been a problem before because the parents have all had custody of their kids. We were getting the kids away from the school and handing them over to their families."

"But not me."

"Not you." Dad stands and begins pacing the kitchen. "The question is whether or not they'll seize all of Isaac's properties, or conduct deep searches. He's under incredible scrutiny. Although, he says the Alliance is strapped for resources, and right now his money is talking."

Ethan shoves his chair away from the table.

I drum my fingers against my cup. "Even if they know I'm with you, they wouldn't find us for a while. I'll be eighteen in a few hours. What if I tell them I ran away? They don't have any proof I didn't."

Dad grabs his soda and takes a sip. "They have Kendrick's notebook. And they're searching for him. If they search Isaac's properties and find him…"

Ethan glares at his half-eaten sandwich and scoots his chair up to the table again, propping his chin against a fist. "So, what do we do? Should we pack up and run somewhere?"

"If we leave, we could be spotted. We wait and pray, right?" I look at Dad, raising my eyebrows. "Until I'm eighteen and old enough to choose."

Dad points to his Bible, which rests on the mantel. "God's will be done."

The minutes go by like hours. We step away from the table and work together to clean the kitchen. Dad decides to tackle a leaky faucet, and Ethan does pushups on the living room floor.

Somewhere after six, Dad ventures to Melvin's house for news. He tells Ethan to inspect all the windows and locks, like it would stop someone from the Alliance from getting to us. As soon as the door closes behind him, Ethan kicks a kitchen chair and knocks it over.

I go to him and jerk the chair upright. "Calm down."

"Easy for you to say. I've lost everything. I'm not going to lose you."

Pinching my lips, I shoot him a direct stare. "Ethan, we haven't even talked about what happened since you kissed me. It's like you're sorry it ever happened."

"Look, I know I have been a jerk to you, and you have no reason to believe I'm telling you the truth. But when you left, my eyes opened. I saw Amber for the whiny brat she was, and I missed you."

"You don't even know me anymore. I've changed so much since then." I bite my lip. "And you said it yourself. I was a kid. You didn't even talk to me more than just stilted sentences the whole time you two dated."

He looks at the floor, and for the first time I notice his thinning hair. When he lifts his gaze, his eyes are bloodshot and droopy.

"You've not been sleeping."

"No." He sits in the chair he kicked and props his chin with his elbows. "Every moment, every thought—it's consumed with you. I'm in love with you, Callie. I always have been. I was stupid then. And it's hard to talk to you about it with your Dad sitting a few feet away."

I clutch my chest, willing my racing pulse to stop betraying me. I've waited to hear this for three years, but since he's said it, I'm not sure I trust his heart.

He reaches for my hands. "If they take you again, I don't know what I'll do."

"What could they do? Make me go to Mom for five or six hours? It wouldn't be worth their time or money."

Ethan slides me into his lap and wraps his arms around me. "I have an idea."

"Okay."

"Let's go to Atlanta."

"Atlanta? Why?"

"CNN. Tell your story. The American people would be outraged and stand up for you. They'd stand up to everyone."

When I open my mouth to protest, he brings his finger to my lips. I shudder, and he laughs. "You still love me. I don't know why you don't admit it."

Amber always used to talk about how her heart would ache before a kiss. Now, I know what she means. I want to scream and run, and I want to get on with it.

His lips are shiny where he's licked them. He brushes my neck with his fingers.

Closing my eyes, I hold my breath as he tugs my head close to his. It's do-or-die time. Pull away or lean in.

I pull away.

Ethan steps closer. He captures my mouth just as Dad yells something from the door. We freeze for a couple of seconds before he releases me.

Standing, I stumble a few steps before heading to the couch. "Dad? Everything okay?"

He strolls into the kitchen. "Forgot the cell phone. Did I miss anything?"

Ethan yawns, stretching his arms over his shoulder.

I don't know how he's so calm. My heart pounds loud enough Dad could have heard it from the driveway.

"We were talking about Atlanta," Ethan says. "I had an idea."

Dad leans against the doorjamb. "I'm listening."

"CNN. After she turns eighteen, we take her straight to their headquarters. Let her sit down with a reporter and explain her side of the story. Let her expose the Alliance for the cult they are."

"I don't know. It might put her at even more risk. They could send someone to retaliate."

"Maybe it won't be necessary," I fiddle with the remote, though I'm sure Dad knows what we were doing. "Let's give it more time."

Dad grabs the phone. "I should return in about thirty minutes." He narrows his eyes at Ethan. "Boy, you'd better keep your hands to yourself. The last thing we need to do is add a baby to this chaos."

Yep. He knows. My cheeks warm, and I concentrate on a small nick in the linoleum.

Ethan chuckles. "No worries, Martin." As Dad closes the door, Ethan moves to the other side of the table. "Sorry, Callie. I shouldn't have kissed you."

"You're right."

"You didn't kiss me, so I guess I know where things stand."

I sigh. "I'm not saying never. Not right now. And not for a long time."

"I can live with waiting." He gives me a sideways grin. "Let's watch some TV or something."

We head into the living room and sit as far away from each other as possible. Ethan switches the TV to some crime scene investigation show, and I cringe as blood spatters across the screen.

He flips to the cooking channel, on the way, passing CNN, and a clip of Adrian, shaking his fist. His fierce eyes bore a hole into my soul.

I force even breaths, in and out, in and out. It sounds like I'm practicing Lamaze or something. When my body takes over breathing again, I wrap myself in my arms. "They're not ever going to stop coming for me. Tomorrow will change nothing."

Chapter Twenty-Three

DAD'S SNORES fill the cabin, though the television blares. I edge the remote from his fingers and pull a blanket from the back of the armchair to cover him. Ethan rubs his eyes with his palms and swallows a yawn. "Well, the good news is it's almost midnight. You'll be eighteen in about forty-five minutes."

"Right." I jump off the couch and pour myself a glass of milk. "You want something?"

"Let's make frozen pizza."

While the oven preheats, we sit at the table holding hands, and for the first time, I'm not nervous. "You know, the day I met you, I thought you were such a jerk."

Ethan brings his hand to his mouth in mock surprise. He relaxes and then wrinkles his forehead. "I was kind of a jerk."

I giggle. "You thought you were so cool, pulling up to the church in your mom's minivan."

"Yeah, well, you thought you were as big as the high school kids. Big eighth grader coming in and showing us up by having all the answers."

"Not showing everybody up. Just you."

"Oh yeah? Prove it. Three men in the fiery furnace."

"Shadrach, Meshach, and Abednego." I smirk. "Zaccheus climbed in what kind of tree?"

Ethan waves his arm across his face. "Easy. Sycamore. Like your street. Jonathan's crippled son."

191

"Mephibosheth. Who said, 'Shall I go and smite these Philistines?'"

"Sampson."

I spit my milk across the room, almost hitting Dad in the face. "David."

Ethan flops over, stopping shy of bumping his head on the table. "Aw, man. Thought I had that one." He reaches into his pocket and pulls out a small white box. "Here. It's not a trophy, but it'll do."

A small ring hides under the lid, white gold, with a heart-shaped pink ice stone. My jaw drops. "What is this?"

"It's for your birthday. I was going to wait, but we can never be sure about tomorrow."

He slips it on my right ring finger, and I lift my hand to my heart, looking down at the stone. "It's pretty."

"Thanks," he says. "It was Mom's. I think she would have wanted you to have it. She always liked you, even though she wasn't nice sometimes. And she used to nag me about picking the wrong sister. I was too dumb to listen."

"Wow." Blinking away tears, I bring the stone closer to my eyes, picturing it on his mother's hand as she smiles and waves at us. "I had no idea." I chuckle. "My mom never liked you."

He shakes his head. "She did try, though. Remember when she decided to make us a pizza out of her awful wheat flour?" Ethan twists his face into a hideous grimace, and I snort my milk.

"And the bean brownies? Amber stunk up the house for days because she ate half the pan before Mom told her."

"Try weeks." He laughs so hard he almost falls out of his chair. "Hey, do you remember the Elderberry Dinner when we serenaded Mr. and Mrs. Whitman on their fifty-sixth wedding anniversary?"

"Ha. How could I forget?"

He launches into an impression of Stevie Wonder's cover of Ella Fitzgerald, and before I know it, I'm spinning across the kitchen floor in his arms while Dad snores on.

This is the Ethan I love—the Ethan who can find the joy in little things and keeps me in sidesplitting laughter for hours. The Ethan who humiliates himself to make an old lady's night brighter, and who wants everyone in the room to share in his smile. I close my eyes, relishing for a moment what might have been. What still could be… if I can trust him.

He spins me against the counter and plants a kiss on my forehead. "We used to do great things together, little sister, before big sister got in our way."

"Amber was your choice." Crossing my arms, I move to the other side of the room and peek out the window. Nothing but trees silhouetted against a charcoal sky. "You said you weren't going to kiss me anymore."

The preheat timer beeps. Grinning, he removes the plastic and places the pizza on the oven rack. "I never said I wouldn't try again, just that I knew where things stood."

I put my hands on my hips. "The next guy I kiss, I'm going to marry. Period."

"I can live with that, too."

Dad's cell dings, and he clears his throat. "Good." No telling how much of our conversation he heard.

Ethan and I both jump, and he meets Dad's gaze, letting out a nervous laugh. "Did you have a nice nap?"

Dad goes to a closet and grabs several heavy-duty backpacks. "No. You guys were too loud. Come here and help me."

I rush to his side, holding my arms out for supplies. "Who texted?"

"James. Adrian has upped security here. Someone tipped him that we've moved to this area. Officers are scouring nearby towns, but they're headed our way. Isaac is under extreme scrutiny, and they have started searching his properties. It's rough territory, and a lot of private land, so we probably have a couple of hours. But we need to move."

The supplies crash to the floor. I bunch my hair into a twisted lump and tug until it hurts, then bend to pick up what I've dropped. This can't be real.

Dad unzips one of the bags and starts shoving cans of food inside. "James says it's time for plan B. Go get a change of clothes, something outdoor appropriate. We can't take suitcases where we're going."

I raise my eyebrows and shut off the oven. "Where are we going?"

"Somewhere safe." He tosses Ethan a backpack. "We have a few hours of darkness before we risk being caught by a local. Move quickly. The back closet is full of camping gear, sleeping bags, and such."

My heart stops. I should help, but I'm frozen. This could be where the road ends for all of us. After a few deep breaths, I force myself to grab a backpack. "What do you need me to do?"

"You'll find medical supplies under the bathroom sink. Take a Ziploc bag from the kitchen and make us a small first aid kit."

When we're all packed, Ethan peeks out the window and swipes away the damp condensation. "What now?"

With a wry grin, Dad points to the door. "We're going for a walk. One of Isaac's friends will meet us in a few miles, and he'll drive us somewhere. And then we're going to disappear."

Dad hands me and Ethan thick canvas jackets lined with soft cotton. Overkill, but I put mine on anyway, stuffing the pockets with random things Dad asks me to carry. We slip the backpacks over our shoulders and head out the front door.

Shining a flashlight, Dad leads the way around a gravel path to the back of Isaac's property. It narrows to a smaller trail and disappears into a grove of trees. "Step on the roots as much as you can," he tells us. "Don't leave prints."

We do as he says, following the beam to a wider path which ends at a road. A dark, rusted van waits under a streetlamp, its engine idling.

The driver's side window lowers, and a pudgy-faced man leans out. "You guys ready?"

Dad nods and opens the sliding door, tossing his pack inside. "Callie, you ride here with me. Ethan, sit in front and pay attention in case we need to find our way back to the cabin."

Once we're all in and the van light goes off, we drive along a winding narrow road heading farther into the country. No one speaks. I figure the driver would at least talk to Dad, but he doesn't.

We twist and turn for about thirty minutes, jostling over gravel and potholes. The driver manages a decent speed, though the engine spits and sputters like it's going to explode. My ears pop as we gain elevation. I clutch the door handle so tight the plastic pulls away. Every inch of my body trembles.

The man pulls over to the gravel shoulder and lets us out. Dad leads us down another narrow trail. Pine scents, chirping crickets, and a melancholy owl welcome us. Mosquitos nip at my chin, and I slap them away. Ethan reaches for my hand, and we follow Dad, walking on roots like he said.

"The bugs are eating me up." I take a couple of paces forward, almost running into Dad, who stops.

"Hush, Callie." His voice is so low it's hard to hear him. "This trail is supposed to be closed right now. We don't want to be discovered."

I clamp my mouth shut, and Ethan squeezes my fingers.

We walk for another hour, and I pause to rub my burning calves. My feet ache from treading on roots, and every step drives my tibia into my kneecap. I'm panting like a dog on a hot summer day, which isn't fair. Dad and Ethan haven't broken a sweat. When I think I can't move further, Dad shines the light a few feet off the path, over a steep-sloped hill.

"This part will be rough, Callie." He tips the flashlight to his face, casting an eerie triangular glow.

Seriously? Rougher than it has been? I brace myself on a moss-covered tree.

"You're going to have to go slow, let me and Ethan move ahead, and bring you down to us. James said it gets slick and one misstep could have you sliding down the whole hill into the creek."

"Okay." My voice sounds tiny, as if someone else is speaking far away.

"It's going to be fine." Ethan drapes his arm over my shoulders.

Everybody says that. Nothing is ever fine, though. How will this be any better?

Dad points into the darkness. "When we get to the bottom of the hill, we're going to cross over to a farm. There's an electric fence, but it's supposed to be turned off right now. Still, you'll have to watch the barbed wire. It can scratch you up bad."

Ethan squeezes me, planting a light kiss on my forehead while Dad has his head turned. "I had to learn the hard way when I was a kid. Listen to your dad."

Dad waves his hand toward a boxy shadow in the distance. "There's a house on the edge of the property. The owners are not home. We're not going to use it, but don't be surprised to see officers there searching. It doesn't have running water or electricity. We'll stay in a nearby cave."

"Cave." I clutch the collar of my jacket. "Like we're going to camp there?"

"For a while," Dad says. "Until we figure something else out. We're still about five miles from Isaac's border property, but we have to cross land belonging to Alliance loyalists to get there." He sidesteps down the hill, reaching for a thin birch trunk. "James is trying to work out another plan."

Ethan secures himself on another trunk to the right of me and eases down a couple of yards, hooking his toes around the base of another small tree. "Okay, Callie. We're going to reach for you. Step down and rest your foot against this lower one."

And so we go, in what feels like a choreographed dance. First Dad slides, then Ethan, and then me. When we reach the bottom, I let out a monstrous yawn.

The moon peeks from a thick line of clouds, illuminating tiny waves and shimmering stones in the creek. My ring glimmers, and I touch the gold band with the tip of my thumb. Ethan's promise.

On the other bank, a barbed-wire fence surrounds a field. The remnants of last year's harvested corn litter the ground, sparkling with dew.

At first, I think we're going to have to go through the water, but then I spot an old wooden bridge to our right. Ethan reclaims my clammy hand as we cross. He snickers and I grimace. It doesn't help I'm sweating like a rock star in this jacket. My body always betrays me.

When we reach the fence, Dad removes his backpack. He retrieves a long, insulated screwdriver. Clutching the plastic handle, he tests for electricity then lifts the upper wire and slips through.

"Hand me the packs."

I do then slither through the barbs to join him, garnering a couple of scratches on my arm. Ethan follows, and we take turns heading into the woods for a quick pit stop.

Three large boulders obscure the cave's mouth. We climb over the flattest one and drop in.

Ethan presses forward, shining his light along the cave walls. "This chamber is level."

Dad peers in after him. "Looks like the path is wide most of the way in. No drops that I can see, but we'll have to watch for stalactites. Ethan, let me go first."

I shiver in the cool, dry air, finally understanding the need for jackets. Zipping mine, I trudge along between them.

Several meters in, a faint glow shines like the one in Isaac's cave. We approach a large room, lit by lanterns and stocked with air mattresses, blankets, and cardboard boxes.

"Wow." I glance at Dad, who's smiling. "Someone thought this out."

"James did. The property belongs to his cousin. You're okay with staying here?"

I shrug. "I have to be, don't I?"

"I'm going to go make a phone call." Dad looks at Ethan. "Keep your hands to yourself."

"Yes, sir."

Heat creeps across my cheeks.

Dad walks back toward the entrance, and Ethan and I inspect the cave walls and ceiling. "Look, there. He gestures. "That rock looks like your sister. A pouty face and protruding nose."

I snap to face him. "Amber looks like a goddess."

"A spoiled one. She's almost too perfect."

My own nose itches, and I raise my hand to scratch it. "I thought I was the one with the protruding snout."

"Yours is natural. Hers is by choice." He leans closer and kisses the tip of my nose. "I happen to like yours."

Backing away, I look at the cave floor. "Ethan, I feel like you're trying to take advantage of this situation. I'm vulnerable, and you're pushing limits again."

He puffs his cheeks, exhaling. "I know you still care about me."

"Maybe I do, but I'm not dumb enough to rush into some kind of false romance. I've said it before. You're interested because I'm here. Let the next pretty girl walk in and you'd be all over her, flirting and making promises you'll never keep."

"When will you believe I've changed?" He stalks over to his backpack and moves it next to one of the mattresses. "I'm going to read a while. I tucked my Bible in here if you want to use it later. Plus a couple of the books Rita sent with you."

"Okay." I claim my air mattress, leaving Dad the one closest to the chamber entrance.

Footsteps echo, and Dad rounds the corner. "Sleep while you can. James says he'll try to get to us tomorrow."

Chapter Twenty-Four

WITH A YAWN, I turn down the blanket on my mattress. A tiny flicker of movement snags my attention. My breath catches, and I ease the blanket back more. A brown leathery tail flitters by, and my scream echoes through the cave.

Cowering on Ethan's mattress, I wrap myself in my arms as a lizard crawls out of the blanket and scuttles over the cave floor, settling at the base of the footwall. Dad and Ethan erupt into knee-slapping guffaws.

I stand, hands on my hips, and glare at them both. "Stop it."

Ethan points to the "beast," who presses its body against a basketball-sized rock. It's redder than brown, about six inches long and, bad as I hate to admit it, adorable.

"You okay?" Dad coaxes me off Ethan's mattress.

"What is that thing?"

"It's a cave salamander. Harmless. They do bite on occasion, but not unless you bother them." He walks over to a loose rock and lifts it. "Sometimes, if you look, you can find their eggs."

Shuddering, I return to my mattress, pinch the blanket between two fingers, and give it a good shake. "I don't want to find any eggs. What other creepy animals live here?"

Dad nods to the ceiling. A cluster of little brown rodents hang upside down.

"Great." I spread the blanket again and brush my fingers over it, checking for insects. "Bats. We'll all catch rabies. What else?"

"Spiders, crickets, and bears—oh my!" Ethan laughs, and I throw a small rock at him, loping it a couple feet short of his hiking boots.

"Not funny." I face Dad. "Do bears live in caves?"

"They come into caves in the winter to hibernate. I think." He winks. "You're safe here. Trust me. Trust God. Speaking of God, Ethan, why don't you lead us in a prayer?"

Ethan reaches for my hand, and we form a circle in the middle of the chamber. He squeezes my fingers and bows his head. "Dear Lord, we come to you today with grateful hearts, thankful for another day, for our health, and for the pleasant weather over the past few hours. We are grateful for Callie's safety and the cover you've provided. Also, Lord, we thank you for the abundance of fish, berries, and clean water, which will nourish our bodies and give us strength."

He breathes heavy. "Lord, we trust your providence. If it's your will, then help us cross the border. And if not, help us understand how you want to use us to further your Word to Alliance citizens. Please give us strength and courage. We feel your presence. Our ultimate goal on this earth is to spread your Good News to every creature. In Jesus' name, amen."

"Amen. Nice job, son." Dad extinguishes the lanterns as Ethan and I settle on our mattresses. "Now get some sleep. Who knows what waits for us in the morning."

How could I possibly sleep? I feel like crying, but I should be happy, shouldn't I? We're together. And free. And Ethan's right. We need to count our blessings. I close my eyes, inhale the musty cave air, and let the crickets lull me to sleep.

I wake to Ethan's and Dad's hushed whispers. Eyes shut, I breathe evenly as possible.

"What time is it? You've already been fishing?" Ethan lets out a long, drawn-out yawn.

Dad snorts. "For three hours. It's almost seven thirty. I thought you guys might need a little extra sleep. I'm meeting James in roughly an hour to discuss our options."

"I still think we should broadcast a message on television." Ethan zips something. "Let her give a message to Adrian and the general public. She's eighteen now, so she can choose. She can tell them she's not in any danger, and let them know what he's really doing to his citizens."

"Maybe. Adrian has painted her as a fugitive, so I'm not sure how that would pan out." Dad peels bark away from a branch with his pocketknife. "I've been waiting to hear from Isaac. The lack of news worries me. Hope he's not in Adrian's custody."

Ethan yawns again. "We should have waited until Callie turned eighteen before helping her escape. Would have saved us all this grief."

"That's what I told James. He said Adrian planned to move her, though, and Hannah wanted to sneak her out under the cover of the big pew shipment. They were trying to do what they thought was best for Callie. Just like having me cross the border to get her. Now we have to get two of us across instead of one." Dad lowers his voice. "James means well, but I'm not sure about his methods sometimes."

"What do the US media outlets say about the Alliance? Are other states still considering secession?"

Dad shakes his head. "It won't happen. People in the Alliance are getting frustrated with their oppressive laws. They've already started writing petitions to rejoin the Union, and leaking it to US reporters. Adrian's army can't be everywhere—they don't have the funding. Or the loyalty. He recruited people through the Internet and handed them a gun. Offered them a lot of things he can't deliver. Some have already started to buck the system."

Ethan's hard exhale echoes through the cavern. "How about Amber? Any word on her?"

Dad coughs, with a hint of a wheeze. "Sorry. This cave air is killing my allergies. We think she's still in rehab. Of course, it's been next to impossible to check."

I peek through slit eyelids. Ethan's shoulders fall in the dim lantern light. As I finger my ring, tears sting my eyes. He can say what he wants about his feelings for me, but the boy still loves my sister.

"I'll cook this fish for breakfast." Dad grabs a backpack and a metal grill. "Why don't you wake Callie?"

Dad's footsteps fade. Ethan kneels beside my air mattress and cups my cheek in his hand.

A trace of his sporty soap lingers, and I inhale longer than I should. I roll my shoulders back, turning my head from side to side and stretching my elbows. When I open my eyes, his face is an inch from mine.

"Hey, beautiful."

"Hey." I can't make myself smile. I always wanted Amber out of the picture. If she'd stayed at college, Ethan might have returned his attention to me. But the ghost of her presence would have haunted us then as it does now.

Ethan's brow furrows. "Isn't it enough I'm giving up everything to be here? I could be walking around free, doing whatever I wanted, sleeping in a real bed." He grasps my hands and helps me sit up. "Even your dad is on my side in this. Why can't you forgive me?"

"Not totally, I bet. You're not doing yourself any favors trying to kiss me all the time in front of him."

Grinning, Ethan glances toward the long tunnel to the cave entrance. "True. But he trusts me it's real. I wish you did."

I stand, smoothing my matted hair. Casting a furtive glance at the bats, I take an indirect path across the room.

Ethan walks me to the cave entrance, where Dad squats beside a small fire.

"I'm going to the bathroom." Ethan nods to the trees.

"Hurry." Dad tosses him a plastic baggie with toilet paper. "Food's almost done."

203

After Ethan finishes, I head into the woods myself, wrinkling my nose as I struggle to stay balanced in a crouch and do my business. I return to bland, but steaming fish on crude plates made from bark, a comfort in the cool morning air. Dad and Ethan settle into easy conversation about salamanders and bats.

"So, what do we do now?" The sun pokes through the clouds, bathing us in the eerie red glow of crepuscular rays. The smell of ozone burns my nose. Red sky at morning. Hope it's not a sign of worse to come.

Dad focuses on the skyline, too, his forehead wrinkled and eyes squinted "You guys just wait here in this clearing. Stay close to the mouth of the cave." He gives me a playful punch on the shoulder. "Keep your eyes open. You might even spot a bear."

Ethan breaks into guffaws again, and I shake my head. "You two are impossible."

"And if it storms, head inside, but don't go too far. We need to conserve the flashlight batteries and lantern oil." Dad scrapes the grill and sets it on rocks to cool.

"We'll sit under that old sugar maple unless it starts thundering." Ethan tosses a rock toward a cluster of thick-trunked trees centered in a small clearing. "We can watch the horizon from there, but it would be hard for anyone to spot us."

"Okay." Dad sprints toward the barbed-wire fence. Ethan and I spread the blanket out under the tree. We sit against the trunk as Dad eases his way up the hill.

For a while, we read in silence, taking turns giving deep, contented sighs as though nothing's wrong. We're sitting on roots, our feet pointing in opposite directions and our shoulders touching. The storm clouds blow over, the sun creeps higher, and the only sounds are nature and our flipping pages.

Again, this is the Ethan I love—the Ethan who never got caught up with the wrong circle, and the Ethan who would rather devour a book than be in the middle of a crowd. It's nice to know he hasn't lost touch with this side of himself.

A couple hours later, Dad still sits at the top of the hill, bent over like he's sleeping. I know better. He's praying because James hasn't shown.

"This has been a surprisingly nice day." I give Ethan a genuine smile, and his deep blue eyes light.

"It has. See, Callie, things can be good with us again. We need to take it one day at a time."

I stretch next to him on my stomach, propping on my elbows. "It's pretty here, too. Under different circumstances…"

"As soon as we cross the border, we're going out on a real date. I'm not taking no for an answer."

With as much coyness as I can muster, I bat my eyes at him. "I'd be much obliged."

A small tail darts into a pile of rocks next to us, and he snickers. "Hey. Did you check the blanket for lizards?"

Sticking my tongue out, I roll over and shove him.

"Careful." He holds his hands up like he's threatening to tickle me.

I do need to be careful. A quick glance up the hill shows Dad staring at us. I roll back to my stomach and try to read, but fall asleep instead.

When I wake, Ethan sits cross-legged on the blanket, watching me. Dad walks toward us, James a few feet in tow. Both men slump forward, their gait slow and dismal.

"Bad news, Callie." Dark circles frame Dad's eyes, and his wrinkles sag into deep lines. "Amber is in an Alliance prison, somewhere in the new capital. Rumor says it's a death sentence."

I drop my book.

"We have to go get her." Ethan's jaw distends.

"We can't. She's stuck for now." James runs a hand through his thick white hair. "There's no way to get close to her."

I turn my gaze from Ethan's deflated shoulders. He's just worried. That's all. "What about us? Are we going to be stuck here?"

James sits on a tree root and picks up a blade of grass, inspecting it before splitting it in two pieces. "The Alliance lost Ohio today. Over the last couple of weeks, Adrian's pulled most of the officers into Virginia to search for Callie, and the Ohio residents acted on a plan they've been developing for months. They've held the officers outside the border and filed a petition to rejoin the union. The US sent in the National Guard and everything. If there are Alliance loyalists remaining, they've been quiet."

"Wow." Are other states close to the same thing? Are people starting to stand up to the crazy Alliance rules? I glance at Dad, who whittles a sharp end on a stick. He may be playing mountain man right now, but he's a writer at heart. And I can tell, he's thinking about the happy ending where the Alliance is no more.

James extends his legs, stretching his feet. "It's led to an influx of citizens trying to leave the Alliance. They have permission—they are technically US citizens, but Adrian is in a panic over it. Until now, he's stalled them with red tape, not letting them get passports and such. But now, the US isn't requiring Alliance-issued passports if people can prove they would have been able to get one from the US before the split. They've made it easy for anyone to cross if they no longer wish to be Alliance citizens."

Dad raises his eyebrows. "Interesting. What does that mean for us? Can we cross without incident, you think?"

James removes a shoe and turns it upside down, shaking it. "It's hard to say. The border officers on the Alliance side are still faithful to Adrian's cause, as far as I know. They are attempting to prevent people from leaving, but once anyone sets foot on US soil, they're fine. So Alliance citizens are going in droves, trying to overwhelm the officers. Adrian has sent more, but they're overworked, underpaid, and exhausted. And easily bribed."

"So, what's happening in this part of the country? Are we in immediate danger?" I grab my book and Ethan helps me stand.

"Officers are combing the area, house by house, although I've worked hard to make sure a lot of them are part of the rebellion." James puts the shoe back on and does the other. "They're warning citizens as they come through. We've had to put several of our successful extractions into hiding, at least the ones in Alliance country. Adrian has been threatening their parents, trying to force kids back into the schools. Unfortunately, these officers are not the border ones."

Ethan picks up the blanket and folds it into quarters. "Well, maybe we just need to be more direct. If the border officers are overwhelmed, they wouldn't have time to inspect every vehicle, right? And they'd wave a high-ranked officer on, wouldn't they?"

"What are you thinking?" Dad takes the blanket from Ethan and winds it into a tight roll.

Ethan shuffles. "What about the Cumberland Gap trails? Didn't you say the national parks are still US territory, but open to Alliance citizens? Don't local people go there all the time? Couldn't I just drive her, like we were on a date or something?"

"True…" Dad studies the trunk of a nearby tree. "But they have high security, and someone might recognize her."

I slide the book into my backpack and fumble with the zipper. "Well, the way I understand things, we're just waiting to get caught. If they catch me, they do. I'm eighteen now. I'm free to make my own choices."

The slightest of smiles plays on Dad's face. "Well, what about your dear old pops here? Can't I have a few months to worry about you since I lost a few?"

I stick my tongue out at him, and we all laugh.

Dad buckles the blanket onto a backpack and tightens the straps. "How about this? I may be a little out of shape, but I'm an excellent climber with great survival skills. I could go through private property until I catch up to the trail, just like I did to get to Isaac's place. Alone, it would be easy to pass through unnoticed."

He turns to James. "Ethan's right. We're doing this all wrong. Sometimes the most obvious route is the best way to sneak across. Why not just drive Ethan and Callie to Kentucky? Wasn't that the plan before you were almost caught? Just tell the border patrol they're teens who snuck off and crossed by accident. They left their backpacks on the trail, so they don't have an ID or luggage. Ethan's right. You rank high enough the border patrolmen wouldn't question you."

Ethan winks. "Callie, did you bring that makeup bag? Let me and your dad paint your face again. Maybe we could do the black lipstick, purple nails, and thick eyeliner Amber did that one Halloween."

"No way. I'm not masking my appearance anymore." Adrenaline pulses through my veins. "Let's do this."

Chapter Twenty-Five

DAD AND ETHAN decide to paint my face anyway. James appraises it. "You guys did great. She doesn't look anything like herself."

I give them a cheeky grin. Guess the earlier practice paid off.

"No, don't smile," James says. "The Alliance loves your smile. That would give you away. Everybody ready?"

The Alliance loves my fake smile. We say a quick prayer, and James, Ethan, and I head to the border.

As we approach, I squeeze his hand, tearing at the sign welcoming us to the United States. We wait behind a line of cars, the pace of my breath quickening as we inch closer.

James rests at the stop sign and looks back at us. "Here goes. Be obnoxious in love."

I scoot closer to Ethan, stretching the seatbelt. He cups my face, and as James drives up to the booth, he plants a kiss on me.

My heart flutters. I clench my fists, pressing my lips against his, but holding back.

James holds our passports up and looks over his shoulder. "Knock it off, you two."

I sit up, cover my mouth, and huff.

The patrol officer shakes his head. "Teenagers."

"Tell me about it." James nods. "Found these two wandering in the park. Thought I'd better return them to their parents and let them know they're safe."

"Have fun." The patrol officer presses a button and the border gate lifts.

Ethan squeezes my hand as we drive through. The whole ordeal took minutes. Anticlimactic. The patrol officer doesn't even look after us.

Once in Kentucky, James drives a few miles and pulls into a grocery parking lot. He buys junk food and water before driving me and Ethan to the Pinnacle Overlook, where Dad said we could meet him. It's been almost too easy.

Dad's had a huge head start, and he should be waiting for us.

Should be.

I cling to the passenger door handle. Maybe it would have been better to wait. My eyes burn, and I rub them, making large circles with my palms. I press so hard my vision blurs when I stop.

Ethan meets my gaze in the side mirror. "You okay?"

I try for a bright smile, but a yawn stifles it. "Yeah, just trying not to worry."

"God's in charge." James signals left. "If you'd like, we can walk out and see the view before we leave. See His beauty and feel His presence. It's not a far hike from where you're standing. It would be a shame to be so close and not experience it."

Grinning, Ethan drapes his arm over my shoulder and squeezes. "That sounds awesome."

I frown. "Is it safe?"

James squints as he makes the turn. "Some of this park used to be across the Virginia line, before the Alliance took over. The US government negotiated the border to keep the park's land together, but ended up giving part of it to the Alliance. Be careful and pay attention to the border lines. As long as you stay on US soil, you'll be safe."

Trees zoom past my window. They sway against the backdrop of occasional bright patches of wildflowers and white rocks. As we twist along, my stomach churns. The looming shoulder drop plummets deeper as we close in on the top. At times, the sky breaks through, the brightest blue I've seen in a while. It reminds me of the rainbow and God's promise. James is right. God is always in charge.

Branches litter the roadside, remnants of the storms that raced across the eastern US these past days. I bow my head and thank God we're not under any weather watches at the moment and beg him to keep Dad safe.

My stomach lurches. I glance in the rearview mirror at James's reflection. "I think…" I take a deep breath. "I think I need to stop."

"I can't stop here." He rounds a hairpin turn.

The contents of my stomach slosh. I cover my mouth.

"Close your eyes." Ethan reaches behind the seat to take my hand. "We're almost there."

Before I can, an oncoming car crosses into our lane. James swerves. The right tires drop off the blacktop, and he scowls as he spins back onto the road.

Mouth still covered, I force timed inhales and exhales as my stomach protests.

A stone building comes into view, offering restrooms. James finds a space close to the trailhead. "Well, we're here."

I jump out of the car and stumble forward as my body adjusts to solid ground.

Dad emerges from a pack of black walnut trees atop a low hill and runs to meet us.

"We made it!" I fall into his arms, only to be smothered by Ethan and James who join in our embrace.

When we pull apart, James retrieves the food from the car, all processed, non-perishable stuff that I haven't had since leaving the Alliance. He leads us up the hill into a small clearing overlooking the trail. Old, tumbled trunks and thorny bushes block us from sight. We settle on a rocky patch of grassless clay. James tears the paper bag from the grocery and spreads it on the ground.

"I've done nothing but pray since I've got here." Dad scratches his beard-covered chin. "Well, that's not entirely true. I did check in with Michael Harding a few minutes ago." He creases his brow. "He said Adrian's paternity test was legit. Mine was too. When they compared our DNA, it was the same."

"That's impossible." I snag a pack of peanut butter crackers and rip it open with my teeth. The smell alone induces comfort. I'm in the US.

James shakes his head and starts handing out water bottles and cans of Vienna sausages. "You know, Martin, I've thought about the resemblance a lot, especially if you'd shave. Your face is rounder, your hair is grayer, but you and Adrian share a lot of features."

Ethan accepts a bag of barbeque chips. "It's true. Take off your glasses."

"I'd thought so myself." Dad removes the glasses.

I gape. James is right. Dad's face is less clear and shiny, and not as tanned, but his square forehead matches Adrian's. I try to imagine Dad a few pounds lighter, wearing Adrian's hair. I can see a familial relationship.

"Twins?" James slides a newspaper clip from his wallet and holds it up to Dad's face. "Or at least brothers. It could be. They say it's hard to tell paternity between twins."

Ethan nods. "Separated at birth? I've heard parents did that a lot in places like Dreyfus back then because they couldn't afford two kids."

Shrugging, Dad twists the cap on a water bottle and downs it in a single drink. "Stranger things have happened. Back in West Fork, where Callie's grandfather grew up, a lady got caught selling her kids. But not my mom." Dad looks at me. "Your grandmother would have never done something like that. At least... I don't think she would have."

"Then what's your explanation? Kidnaping?" Frowning, I brush cracker crumbs from my pants. Their DNA matching still doesn't answer the question of which one of them would be my father.

"I don't know." He leans against an old tree and taps his head against the trunk. "Although, it would explain why he picked our family to destroy. Why he stalked Ella for years… If your grandmother chose to keep me and let him go, he'd have reason to resent me."

He rolls his blanket tight, and ties a knot around it. "Guess it's time to go back to your grandma's house and find out. Surely something in the genealogical records will give us an answer."

Ethan scarfs down the rest of his chips and nods toward the stone building. "I'm going to the bathroom."

"I'll go, too." James hops up. They head down the hill and cross the lot.

"We'll wait." Dad sits on a stump. "Unless you need to go."

"I will in a few minutes." I drop to my knees next to him. Black ants crawl across his shoes. "Just so you know, I don't care what the DNA says. You're always going to be Dad."

He leans over, hugs my shoulders, and kisses my forehead. "I know, Callie. Your mother and I were so happy in the nine months before you were born. I can't imagine her having an affair during that time. Later, absolutely, but not then." Twisting his empty water bottle into a crumpled lump of plastic, he caps it and tosses it into a bag. "But then again, guess I could have been blind to it. Guess I was blind to a lot of things."

He stands, and I link arms with him. "So, all this survivalist stuff. I didn't even know you liked to hike."

Dad gives me a sad smile. "There are so many things I wanted to teach you. So many opportunities I missed out on. But your mother could be very insistent."

"What were things like between you and Mom over the last few years? The truth." I swallow. "Like the things Amber and I didn't know about."

He turns his head. "Our relationship was strained. We put on a good face for you."

"Did you know about Adrian?"

He kneels by a huge tree stump and sifts the dirt at its base. "I caught her with someone once about ten years ago, a squirrelly guy with greasy blond-streaked hair. It could have been Adrian, I guess. I didn't get the best look." He coughs and blinks. "The guy ran away, and I gave her a black eye."

"You hit Mom?"

"She started screaming and kicking at me. She was pounding my chest and coming at me from all angles." Looking away, he throws a branch fragment several feet. "I was drunk. I lost it and smacked her across the room."

"You drank?" How many other things have I not noticed over the years?

"I did. Then, not now." He loosens a rock from the stone wall surrounding the base of the hill and tosses it down a nearby path. It bounces between thin tree stumps and lands in a pile of poison ivy. "Not often. But when I did..."

He reaches for my hands. "We were both imperfect. Your mom caught me a few months into our marriage sneaking around with one of my grad students. Nothing happened, but it could have. Your mother was jealous of the time I spent at the university, even though she forgave me and I forgave her. Granted, I did spend too much time there."

Frowning, he looks toward the stone building where Ethan and James have disappeared. "Speaking of jealousy, did I detect it coming from you a little while ago?"

"No." My shoulders slump, and I exhale, air vibrating through my lips like a horse. Denial. Might as well own up to it. "I've always been jealous of Amber. She's the pretty one, she's the popular one, and she's the one who dated the only boy I've ever even had a crush on."

"Ethan loved her. Maybe he still does love her a bit. But you shouldn't compare yourself to her. You're as pretty and much kinder."

"He claims to be over her. And their relationship must have been superficial. All I ever saw them do was sneak around and make out."

Dad's eyes briefly harden, but he doesn't seem surprised. "Ethan's changed a lot since his parents died. And he does love you."

"So he says."

He touches my shoulder. "He's a good guy, Callie, but confused. Cut him a little slack. He's lost both parents, been abandoned by his siblings. I'm not saying you need to date him—in fact, I'd rather you didn't until you're both more settled—but remember we're all he has right now."

"Okay. I'll try."

Dad winks. "And he is a Christian, so you have my approval when you decide to take that leap."

"You're impossible."

When Ethan and James return, Dad starts piling our backpacks in the trunk. "James, how's your wife?"

"The same. It's doubtful she'll ever fully recover." James gathers our trash and carries it to a receptacle.

I scrape my tongue across my teeth. "What happened to her?"

"Just before the presidential assassination—a freak accident. She was riding her bike along an eastern Kentucky road. A tree top fell and struck her head." He dumps the trash, his voice lowering. "She's been a vegetable ever since. I took the job as an officer to pay her medical bills. I never knew it would turn into something like this."

A pang of guilt hits me. "You know, I never thanked you for getting me out. I feel terrible. It could cost you everything."

James shrugs. "It's nothing. I did it for a lot of others. And I have life insurance to take care of Marilyn. We should have waited until you turned eighteen. Hannah and I didn't think we'd get another opportunity for a while, so we seized the moment."

He shoves his hands in his pocket. "I've made a lot of bad choices these days. I'm so, so sorry for what you're been through."

"It's fine." I take my turn in the bathroom, washing off the heavy black makeup and applying a light coat of blush and lip gloss. The dye is starting to fade from my hair. Good. Ethan will see *me*.

When I get back to the hill, Ethan points to a trail sign. "Hey, Callie, do you want to check out the overlook before we go? The sign says you can see Kentucky, Tennessee, and Virginia from there."

"Yeah. It's pretty awesome. Dad brought us here once before." My heart races, but I let him lead me along the trail.

"Don't stay too long." Dad's voice is wistful. I'm sure he's thinking about sharing the same moment with Mom.

As we get closer to the overlook, faint singing grows louder, several voices blending into one. Ethan and I tiptoe to join the group, which looks to be a bunch of college students.

The students sing on, beautiful songs of devotion with voices harmonized in parts. Ethan catches part of a tune and hums along. There's a pause after the song finishes, and a guy bumbles to the front of the group, gnawing on his lip and tugging a pretty brunette behind him.

"Before we go on," the guy says, "I need to do something." He drops to one knee and pulls out a small black box.

The brunette gasps, waving her hands in front of her face. "Oh, oh!"

Claps and sighs emerge from the students. When then they quiet, the guy opens the box and holds it out to her. "Jill, I've loved you since the day I met you. Be my wife."

Cheers cover her yes. They kiss, drawing hoots from their friends.

Ethan and I squeeze by, making our way to the stone porch that extends from the mountain. I grip the rail, leaning slightly over the edge, shivering when he wraps his arms around my waist and straightens me.

"It's nice to see a couple in love—in a Godly love, that is." He glances back to the group, where the girl maneuvers through the students, accepting their congratulations and hugs. "That could be us, you know."

With tears blinding my sight, I duck under Ethan's arms and move to the Kentucky overlook. "Amber is always going to be in our way."

"Will you stop with the excuses?" His nostrils flare. "Love doesn't have to be some complicated, planned, perfectly-executed adventure. My soul burns for you, Callie. I want to share every living breath with you. Why can't that be enough?"

"I—"

"Hear me out. I want us to be in church together every time the doors are open. I'll go back to college and study counseling, to help people who've been traumatized by the Alliance. After that, I want to get married and have a couple of kids and live happily ever after. I want to build things like Michael Harding and serve others the way Angela does." He grins. "I want to be a grumpy old codger like Mr. Whitman, driving the getaway car when my well-meaning wife drops dry bread off to some unsuspecting invalid."

He takes both my hands. "Tell me, Callie, can't you see yourself fitting into that life? Isn't that what you want, too?"

"Yes," I whisper. "Yes, it is."

The lush, green valley blurs as I lean into his kiss, this time slow and sweet, and not at all demanding. He sweeps me in his arms, and I melt into him, the last of my icy heart subliming to vapor.

Backing away, he grins. "Tell me you love me." He gestures to the horizon. "Tell the world."

I pivot, leaning against the railing with outstretched arms, and shout at the top of my lungs. "I love you, Ethan Thomas!"

My words dance across the treetops, and he grins, swinging me around, trading places. "I love you, Callie Noland!"

A collective gasp escapes from the crowd of students. Ethan covers his mouth with his hand.

Someone says the words we've dreaded to hear. "It's that girl. The one on TV."

Ethan locks his fingers in mine, and we push past their querying stares. One girl shoves her phone at me, probably snapping a picture. "Please don't." I hold my hand in front of my face, turning toward the edge of the path. "You don't know the whole story. Please respect my privacy."

"I'm sorry," she says. "I've already posted it."

Chapter Twenty-Six

ETHAN AND I run to the end of the trail and bound uphill to Dad and James.

"We have to go now." Ethan clutches his chest, wheezing. "We've been recognized."

Dad's face turns ashen. "Let's go."

We duck behind trees as the students emerge from the scenery. They don't seem to be looking for us, so we stay hidden then move to the car after they leave. James scans the parking lot and frowns. "Where to, Martin?"

"You've done enough. Drive us to the bottom and drop us off somewhere. We'll find our way home. You go back to your life. No point in hiding out now." Dad reaches for my hand. "If they follow us, they follow us. But first, let's pray."

This time each of us lifts a silent plea to God. When I open my eyes, Dad's tearstained face pains me. I drop to my knees, drenched in sobs.

Ethan kneels, wrapping his arms around me. Dad does, too, and we cling to each other, my tears wetting both their cheeks.

"Who cares who knows? You're safe now," Dad whispers. "You're free."

"Right." Ethan rubs his thumb against my arm. "We're going to take you home and help you rebuild your life."

A menacing cloud covers us. Thick raindrops pelt our backs as we race to the car and shove our stuff in the trunk.

James crouches, rubbing the oil-slick blacktop. "Going to be a tough ride to the bottom. Let's go before it gets worse."

I keep my eyes closed at first, trying to blot out the roaring thunder. Trust God. Have faith. Be courageous. Trust God. Have faith. Be courageous.

The hairpin turns jolt my stomach, and I peek. An elm's huge trunk passes inches from the car. I squeeze the door handle with one hand and Ethan's arm with the other.

Forcing out even breaths, I tune into details. Out my window, wet leaves clump. The trees look misshapen and eerie, as if they have fists. Fragmented rock juts out of the opposite hill like sharp blades thrusting toward the car.

Ethan meets my eyes. "Get a grip, Callie. We're going to be okay."

I rest my head on his shoulder and resume my chant. Trust God. Have faith. Be courageous.

By the time we reach the end of the road, the sky has cleared.

At Dad's insistence, James drops us off at the visitor's center, just off US-25. Ethan and I separate, mingling with umbrella-toting tourists and pretending to read pamphlets while Dad calls Michael Harding to plan our next move. Then, he and Ethan go shave. I slip into the women's restroom so I'm not just standing out in public. I wince at my reflection, my sweaty hair—clumped, oily fragments sticking out in all directions. I just checked it in the other bathroom mirror. How did it get so messy so fast? Just from us running? If I'm caught, I do not want to look like this.

I shampoo my hair with the wall-mounted soap and dry it with the hand dryer.

After watching me unsuccessfully dig through my backpack for my brush, a college-aged girl gives me one. "I have two," she says. "You look like you need a break."

"Yeah. You have no idea." Tears spill from my eyes, and I grip the brush with trembling hands.

She hugs me. "What can I do?"

I catch my blotchy reflection in the mirror and peer into the cosmetic bag Emily gave me. "How are you at makeup?"

Thirty minutes later, I step out of the bathroom with sultry eyes and dark lips, meeting Dad's creased brow. He has taken James and Ethan's advice and lost his beard. With his clean-shaven, thinner face, Dad looks startlingly like Adrian.

I move around the corner, my heart pausing as I meet Ethan's gaze. He gapes.

"We thought we were going to have to come in after you." Dad glances at the sky. "I called the rental place, and they're bringing us a car. We'll be home in a couple hours."

"But you look fantastic." Ethan grins.

We head toward benches to wait for the rental car, almost running into a man dressed in a black suit and sunglasses. My heart plummets.

He stops short. "Hello, Callie. *Agent* Kevin Wiseman. Remember me? Although I'm not an agent anymore."

"Were you ever?" Ethan lunges toward Wiseman, fists clenched. Dad restrains him, but not before Ethan manages a square connection with Wiseman's jaw.

Instead of fighting, Wiseman holds up his palms. "I come in peace, man. Please, hold your fire."

Ethan's eyes blaze.

"What do you want?" Dad straightens, folding muscular arms across his chest.

Wiseman smirks. "I have a message for you. From Lord Lamb."

Lord Lamb. Ridiculous. I shudder, and Ethan tightens his grip.

Wiseman reaches into his suit coat and withdraws a red envelope from an inner pocket. He passes it to Dad, who opens it and winces.

"Amber."

He drops the envelope and pictures spill on the sidewalk. Her face is mutilated—bruised, cut, and swollen. Clinging to Ethan, I peek at the pictures and resist the urge to bury my face in his chest.

Dad blanches, turns away, and covers his mouth.

Wiseman sidesteps, forcing Dad to face him.

The veins in Dad's neck bulge. "What's the meaning of this?"

"Adrian wants a tradeoff. Callie turns herself in, and he releases her sister. Otherwise, Amber will receive the full execution of the law. And I do mean *execution*."

"Why?" Ethan dives to the pictures, scrambling to pick them up.

"She sinned against the Allied States. Others before her have had worse punishments than death. Why is Amber special?" Wiseman shrugs and backs toward his car. "But don't shoot me. I'm the messenger. If you want to negotiate, Adrian will be waiting at the Tri-State Peak at noon tomorrow. Come alone—just you, the boy, and Callie. No police." He winks. "After all, Martin, isn't that where you last crossed the border?"

Wiseman walks away, and I fall into a stupor, stumbling behind Dad and Ethan, whose steps falter as well. Dad mumbles something about a hotel and starting early in the morning, and somehow I awaken in a bleach-white bed to their hushed whispers. After bumbling showers and pushing hotel eggs around on a plate, we set out for the peak.

The trail is just a few miles, and we walk it in a prayerful blur. Dad presses forward, keeping us moving at such a rapid pace my lungs burn. Ethan squeezes my hand every so often and kisses my forehead, but mostly he tugs me along the path. Our plan is to get there first and wait for Adrian so we can strategize. But when we reach the peak, Adrian sits in a folding chair, right across the Virginia line.

I hesitate. Ethan wraps protective arms around my waist, but Dad steps forward. At first, I think he might punch Adrian. Instead, he extends his hand. "Hello, brother."

Adrian raises his eyebrows, his lips slightly upturned.

"How's my Ella?" Dad somehow smiles. "Would you care to let her know how much I've missed her?"

Snorting, Adrian slaps his leg. "Sure. Would you like me to pass your message on to your junkie daughter as well?"

"So you lay no claim to Amber?"

"She's nothing to me. Useless." Standing, Adrian steadies himself against a thin tree trunk. "But Callie..." He pushes his lips into a pout. "I must admit, dear, I'm hurt by your decision to run away."

"I want no part of your world."

Stretching to reach across the border without moving his feet, he traces my choker with his crooked pointer finger, pulling the edge away from my neck. "However, I'm thrilled you haven't done like some of the other rebel children and you've kept your butterfly. Am I to dare hope it's not a complete betrayal?"

I scan the forest behind him for flashes of red between the thicket of greens and browns. Is he alone? Surely officers wait with their guns to goad us into compliance.

Adrian places a toe on the path. "It's a funny thing, Martin. I can't cross here. I've renounced my citizenship, and crossing the border would be... illegal." He chuckles, inching his toe further. "Shameful, right?"

Ethan presses his lips together. "I thought the park was all US land."

A slow grin crosses Adrian's face. "Except this small portion. A piece I held on to, just in case. Is it not the perfect meeting place? I can even drive up to it with an access road. Poor Martin, you had to hike all that way." He nudges a pebble with the toe of his shoe. "Now, about our business. It's simple. Callie comes home and Amber goes free."

"Callie is home." Dad's eyes narrow.

Hands on my hips, I spit in Adrian's eyes. "You're a fool. I'm not going anywhere with you."

"You belligerent girl." Adrian wipes away the spit with his knuckles and glares at me. "You'd choose death for your sister to save your own hide. And yet..." He nods. "Yes, a girl after my own heart."

I am *not* a girl after Adrian's heart. No.

Dad steps closer, his fists clenched. "Last night, I faxed those photos to every government agency I could think of, with a long statement detailing your abuse of my family."

Adrian sits again, like he's trying to act bored. He tilts so far to the right I think his chair might tip over then straightens himself with his walking stick.

"With God as my witness, I'll kill you with my bare hands before I'll let you take my daughter." At Dad's low chilling tone, goose bumps pucker my skin. "And make no mistake, you'll be sending Amber to the US within the next few weeks, or I'll send an army in after her."

Adrian sneers. "You have no power over me." He swings the walking stick wide, catching the back of Dad's knees, causing him to stumble across the path and land in the Virginia soil at Adrian's feet.

Jaws tight, Dad tries to pull himself upright as Adrian cries out, "Seize him!" Two camouflaged officers emerge from the trees and shove Dad to the ground. "You're in my territory now, Martin. Undocumented, right? How do you plan to protect your daughters from an Alliance prison cell?"

Dad squirms until one of the officers holds a needle to his neck.

I faint. Rough rocks from the path dig into my skin. I think I scream and lunge toward Dad, but Ethan restrains me. "Callie, wait. He'll trick you, too."

Adrian whips out two stacks of hundred dollar bills from a fanny pack and throws them on the path. "I don't think I've paid you lately for your service, Mr... Thomas, is it? Declaring your love at the

Pinnacles. How romantic. And yet, how convenient for me. Just a matter of communications to track your location."

Ethan kicks the stacks a few feet down the trail. "I don't want anything from you."

Through tears thick as blood, I grope for the money and wrap my fingers around it, lifting it over my head.

"Never mind, Mr. Thomas. Let Ms. *Noland* here have it. She can spend it while she contemplates her father's fate, rotting away in an Alliance dungeon." Adrian's maniacal laugh echoes through the trees. "Well, a storm cellar perhaps, but you get the idea."

I sling the money at Adrian's forehead with all my might. "I hate you! I hate you!" I pound my fists into the air. If only I could cross and pound him instead.

Ethan and Adrian stare at each other for several seconds, then Ethan pivots. "Come on, Callie. Let's go report this kidnaping." He helps me stand and faces Adrian. "You're a pig. How can you live with yourself, ruling with trickery and deceit? What has this family ever done to you?"

More officers emerge from the trees. Ignoring state boundaries, they cross the border to restrain Ethan.

"Cuff the upstart. Put him in the cell next to Martin." Adrian scratches his chin. "No, wait. Put them both in isolation."

He folds his chair, then motions for the officers to follow. "Let's go, boys. Drop the prisoners at Monongahela." He leers at me one last time. "You'll know where to find us, Callie. Right where you started. We've converted your school into a prison. The stakes are higher now. Join us, and free your Dad, sister, and Mr. Thomas."

I cling to the grass inches from his feet, covering it with my tears.

"I didn't take you for such a weakling." Adrian kicks the ground beside my mouth.

Palming my face with dirt-stained hands, I meet Ethan's gaze, resisting the urge to run to him as if I had any hope to save him. "Please. Why can't you just let us go free?"

"She abandoned both of us, you know."

"I don't know. Who? Mom?" My knees knock like I'm at the edge of a cliff.

"Your grandmother."

"Not true. My grandmother loved Dad. She loved all of us."

"She didn't love you enough to tell you the truth."

"What truth?"

"That she only wanted one child. And she chose him. And you're asking me to not retaliate." Adrian waves his hand.

I let out a slow breath. What can I say to reason with him? "Hasn't Dad paid enough?"

"It's nothing of consequence." He spins and strides down the path, the officers towing Ethan and Dad along behind them.

"Wait!" I rub my temples and close my eyes. *Lord, please help me find the words. Give me strength. Help me know what to do.*

When I open them, Adrian pauses at the base of a large tree, several feet downhill. "You're wasting our time."

"What if I go with you? I'll be your First Daughter, like you wanted me to."

"No!" Ethan jerks toward me, but the officers rein him in.

Adrian smirks. "Now you're talking. I'm listening."

I dry my eyes on my shirt. "Would you let them go, like you've promised? All of them? Dad, Ethan, and Amber? And Mom?"

"Other than your mother, I'd happily ban them from the country so they can't cause any more trouble. How about this? I'll keep them as prisoner until you take your stand by my side and declare your allegiance to the Alliance. Just for insurance. Then, I'll let them go."

"No. Let them go now."

Adrian continues along the path, away from me. "Deal or not a deal, sugar. If you want their freedom, you all come with me now."

I meet Ethan's gaze. He shakes his head, but I cross the line anyway. "Then I'll do it. We'll go with you now, and I'll stand up as your First Daughter. But only after you release them."

Chapter Twenty-Seven

WE CLIMB into a tricked-out, fifteen-passenger van with red velvet upholstery and brass trim. A lively classical arrangement pulses through speakers. Dad and Ethan ride cuffed and drugged in the back seat. Adrian put me in the middle beside him, clutching my arm. And in case that isn't enough to hold me, a young officer sits on my left, keeping his gaze out the window. I don't know what Adrian thinks I can do.

He prattles on about his plans for the nation, and I tune most of it out.

"By this time next year, we will have academies for our early grades, too. We're going to start them in archery in third grade and train them to be soldiers." Whistling, he slaps the shoulder of the officer in the front passenger seat. "I bet you're asking yourself if they'll be residential schools." He cackles. "They will, they will!"

Weirdo. I stare at him through glossy lenses. "Wouldn't it be better for them to stay with their mothers?"

Adrian nods, grinning. "Yes, yes. That's the beauty. Their mothers come live with them until they're old enough to attend the intermediate schools."

"You're ripping apart families."

The faintest scowl crosses his face. "I'm building stronger families by helping them raise better children."

I glance at Dad and Ethan through the rearview mirror, both slumped against cup holders. Trembling, I slide my hands under my knees and pinch the skin beneath my jeans. Gotta bite my tongue and do what's best for them.

"What else will they learn?" I lean toward him. *Please, let him think I'm interested.* "How will you teach them better behavior?"

"It's simple…" He drapes his arm over my shoulder, twisting the hair away from my neck. "Take off the necklace. I can't see your tattoo."

I do, resting the choker in my lap, clinging so hard it digs into my fingers.

"In youth, I was ruled by two things—the paddle and the fist. Modern parents let their kids go to ruin. They don't spank them, and expectations for behavior are far too low."

Of course. Why wouldn't he beat a little kid if he'll beat a grown man—or a girl like Amber?

"We have quite a few medicinal treatments as well."

I frown. "Couldn't that be dangerous for children?"

He shrugs. "I have doctors who will test the dosages. It's for the greater good."

My tattoo itches, and as I reach to scratch it, the ink under his sleeve snags my gaze. Maybe I need to get to know him better. Pretend to fully go along with his plan. Find something to use against him. I smile and sit straighter. "Will you tell me about your tattoos?"

Adrian slips out of his jacket, extending his arm into my lap. Two-inch scars haphazardly cross the flesh beneath the huge butterfly. Was he a cutter?

I raise my brows. "Why the butterflies?" Wings span his elbow and wrist.

He strokes his chin and looks toward the van ceiling. "Have you heard the Serenity Prayer? You know, the one alcoholics use?"

"I think we read it in health class once."

"Right. Well, it asks God to help us accept the things we cannot change. But I don't believe there's anything we cannot change.

Life is a continual metamorphosis." He pushes his fists together, intertwining his thumbs and opening his palms into the shape of a butterfly. He wiggles his fingers. "I started taking charge of my life when I was eleven, the year I ran away from my foster home."

I glance at the officers. Is he going to tell his whole life story in front of all of them?

Gritting his teeth, he pulls the seatbelt away from his shoulder and lets it snap back into place. "Can you imagine being told your parents didn't want you—and further, you had a twin brother they decided to keep? A twin they loved and doted on?"

"No." I lower my gaze. Could he be telling the truth? "It must have hurt terribly."

He points to the smaller butterfly tattoos surrounding his larger one. "Each represents a different time I tried to go back to your grandmother. For every time she turned me away."

I swallow, and my chest constricts. Could the grandmother I've always known and loved possibly have been so heartless? I can't imagine it. And yet...

Tracing his finger over red and green wings, he hums a few bars to "O Come, All Ye Faithful" and laughs. "That first year, age eleven, I ran to them and watched the family Christmas through the window. Like Ebenezer Scrooge, watching my life as it could have been."

"I'm so sorry."

The driver meets my gaze in the rearview mirror. His brow creases, and his jaw sets in a frown. Worried? Annoyed? Has he heard this story before?

Adrian refolds his hands, prayer-like, and rests his chin on his fingertips. "The last time I went and begged, she said I was an abomination. Can you believe that? An abomination."

"How awful." Grandma did use that word a lot.

"Amazingly, the tattoos ease the pain. You don't feel it in your heart."

I clutch the edge of my seat. I know what he means.

When we arrive at Adrian's mansion, he helps me out and walks me through shadows and streetlights to the front door. "I want you to experience the full effect."

"Sure." I shove my hands in my pockets and follow. Thick columns prop a gabled roof and balconied windows crown white double doors. He lifts the doorknocker, and when it falls, I jump.

"Callie, I have to admit I worried there for a bit. But I'm glad you remember who you are."

I force myself to lean closer so he'll think I'm sincere. Swallowing bile, I touch his forearm. "I'm glad, too… Dad."

A silver-haired woman in a flowing red dress opens the door, flooding his face with incandescent light. "Welcome, Callie."

"Meredith will show you around your new home. She was a tour guide, pre-Alliance. And I'll accompany you, of course." Adrian kisses my hand. Ugh.

"Of course." I shiver and focus on a copper plaque beside the front entrance. A relief sculpture of Adrian's face, complete with cheeky grin and clownish brows, stares back. What a perfect rendition of his creepiness.

Meredith beckons me. "This home was—"

"Georgia-revival style, built in the early 1920s." Adrian leads me across the threshold to a split staircase. "Note the mahogany wood and crystal finials."

Frowning, Meredith points to the checkered tile floor. "The black tiles are Belgium marble, and the white are Tennessean."

"And look at those magnificent, painted walls. Bet you thought they were papered." Pivoting, he brushes his fingers over at an antique couch. "Empire sofas from the first governor's residence. Beautiful. Yes?"

Seriously? Did he memorize the tour?

He walks me through each room—the library, the ballroom, the kitchen—interrupting Meredith with random details about every feature. This nineteenth-century rug, that Old Berlin clock.

We stop in an enormous great room where a twenty-foot high ceiling culminates in a dome. Mom stands in the room's center, holding a bouquet of flowers. "Callie, you're back."

Her voice quivers.

"Meredith, you may leave us now." Adrian brushes his fingers over a statue of a disc-headed woman with contorted features.

"This piece is a fertility figure, an akuaba, from the African culture. I wanted your mother to conceive, and she couldn't. I had it shipped to me right away."

I squint at the print below the piece. "You wanted her to have a baby? Isn't she too old?"

He jabs my side, and my skin crawls. "No, silly, I wanted her to conceive you." His laugh echoes in the vaulted room. "I just brought it here to remind her."

Mom, who has been trudging along beside us, gives him a forced smile. "He made me wear it on my back, just like the Ashanti. It was supposed to make you beautiful." She steps in front of me and takes both of my hands. "And it did, sweetheart. Your beauty grows every day."

"Amber was the beauty," I stare straight into her eyes. "And I have Dad's freckles."

She winces.

"Never mind." Adrian whisks us away, to a flight of carpeted stairs. "The bedrooms are this way."

My gaze darts. The stairs lead up two floors and down one. At least four stories. "Where is Dad? And Ethan and Amber? I want to see them."

Adrian purses his lips. "They're safe."

Crossing my arms, I face him. "Are they here?"

He links my arm and drags me to a door. After shoving me inside, he locks it behind me. Mom cries, and Adrian's shouts vibrate the door. "You stay out of this, Ella!"

Her muffled reply fades beneath a terrible crack, like a whip. Her scream follows. "No, no, no! I will not let you destroy my daughter!"

"She's my daughter," Adrian bellows, and I clutch my chest.

"She'll never be yours!" More of her screaming, then quiet sobs, and finally silence.

I turn out the light and grope my way to silk sheets, burying my tears in their comfort. I have to save Mom, too.

Sunrise brings a day of brainwashing, though a visit from James assures me Ethan, Dad, and Amber are safe. I spend hours listening to propaganda while they stay locked up enduring who knows what.

Day after day of preparation passes. Adrian hovers over me, micromanaging the details of my final Redemption ceremony, where I'll be sworn in as First Daughter.

The lies come so easily to him. He repeats them, again and again, smooth as the silk of my sheets. The Lord sent me back, a repentant servant of the Alliance, to do Adrian's will and further the cause.

He pushes me through continual tests, and the lies come pretty easy to me as well. I will serve him. I will obey him. I will help others follow him.

The morning of my final Redemption, James stands guard at my door. "I've arranged everything." His whisper comes through clenched teeth. "Amber, Ethan, and your dad will be permitted to watch your speech from the crowd, and they'll leave as soon as it's over."

I shake my head. "I want them to leave before. There's no evidence Adrian can be trusted."

He raises his pointer finger, and I grab it.

"No. Get them out at the beginning. Help them find safety."

"Rebels have infiltrated most of the inner guard. Your family will easily escape. And Ethan."

I hope so.

Moments later, Adrian raps at my door. When James opens it, Adrian leans against the frame, wearing a cheeky smirk. "Quote me a passage of scripture, Callie. How about something from… James."

James shifts and moves the rifle from his left shoulder to right.

My heart pounds. Does Adrian know he's not loyal?

I chew my lower lip. "Blessed is the man who endures temptation; for when he has been approved, he will receive the crown of life which the Lord has promised."

"And who is that Lord?"

I swallow hard. "You are."

"Oh, Callie," he claps his hands, "you have come so far."

"Yes, *Father*."

His eyes widen.

A laugh chokes my throat. "I'm just trying it out. Sounds more formal than Dad, right? The citizens will like it."

"Yes, yes." He bobs his head up and down with gusto. "I think it's perfect. By the way, Adriana will help with your final dress fitting this morning."

Adriana. His latest conquest, and my personal maid. She even looks a little like him, with curly dark hair and a smooth complexion. It's so scary how he tries to make everyone his twin. "I'll be ready."

"Say it again. Please. Let me hear it again."

Grinning, I bare my teeth. "I'll be ready, *Father*."

He claps again. "Oh, I do love it. Today is going to be such a fantastic day."

I've come to believe Adrian has a full-blown case of identity disorder. Today, he's childlike. Tomorrow, he could be murderous. Hopefully, tomorrow, I'll be far, far away.

Chapter Twenty-Eight

ADRIAN'S COLOGNE encompasses the room before his footsteps shuffle behind me.

"Ooh. Is that your speech?"

Dropping the pencil, I shove the paper to the edge of the desk and face him. "I'm looking over it one more time. Made the changes, just like you wanted."

"Let me see, let me see!"

Nodding, he traces the lines with his finger. "Yes, yes." He grabs my shoulders, giving them a slight shake. "This is perfect, Callie. I knew you'd come around."

Sure. Whatever. Poison to sugar. I can do this. "Would you like me to say it for you?"

"No time." He pouts, catches his reflection in the mirror, and then tugs at a wayward nose hair. "I probably won't see you again until you're onstage. I'm leaving the mansion for the arena soon."

"Do you mind if I visit Amber? And Martin and Ethan? I want to tell them goodbye."

He stares at me for a full minute with an expression I can't read. Please don't tell me he's changed his mind. He will free them. I won't speak otherwise. I made myself clear.

"No harm in it, I guess. Just be ready when I send for you."

"I will. Thanks again for letting them go."

He shrugs and waves a dismissive hand as he steps out the door. "They're useless to me. Wasted Alliance space and resources."

Yeah. He's said that. But can I trust him not to kill them?

When he's gone, I stuff the speech in my pocket and run to the room where he's holding Amber. The guard opens the door for me, and I puff my cheeks before walking inside. Who would have thought my heart might break as I tell her goodbye.

She stands in front of a mirror, twisting her hair into a formal braid. Black knit pants stick out beneath the hem of her dress.

"Callie." When she faces me, she drops the braid. Her hair untwists, spilling around her shoulders. Plain-faced, with blotchy eyes, she looks just like me. "You didn't have to do this."

"It's for the best. Dad shouldn't be alone." I move to her side. "Amber, you have to be responsible. No partying. No drugs."

Tears slide down her cheeks. I stand with my arms crossed. I should hug her or something. "I've got my speech. Do you want to see it? You always were better in English than me."

Sniffling, she wipes her tears with her sleeve and accepts the paper. After several painful minutes, she blinks and shoves it back at me. "This is ridiculous. Don't stand up there and say all this nonsense. I know you. It's not what's in your heart."

I nod toward the guard.

"He's on our side." Amber flicks him a glance then leads me to the window and points across the highway at the crowd amassing outside the arena. "You have an opportunity to speak to them. All of them. Thousands of people waiting for the opportunity—the signal to take a stand. They want to fight. They just need an excuse."

Mr. Sanders, Reva, and Hannah—all these people were doing what Adrian wanted because of fear. Amber is right. I need to show them it's okay to not be afraid.

A shiver runs up my spine. No matter the cost.

To live is Christ and to die is gain.

My gaze flickers to the ceiling. I could do this. I have to do this. But…

Breath held, I spin to her. "What about you? No way he'll let you go if I take a stand."

Amber smiles, bends, and grabs the hem of her right pant leg. She folds it to her thigh, hiding it completely beneath her skirt. "Ethan and I have a plan to get us all out of there—you, Mom, Dad. We're going to disappear before you start the speech. James will help you escape afterward." She hugs me. "We've prayed about it. We didn't tell you because we couldn't risk Adrian finding out. God will be on our side in this, I just know it."

I lean into her, resting my cheek against hers. When did she grow up? Out the window, rows and rows of cars line up against barricades. Chain-link fences surround officers by the hundreds. No possible route of escape, but God does have a way of making the impossible possible.

"Okay." I chew my lower lip. "What should I do?"

She speaks in my ear, and I stand straighter. "You're right. That's the perfect verse."

"Go, get dressed early so you'll have time to rehearse. You'll do great."

Lord willing.

On the way to my room, I stop by to see Dad and Ethan. The guards smile. They must be on our side, too.

Dad embraces me and kisses my forehead.

My body sinks into his arms, and I have to force myself to support my own weight. "I just talked to Amber. About my speech."

Pulling back, he gives me an intense stare, filled with more words than he could possibly say in the time we have. But I hear every one. A resounding message of hope.

He moves to the door and speaks quietly to the guard, who takes him by the arm and leads him down the hall, leaving me and Ethan alone. The second guard closes the door, promising a few precious moments of true privacy.

Ethan grasps both my hands and tugs me to a leather couch, and as we sit, the rest of the room disappears. Heat rushes from my neck to my forehead and down my spine, and I tremble. If they can help me escape Adrian for good, there's so much I need to tell him.

"When this is over…"

In my pause, Ethan's hand slides into my hair, tracing my tresses to the tips and letting them fall over my ears. He cups my chin and rubs his thumb against my cheek. "We'll have some catching up to do."

His lips meet mine before I can answer, salty with a faint hint of chocolate. How is that possible? As the taste fades, I sink into the soft leather, and he slides his arm around my waist.

I should close my eyes, lose myself in the embrace, and yet even as I yield, I'm acutely aware this could be our last.

He moves away for a second, and I struggle to breathe.

"You okay?"

Managing a slight nod, I close my eyes and part my lips a sliver, but he doesn't kiss me again. When I open my eyes, he's looking across the room at a beige halter top.

"What is that?"

He smiles. "Bullet proof. Goes under your dress. It doesn't cover everything, but protects vital organs. Your dad ordered it from an armor company and had it shipped here overnight."

"Seriously? How did he do that?"

"No time for details. We were going to send it to your dressing room, but you could go on and take it." He grins, holding out a dish. "Want some candy?"

"You're sure you can get me out."

Ethan grabs a handful of M&Ms and pops them into his mouth. "These days, we can pretty much do what we want. Thanks to James, we've completely infiltrated the officers who serve in Adrian's outer guard. It'll be easy."

A butterfly dances around the windowsill, and I touch my neck, feeling the slight ridges on my still-tender tattoo. Ethan was wrong. There will always be a scar. But only a small one, a scar I've chosen to keep. "Then we'll be free. What next?"

He nibbles the tattoo ridges, sending tingles to my toes. "I'll never leave your side."

The guard opens the door, and Dad steps in, walks straight to the bulletproof top, and slides it off the hanger. He sends me to their bathroom, and I slip it on under my shirt, catching my reflection in the mirror.

My flushed cheeks and bright eyes will bring the vibrant edge to my appearance that Adrian expects. Maybe I can pull this off.

I cling to Dad and Ethan once more and then return to my room.

Mom sits on my bed, a silk dress folded over her lap. Cream, of course. To accentuate the spray tan Adrian insisted I get.

"He's so ridiculous."

"I wish I'd never met him." Mom lets tears drip onto her dress, leaving tiny beige spots from her makeup. "I'm so sorry for putting you through all this."

"Coming back was my choice."

"It's a brave choice, but a choice you wouldn't have had to make if not for me." She averts her gaze.

"Just go, Mom. I'll be fine, and you need to get yourself together."

"I'll be watching from the front row today. Adrian didn't want me onstage."

I snort. "Let me guess. He was afraid your beauty would outshine mine."

"Something like that." Her eyes darken. She kisses my cheek as the prep team arrives to do my hair and makeup. "Bye, Callie. I love you."

Swallowing hard, I reach after her. "I love you, too, Mom."

Two hours later, officers escort me across the street, through the arena's back door to the stage. The monstrous structure has been hastily constructed, evident from visible zip ties and half-painted columns. Adrian probably doesn't care as long as it looks good from the audience.

Alliance citizens, dressed in their Sunday best, stream in from the front. No way will they all fit into the building. Who knows why Adrian chose this location. Then again, who knows why Adrian does anything.

I go through the motions, greeting people and shaking hands, and join Adrian at the edge of a velvety curtain.

He points to the other side of the stage, where Dad leans against a thick, faux-marble column. "There you go. Martin, your sister, and your boyfriend, free as promised."

I blink back tears as the officers guarding Dad step aside.

He waves and descends stairs, blending into the crowd, who all wear black baseball caps in support of Adrian. Dad dons one and disappears.

Ethan meets my eyes and mouths, "I love you."

The soundless words swarm my ears and blanket me in bittersweet warmth. I tilt toward him, reaching involuntarily.

"We're on." Adrian smirks and steps between us. I peek past him. Ethan faces the crowd, also having donned a hat.

Classical music streams from overhead speakers. When we reach the glass podium, it stops. Adrian draws the microphone closer to his lips. "Friends and neighbors."

The crowd waves their arms and screams, wide grins crossing their faces. Probably because Adrian has permitted them champagne. He stands on his tiptoes, and I briefly consider shoving him to the ground. Instead, I note officers with rifles on either side of the stage. Five I don't recognize, plus James.

Mom waves from the front row, surrounded by four officers of her own. Adrian averts his gaze from hers, which makes me fear for her safety even more.

He halts the applause with his hand. "Friends and neighbors, we have gathered here today to rejoice over my prodigal daughter's return. She has sown her wayward seeds, as have many of us, and is now ready to serve the Alliance wholeheartedly."

As he links my arm, I force a smile.

"Isn't she beautiful?"

Cheers erupt again. My head aches from the tightly twisted braids encircling my scalp and culminating in a poofy up-do like something from the sixties. I free my hand from Adrian's and wave, and the cheers amplify.

When I bring my hand to my side, I close my fist. I clutch true power—God's power. This will work. Dad and Ethan have a plan. We'll all be free. We have to. And if not, it's God's will.

A dismissive wave settles the cheering. Adrian tiptoes again and leans closer to the microphone. "Would you like to hear her speak?"

Off they go again. He nudges me and steps to my right.

Shakily, I retrieve my speech from the blue folder on the podium. The paper slips from my hand, and I contemplate leaving it on the ground. It's not like I plan to use it anyway.

Ethan and Amber slip to the edge of the crowd, hand in hand. Good. They've already started their escape. Maybe if all this doesn't work out, at least they can find happiness together. Clenching my jaw, I pick up the paper and set it on the podium.

"Good people!"

The crowd roars. I blink, almost stepping back. How can two words set them in a frenzy? I raise my hand like Adrian did, and they quieten. "We are gathered today to celebrate our great nation."

He stands a few feet away, smiling like he's won a trophy.

"In expeditions led by great men—Vespucci, Columbus, Magellan, many others—humanity came to occupy all corners of this world. Wars were fought, victories won, land attained, exchanged, and purchased. And I think all for a common purpose, at least in the beginning. To make life better for the ones we love."

I exhale and close my eyes. "I love the people in this arena. People whom I'd give my heart and soul to protect. People who will hopefully forgive me."

"We forgive you!" Applause quickly drowns the voice from a few rows back in the crowd.

"But I have a deeper purpose than seeking your forgiveness." I'm still sticking to the script. Adrian mouths the words along with me as he reads from his copy. "America was founded upon ideals such as perfect union, justice, domestic tranquility—those things stated in the preamble to the constitution—and the Alliance leadership chose to act because those ideals were becoming irrelevant. They felt the America we knew and loved was broken, and States peacefully seceded in an effort to restore some of those ideals."

Adrian claps, his copy falling to the stage. "Yes, yes!"

The crowd applauds as well, and this time almost a full minute passes before I speak again.

"Our education system was flailing, our children overfed, and our citizens bickered and spread hate and fear between us."

I reach into my sleeve and withdraw the folded poster, opening it for the crowd to see. The same propaganda I saw the day I started the journey—the woman struggling to feed both babies and being held back by a faulty system. They gasp, and I throw it into the mob. "Ask yourself! Are your bellies full, when they were once empty? Is your financial path clearer, where it was once muddled?"

From the midst of the crowd, a man raises his fist, his jaw set in a frumpy smile. "Yes, yes!"

The crowd follows suit.

"Of course they're not!"

My words go unnoticed. They're too busy mimicking Adrian. Sick. Is this really the right moment to take my stand?

I glance at Adrian, who nods for me to continue. Even he didn't notice. It's definitely the moment.

"And to whose benefit? Yours?" I scan the crowd. "Your neighbor's? His?" My fingers line up directly with Adrian's nose, and then I raise them to the sky. "Or His?"

Adrian doesn't react to what I've said, but the crowd gasps and covers their lips.

"I pledge allegiance to the America of our forefathers, where we were given the freedom to worship our true Lord and Master, the one whose heavenly power far outshines…" I sweep my arm toward Adrian. "…this man's earthly wit."

Another collective gasp crosses the auditorium, and Adrian glares at me.

I stand straighter. "Through that true Lord's great providence I stand before you now, a willing slave, abducted from my true biological father by Adrian Lamb."

"Silence her." Adrian motions to James, who raises his rifle. "She is my daughter. She is!"

James doesn't fire, but someone else does. Blood trickles from a hole in my left side and spreads through the creamy white silk.

Pain shoots through every fiber of my being. I grit my teeth. Everything vital is protected. I can be strong. Dad and Ethan have a plan.

My vision glazes. Mom lunges toward Adrian, but the officers restrain her. I grip the podium and inhale as much as I can manage. "Remember Joshua. Choose you this day whom you will serve: whether this man who considers himself a god, or the selfish desires that led us to this moment."

The second shot skims my right knee just as I move my leg forward. I tumble to the stage, dragging the microphone with me. "As for me and my house…" I look directly into my mom's tear-filled eyes. "We will serve the Lord."

She brings her hand to her lips and kisses it, then holds it out to me. One more lunge, and she grapples for the mic, stretching the cord to its max. "Far be it from me to forsake the Lord to serve this man!" Her shout rings through the quieted crowd. "Jesus, sweet Jesus! If you have any forgiveness left for me, please purge my sins and restore me to your fold!"

Blood trickles from her chest, but her words resonate. The crowd shouts them over and over. "Far be it from us to forsake the Lord to serve this man. We will serve the Lord."

Quivering, I muster another breath and sing as loud as I can. "Mine eyes have seen the glory…"

The chanting people pick up the song where I leave off, and the officers aim into the crowd.

I open my mouth to scream no! The word never makes it past my lips.

The blue sky turns gray as the crowd sings amidst rifle shots. I scan the front rows through hazy eyes. No sign of Ethan or Amber. They've escaped. At least I hope so.

Then the world fades to black.

THE END

Epilogue

INIQUITY.

I scratch the letters into the oak table with a drywall nail. Words now cover half its surface, from the base of the wobbly legs to the peeling polyurethane top. I've only been here six weeks, but it's been long enough for Adrian's daily visits to grate my nerves.

Five months, most of them in an Alliance hospital, have passed since I betrayed him.

Though my physical wounds healed, my body aches from head to toe. Mostly my heart. The not knowing whether or not Dad and Ethan escaped with Amber or Mom…

My prison is nothing more than a basement in an old Monongahela School. A wooden frame with remnants of drywall covers moldy concrete walls. In the corner, dry-rotted panels separate a toilet and sink from the main room. It smells like old dirty socks down here, but Adrian doesn't seem to mind. In fact, I think he thrives on it. And for whatever reason, he tolerates my etching.

I've considered ways to escape, but they're pointless. Guards and electric fences still surround the facility. From what I've gathered, Adrian's put so many people in jail they've started filling the churches and schools, which encourages me. The rebellion is alive.

I glance at a wad of paper on the floor by my feet. Adrian sits across the room on a worn leather couch, his legs crossed like a woman's. His heart throbs through his skin-tight shirt and his waxy curls bounce from the pulse on his temple.

Let him be mad. I'm not picking it up. It's a forgery.

"Aren't you even curious?" He smirks. "The boy is, after all, the love of your life."

"He's free." I carve a loop near the top corner of the left table leg. Adrian wants me to think he caught Ethan, but he refuses to look me in the eye. So I have faith.

"Free with your sister."

Pangs sear my chest. I etch them away. "Don't you have any original material for torture?" I lean closer to the table, scraping a small circle to dot the *I*. "This is growing tiresome. You talk about Amber and Ethan to get a rise from me; I don't care, which frustrates you. Your blood pressure soars, and you go home to pop pills. Surely you have more important things to do than sit around this cell with me."

A centipede pokes its head out of a crack in the concrete wall. I shuffle over and catch it on my nail. Beside me, a huge spider hovers. I drop the centipede on its web. "Eat away, little buddy." And stay away from my cot. I turn to Adrian. "Are you hungry? I could catch you one, too."

Adrian coughs and raises his feet from the floor. He scratches his chin. Bet he's thinking about his next fix.

I return to the centipede's crevice, running my fingers along the surrounding wood beams that once held plastered walls. Tracing my etchings, I murmur, "I am convinced that neither death nor life, neither angels nor demons, neither the present nor the future, nor any powers, neither height nor depth, nor anything else in all creation, will be able to separate us from the love of God that is in Christ Jesus our Lord."

"You're wasting your time with those verses. We're going to burn this place in a few weeks anyway, after we move the prisoners into our new facility. Construction will be complete soon."

My pulse races. "Don't care." I return to the table and etch some more. "Shouldn't you go run your little country?"

"I have men who do that."

I shrug, though my hand shakes. "Yes, you've told me."

He stands then paces by the heavy steel door barring me from the world. "I visited your mother. She's healing nicely from her last punishment. I think she lifted her arms over her head with no pain."

My heart freezes, and I have to force my lips to speak. "Good."

"She says hello. And that you should ask forgiveness for betraying me. Three little words, and I'll let you come back to the mansion."

"Not happening." I finish the last curve on the S and inspect my work, scratching a little deeper over the letters. Does he honestly think I'd want to go back?

His face contorts. After a pause, he smiles. "How's your knee? You're not getting around so well today. Is your shoe on too tight?"

I stifle a grimace. My knee throbs, actually. Speaking of shoes… His question makes me think of an old Bible joke Dad and I shared. "You ever hear of Bildad the Shu-hite?"

Adrian tosses a glance at the ceiling. "The name doesn't ring a bell."

It wouldn't. "Shortest man in the Bible." I snort as Adrian scowls. "The book of Job. Bildad, who accused Job wrongfully of wickedness the way you are accusing me. It's interesting, what he said, how dominion and fear belong to God."

Pressing his hands against his thighs, Adrian draws in the musty air. "I fail to understand how you could have lost everything and still choose to believe. It disgusts me."

"So kill me. Put me out of my misery." I rest my elbows on the table and fold my hands together. "Oh, that my words were written! Oh, that they were inscribed in a book! That they were engraved on a rock with an iron pen and lead forever! For I know that my redeemer lives, and that he shall stand last on the Earth. And after my skin is destroyed, this I know. That in my flesh I shall see God."

Adrian scoffs, his pacing growing more frenzied. "You're a lunatic."

Says the lunatic. I tap my knuckles against the table. "Xanax today? Need something for those nerves?"

He stops short, grinding his teeth. Beads of sweat sprinkle his forehead. "I hate you, Callie."

"I forgive you, Adrian." I cast him a cheeky smile. "I still don't understand why you keep me around. Ultimate betrayal and all. And if it's true, what you say… you know, how everyone thinks I'm dead. That's a lot of expense for a funeral for someone who you didn't manage to kill."

His breath quickens. He spins on his heels and grabs the doorknob. "Killing you would end your suffering. I'd rather it go on."

"As the Apostle Paul said, 'I've learned to be content in whatever state I am.' You're wasting your time."

Adrian harrumphs and storms through the door. When it slams, a piece of the wooden frame clatters to the concrete floor.

I crouch beside the table, wincing as pain shoots through my knee and up my thigh. Finding an empty spot on one of the legs, I dig the nail into the soft wood. The hair on my skin prickles as my eyes fill. Shallow breaths quell my trembling. I etch a line across the leg, separating the last verse from the new one.

Adrian's empty words still haunt me. The same message, day after day. The Alliance is strong as ever. America has had a financial breakdown, and nine other states are prepared to secede and form their own nation on the Pacific coast, splitting the US into thirds. Parents are sending their kids to the Alliance schools in droves, and the Alliance government has constructed more to accommodate the demand. And Isaac's operation has been cut off, so there's no one to save them. Probably lies, but I have no way of knowing.

Every day he promises to set fire to this place and destroy it. Will he destroy me, too? Shivers race up my spine. I'm fine with dying, but I don't want to burn.

A roach skitters by, racing from the table to the wobbly bookshelf housing Adrian's trinkets. Six months of gifts. A silver crown, studded with diamonds, rests in velvet on the top shelf, his reminder of what could have been. On the shelf below it, the Alliance Bible gathers dust, surrounded by little tchotchkes and figurines like the ones he'd given Mom.

Thoughts of Ethan encompass me. I taste the chocolate and peanuts from his last kiss and feel his smooth lips pressed against mine. Rubbing my arms, I squeeze, pretending he's holding me instead. Whether this is self-inflicted torture or guilty pleasure, I haven't decided, but it's become part of my routine. It keeps me sane, as does praying and reciting Scripture.

But today, I tremble.

Be still, and know that I am God.

I pull myself to a stand and hobble to my cot, tears trickling down my cheeks. Be still. I'm listening.

Curling in a ball, I slide under the thin sheet and wrap myself in my arms. Other than praying, being still is all I can do right now.

That, and wait.

$\mathcal{T}$he $\mathcal{S}$eries

CAVERNOUS

*A Christian teen battles for her soul against an extremist leader—
her father.*

In a divided America, several secessions lead to the formation of a
new nation, the Alliance of American States. Fueled by extremists
who solicit members via social media, the Alliance has one weak
point: Callie Noland, daughter of deceptive leader Adrian Lamb.
When he snatches her from the man she's always called dad, he
forces her into a suppressive life, training to serve in the Alliance
military. Can she maintain her faith in God and stand up to the man
who calls himself Lord and Master?

COCOONED—Fall 2016

A Christian teen clings to her faith in God's providence while the boy she loves fights to secure her freedom.

Pressured by the rebellion incited by Callie Noland, Alliance leader Adrian Lamb reaches critical mass. Callie Noland sits in an Alliance prison, recovering from wounds she received during a public stand for her faith which cost her status as First Daughter.

Circumstances place Ethan Thomas in a homegrown terrorist organization bent on destroying the Alliance. In his desperation he elicits their help to find and rescue her.

Meanwhile, Callie draws inspiration from Psalms 94:16: *Who will rise up for me against the wicked? Who will protect me against the evildoers?* It's as if God is saying the words directly to her. It's time to take a stand against extremist leader Adrian Lamb. The Alliance people need to know she did not die.

CONCEDED—Coming Fall 2017

A Christian teen yields completely to God's will and devotes her life to spreading His truth.
When the Alliance is taken down by the American military, a Christian, Michael Harding, decides to run for president as an independent candidate. He enlists the help of Ethan Thomas and Callie Noland, who have newfound zeal following their triumph over Adrian Lamb's persecution.

They launch a campaign built on benevolence, service, faith, and Scriptures. Though their personal stand brings scrutiny and judgment, a broken America clings to their promise of hope.

Can Callie convince her divided nation that submission to Christ brings the ultimate freedom?

Cocooned Excerpt

Please enjoy this sneak peek from my upcoming full-length novel, *Cocooned*, book two of the *Cavernous Trilogy*, coming Fall 2016.

BRIEF PAIN sears my cheek, and I press my face against the dry-rotted foam pillow. The brimstone scent conjures images of campfires and roasting marshmallows with Ethan, and for a moment, grogginess pulls me back into dreams.

Another sharp jolt scorches my shoulder. As I sputter and cough, my eyes open to swelling embers and a cloud of smoke above my head. My prison cell glows an eerie orange, and flames lick through the foam ceiling.

I throw my wool blanket aside and dive away from dropping ash. My gaze lands first on the high windows lining the wall above me, far out of my reach. Next, I spin to the thick steel door to my left, bracing for pain when I touch the metal. It's locked, as I knew it would be, but at least it's cool. Tears sting my eyes, and I cover my mouth and nose with my shirt collar. Please, Lord. If this is your will, help me yield to it.

An overhead beam crackles. A chunk falls to my bed, igniting the sheets. Shudders pulse through my body. I crawl to the blanket and pull it to the floor. Maybe if I roll it tight around me… Or would it make things worse?

I edge back to the door, ball up under the blanket, and sing in a shaky voice. "Amazing grace, how sweet the sound, that saved—"

The lock clicks, and the door handle turns. My shoulders stiffen, and I stand as a crack forms between the door and the frame. Screams and shouts from the open room outside my cell give me hope. Someone is setting us all free. Maybe one of the guards has shown compassion. Clutching the blanket so tight the fibers dig into my fingers, I wait for my savior to burst into the room.

Feet shuffle, and a low cough punctuates the popping and cracking.

Why haven't they come in yet? Should I go out? Will they lock the door back if I don't?

I ease it open wider, drawing in fresher air, if you could call it that. The smoke barely obscures the constant mustiness I've endured since Adrian snatched me away from my beloved sycamores and forced me into Alliance custody. The influx of light reveals ash spots on my blanket. If I'd slept any longer… Chills shoot down my spine.

Maybe… dare I hope Ethan could be here? I've dreamed for so long that he'd come to save me. But Ethan would have burst in and embraced me. Wouldn't he?

"Thank you." My shaky whisper is lost to the void as I shove the door to its full span. "Now, who are you? Friend or foe?"

Dim sunbeams streams from the ceiling windows into an empty room with cracking mortar and stray crates and boxes. Rough patches mar the dulled concrete floor, but no embers. Disoriented prisoners dash in uncertain paths, but still no savior. And no clear escape path. A salty tear rolls over my lips, and I shove it away with the back of my hand. If Adrian's watching, and this is some kind of twisted game, no way will I let him see me cry.

Six red garage doors line the far wall. One rises, and I duck behind a pallet of crates, then creep past fork lifts toward a smaller, nearby door. Surely someone wouldn't afford us this opportunity only to give us away.

Following skid marks from the rubber tires, I edge closer as the opening garage exposes two pairs of Kevlar-covered legs in Alliance red. As the other prisoners charge toward them, they are met with a spray of rifle fire.

I shield myself with the blanket like it could render me invisible, still seeing no sign of a savior. Hope this person is a friend.

But what if they're not? I reach for the door knob, praying my jagged breath doesn't give me away.

A hand clamps my mouth, and another grips my left shoulder. Tremors pulse my spine as I try to turn.

"Wait." Breath from the whisper tickles my neck, and the hand drops to my forearm. Two dark-haired men clad in full rescue gear burst through the garage door, their faces obscured by oxygen masks, and rifles propped on their right shoulders. They rush to my cell, and the hand squeezes my arm. "Now!"

A lanky figure, perhaps old enough to be a man, steps in front of me, his face hidden by a knitted ski mask. He bumps the side door with his hips and drags me outside, then eases it closed again. We dash a few feet forward into rows of rusting café tables and chairs.

His gaze darts to the right and left. "This way."

Across an alley street, we duck into a thicket of thorny bushes. As he clears a path for me, shouts echo from the warehouse and sirens wail in the distance.

"She's not here!"

"Impossible!"

Exiting the thicket, we come to a neighborhood of deteriorating houses. Tiny gravels dig into my bare feet as we flee over a crumbling sidewalk.

He stops suddenly, removes his mask, and pulls me onto the cover of a closed-in porch. "My name is Luke. Do you remember me?"

My heart sinks. His hair, curled and gelled, resembles Adrian's, just like the men in the warehouse. Is he a loyalist? His face does look familiar, but I can't think of anyone named Luke. "I don't. Sorry."

"My dad, Larry, helped you escape Virginia. And with my brothers, I'm helping you now."

I swallow a shiver. "You look like him."

Luke grins. "Dad?"

"No." Bile sticks in my throat. "Adrian."

A scowl flickers across his face. "We have to pretend to be followers. It's the only way to secure our freedom."

"So you lie."

"We pretend." He picks the lock on the back door and leads me into the house. Thick dust layers kitchen countertops, and a musty smell fills my lungs. Water stains the ceiling.

"Here." He grabs a camouflage backpack from a dingy leather couch. "A change of clothes. You can use that restroom, but there's not any running water. Put the hood over your head."

The jeans, mock turtleneck, and oversized hoodie swallow my malnourished frame. A ponytail holder loops around one of the tennis shoe strings, and a brief memory flashes, of Mom brushing my hair as we watch the evening news. I can almost hear Dad reading scripture in the background, and Amber huffing as she washes the dishes.

After changing, I join Luke, who peeks out a curtain at the front of the house.

He winks as a black sedan pulls into the drive. "Good timing."

We rush outside, and he opens the back car door. Another Adrian twin waves from the driver's seat. "Hi, Callie."

I chew my lip. He must be Luke's brother. Their eyes are the same perfect shade of hunter green, and they share a pepper of freckles across the bridge of their noses. "Hi."

He chuckles. "I'm Tristan. You don't remember us, do you?"

"I remember seeing you guys in the cave. It's just unsettling to see you looking like Adrian."

Luke slides into the front seat. "Yeah, we know."

I crawl in the back.

"Duck down into the floorboards, but brace yourself. This might be kind of a wild ride."

The car jerks into motion, throwing me against the front seat. Tristan whips out of the drive and speeds through the neighborhood streets as I lower myself into the foot space.

"Won't they be searching cars?" Butterflies swarm my stomach like a hurricane.

Tristan signals. "I forgot. You haven't been out lately. In about two minutes, we're going to blend with hundreds of cars exactly like this one. And all the drivers will look exactly alike. So, no. I think they'll find searching cars useless."

He makes a sharp right turn. "Besides, Adrian hired lackeys to guard you instead of professionals. Those goons are probably still looking through the burning warehouse trying to find you."

I snort. "I thought Adrian set the fire."

"Nope." Another sharp turn. "We did, as a distraction. But we didn't expect it to spread so fast. Sorry about that." Tristan twists the steering wheel with stunt-driver expertise that sets my heart pounding.

"Weren't their other prisoners?" I lurch forward.

Luke reaches to steady me while Tristan jerks the car to the right. "Not that we could see. They'd moved all the others already. We're merging into traffic now."

My stomach lurches as Tristan weaves between lanes. When I think I can't take anymore, the car halts.

"Up and out." Luke opens the car door, and I step into a narrow alley between dirty brick buildings.

Tristan tries a number of steel doors as we walk through the alley. At last, one opens, leading us to a long, dim hall. He raises a finger, furrows his brow, and presses his ear against several interior doors.

"Don't you know where we're going?" My whisper almost shouts. "What are you listening for?"

"The hum of machines." He selects a door and raps five times. "We had to make a change of plans."

A short, gray-haired woman sweeps it open. "May I help you?"

"It's me." Luke stands straighter. "I need you to hide someone."

She appraises me, wrinkling her nose when she peeks beneath my hood. "This is another teenager. I'm already having trouble managing the others. What good is she to me?"

"I know this one personally. She will work hard." He pulls the hood back, uncovering my butterfly tattoo.

Her eyes widen as she studies my face and the color drains from hers. "It can't be."

Luke points to my abdomen. "Show her your scars."

I lift my sweatshirt, exposing the purplish streaks surrounding the sphere where the bullet pierced my side.

She steadies herself against the cracked wall. "Not such an unusual wound. Are you sure it's her?"

Dropping the shirt, I raise my right pant leg to the knee. "Maybe this scar is more unusual?"

Her chest deflates. "Does it hurt you? Will it keep you from standing on your feet?"

I nod. "It's arthritic, I think. I'll need to rest or sit sometimes. But I can still work hard with my hands."

She turns to Luke. "Do you realize the risk? If we are discovered... Our whole operation will be compromised."

"You won't be. We'll be back for her as soon as the escape route has been cleared."

A sad smile flickers his face, one that doesn't reach his eyes. "Callie, I have to go. You'll be safe here. Erma will treat you well. Hopefully Tristan and I will be back in a few days."

I eye the sharp-nosed woman and lick my lips. What can I say? "Okay."

Erma and I stand mute until he passes through the exterior door into the sunlight.

She sighs. "Let's get you changed."

We head to a room with a salon chair and sink. She opens a drawer and removes a basket of curlers. "This will take a couple of hours, so feel free to get some shut-eye when I set the timers."

With a fine-toothed comb, she separates my hair into small sections and wraps them around the rollers.

"You're giving me a perm."

"I'm changing your appearance so no one will recognize you." She frowns. "Though, I'm going to have to leave it longer to hide your butterfly."

"I don't want to hide my butterfly. And I don't want a perm."

She releases a roller, the elastic snap striking my cheek. "Do you want to get caught?"

"No." I chew on my lower lip, blinking away tears. Not fair.

As she finishes the rollers on the back of my head, a nagging thought presses to the forefront of my mind. I survived two gunshots and a fire. I have been an Alliance prisoner for months, and I'm now free… I need to be thankful, not stubborn.

Erma tucks cotton around my forehead and squirts warm liquid over the curlers, then nudges my head against the leather seat. She sets a timer, and my eyes flicker shut. Dear Lord, please forgive my attitude. I am blessed to be here today, free and hidden.

The room blurs, and dreams fill my thoughts.

Erma wakes me, this time squirting a cool liquid over my head. A few minutes later, she rinses my hair, pulling springy curls and letting them bounce back. "I suppose we could leave it long for now." She scrunches the hair in her fingers and squeezes excess water. "And maybe we could remove the tattoo if you're ready."

"No. I'm keeping the tattoo. It's a memory of how I overcame a challenging time in my life."

Clucking her tongue, she dabs makeup over my tattoo, then twists my hair into a loose side ponytail that she secures at the base of my neck and pulls toward my collarbone. "I guess this will do."

She spins the chair so I can see the mirror. Eerie how much I look like Adrian with curly hair. But I belong to Dad.

"I understand you are quite the rebel." Her piercing reflection prickles my arm hair. "There will be no talk of rebellion. The Christians have a secret meeting on Sundays, and you may deliver your doctrine to them if you so wish. But never a mention of it on the floor."

"Yes, ma'am."

Her swallow seems to stick, and she clears her throat. "You may find circumstances here shocking. You should know that we emulate all Alliance circumstance and follow those rules. It allows us to operate in secret. Do not risk our exposure by questioning what you do not understand."

"I won't question anything." The pit in my stomach plummets.

"Let's go."

She takes me to another room and gives me a gray uniform. Then we head toward a roaring sound. By the time we reach the huge, open room, my ears ache.

"The dishwashing area," she shouts, leading me past steaming steel structures where rows of mason jars drift by on a conveyer belt.

We leave the room and enter another. A line of Adrian-haired women sit at cutting-board tables peeling and chopping vegetables. When the door closes behind us, the noise dies to a dull whir.

"These ladies provide clean, organic food to Alliance citizens using traditional canning means."

"Why?"

"They reduce our exposure to the chemicals we once feared in the plastic liners."

I guess it makes sense.

Erma speaks in my ear, a soft whisper I have to strain to hear. "Though the hours are long and the pay is small, we wire an overtime salary to an account in the United States with your name. Should you ever escape, the money will be waiting for you."

"And if not?" I fumble with the hem of my shirt.

"You will receive your regular salary like everyone else. If you die before returning, the money will be given to someone else who needs to start over when they escape."

She walks me past a line of women peeling carrots with paring knives, to a line of old-school stoves with huge boiling pots with clamped lids. Steam hisses from vents on the top, and some of the pots rattle so hard they might explode. Women move the pots from one burner to another like bees hopping between flowers, easing the rattling to small jiggles. "One day I'll put you with the pressure cookers, but for today, you're going to peel potatoes."

I clench my jaw. Luke said a few days. I'm not going to be here long enough for the pressure cookers. I smile and nod and follow her to the potato counter.

"Meet Harmony." Erma nods to me, and the Adrian lookalikes face me. Teenagers and women, they all wear worry lines on their foreheads and exhaustion in their eyes.

She nudges me toward a stool and hands me a paring knife. The girl next to me peels in one continuous spiral, and I try to mimic her.

For five hours, I peel with no mention of a break. The other girls at the table stare at their potatoes, not venturing a glance in any direction. Though blisters form on my tender hands and aches spread through my fingers, I do the same.

The hands on the wall clock move into the sixth hour, and a bell chimes. All the girls set their potatoes on the counter and stand. They file out of the room one by one, and I fall into the last place in line. We move one at a time through a narrow hallway. The women disappear into a small room and come out with dripping hands. A restroom, I guess. The finished ones walk past and return to the peeling room.

A girl gasps as she passes. She slips in line behind me and plants her lips against to my ear. "Callie? I thought you were dead."

Bible Studies for Ladies
Ungodly Clutter

UnGODly Clutter
MONICA MYNK

HOW CAN A CHRISTIAN LIVE A GODLY LIFE IN A MESSY WORLD?

Have you ever been embarrassed to invite someone into your home? Cobwebs in the corners? Laundry piled to the ceiling? Mile-high dishes in the sink? If it's true that cleanliness is next to godliness, does that mean those of us too stressed and over-worked to maintain a clean home are ungodly?

Perhaps, God would be appalled to enter many of our homes... but not for the reasons we might think! Today's world is full of distractions and many litter our living space without us giving them a second thought.

How can Christian women cleanse their homes of the idols and temptations that hinder salvation?

Available for print and Amazon Kindle. More information at https:// monicamynk.com

Contemporary Women's Fiction
Romantic Suspense
Goddess to Daughter Series

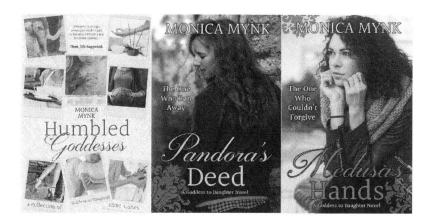

Years ago in rural Dreyfus, Kentucky, seven fourth grade girls studied mythology at a small Christian school. Three bore names of goddesses, and the others took on goddess nicknames.

Pretending divinity made them feel powerful until their teacher explained they could only attain true power through Christ. They promised to always be friends, following Jesus together. Then, they went their separate ways and fell deep into sin.

The Goddess to Daughter Series explores their stories of redemption and love. Available in print and on Amazon Kindle. Find more information at https://monicamynk.com

About the Author

MONICA MYNK is a high school Chemistry teacher and author from Eastern Kentucky. She spent her early years reading books with her mother, acting out plays with her brother and sister, climbing in corncribs, and helping her dad on the farm. Periodically, she loves to tell corny science jokes

Monica comes from a long line of preachers, elders, deacons, and Bible class teachers, and hopes to live up to their example. She clings to the hope that God's promises are new every morning. A favorite hobby is writing devotionals, which can be found on her blog.

In her spare time, Monica loves spending time with family, especially her husband and beautiful children. They've been known to hang out at the soccer field, and they are active participants in the Lads to Leaders program She is an active member of the American Christian Fiction Writers (ACFW).

NEED A SPEAKER?

Monica enjoys conducting ladies days and writing/editing seminars for women. If you're interested in booking, more information is available on her website.

https://monicamynk.com/speaking/

Letter to the Reader

Dear Reader,

Thank you so much for allowing me to share my stories with you. If you've enjoyed them, I would love to hear from you. Please, visit my social media links and connect so I can keep you informed of new releases.

I wrote this book because I am concerned that not enough Christians are committing Scripture to memory. One day, I sat in a coffee shop with a friend talking about writing and life. Across the room, the owners had placed a wall decal of Hosea 4:6, and the words struck a cord in my heart.

"My people are destroyed for lack of knowledge..."

It's my prayer that everyone who reads Callie's story will understand the importance of reading and memorizing God's word.

Blessings,

Monica

Twitter: @mgmwrites

Facebook: www.facebook.com/mgmynk

Website: https://monicamynk.com

Devotional and Writing Blog: https://mynkmusings.com

Acknowledgements

Thanks to Deirdre Lockhart, for "Brilliant editing."

To Christa Holland of Paper and Sage Design. Thanks for making my Callie come to life.

Thanks to Kathy Cretsinger and Diane Turpin.

To my Scribes girls. Forever friends and critique partners.

To my ACFW friends for advice and guidance.

To Callie, student teacher extraordinaire, for your friendship, legal advice, and lending me the use of your name.

To Jeannie, for listening, reading, and believing.

To my beta readers—my sisters—for helping make that final polish perfect. I've so enjoyed our discussions. I love and appreciate all of you!

To those on writing forums and social media. Through your brutal honesty, I've been able to turn a dream into a reality. Special thanks to Rebecca, Paylor, Jordan, Viktor, and Patrick.

To friends and family, especially my brother Nick and sister Micki, who were great partners in pretending, and my wonderful in-laws, Terry, Sue, Lindsay and Joseph. Love you all!

To my parents—my heroes. Mom, who nicknamed me Florence, and Dad, who taught me to always search the Scriptures.

To Lane, Matt, and Dana Kate, my beautiful family. Every day, my love for you grows even more.

To God, for His enduring patience and benevolent forgiveness. I pray that my stories will inspire others to delve into Your truth.

Made in the USA
Columbia, SC
17 December 2020